DEDICATION

This book is dedicated to my brother William E. Peters,
who was taken from us much too soon.

And, as always, to my wife Donna Walker-Nixon
for her continued encouragement and support.

The Pumpkin Seed

BY

TIMOTHY C. HOBBS

Visionary Press Cooperative

This book is a work of fiction. All characters, situation and dialogue are products of the author's imagination. Any semblance to actual events or persons, living or dead, is entirely coincidental.

THE PUMPKIN SEED

PRINTING HISTORY
Visionary Press Cooperative edition / 2012
Vamplit Publishing edition / 2009

ISBN-13: 978-1482653175
ISBN-10: 1482653176

PUBLISHED BY
VSIONARY PRESS COOPERATIVE
DENVER, CO

Visit our website at:
www.visionarypresscoop.com

PROLOGUE

Pasha, India-near the Nepal and India border-July 1798

The dead walk the streets of Pasha.

The leper repeated this through the matted wraps covering his face.

The British officer turned to his interpreter. "Ask him again. Does he have any information concerning a James Wilkins and his family?"

The leper shook his head and said, "The dead walk the streets of Pasha," then turned away toward a collection of small huts recessed into the walls of a cliff.

"Poor soul. The disease has affected his brain," the Indian interpreter commented. "I'm afraid, sir, he will be of no help."

There were only fifteen soldiers remaining. They had started with twenty-five from their landing at Calcutta over a month ago. The weather, dysentery, and rogue bandits were responsible for their losses.

"Hang it all!" the officer swore. "Sergeant Hookes, a moment please."

"Sir!"

"Bring that Weathers chap here. The one from the Company."

"He's gone over the hill, Sir. His shits has hit again."

"Then, go and find him, tell him to wipe his arse and bring the fellow here."

"Sir!"

"Oh, Sergeant, better take a few lads with you. We don't know what lies beyond that crest."

"Sir!"

The sun was approaching its westward plunge, and twilight shadowed the small village. The officer hailed his remaining men for a search of the huts. No one save the leper was found. The meager shacks held nothing more than broken furniture and discarded bowls. Something had sucked the life from the village of Pasha.

A young private came running over the hill. "Sir!" he hailed. "Come quickly. We've found some bodies."

Just over the ridge the remains of an ancient temple spread out. The officer found his sergeant and a pale Mr. Weathers standing at the top of a descending stone staircase.

"Sir, the rest of the men are down already," the sergeant explained as they moved down the stairs. Flickers of light could be seen from inside the temple. "We found these torches, Sir. They were still sticky with tar and lit up fine." Inside, the air was cold and spoke of decomposition. In the center of the room was a large statue. The soldiers gathered there. "We also found these," the sergeant said, pointing to a pile of bodies at the base of the statue. "Looks like maybe twenty dead, Sir."

The officer covered his mouth. "My God, what a stench!"

"Heaven help us," the interpreter whispered as he knelt before the bodies and the statue.

"For God's sake, man, get up off your knees," the officer chided, "unless you worship the rotting dead. It must have been a plague of some sort."

"No, sir," the kneeling man said. "It is Kali"

"Who?

"The dead walk the streets of Pasha." The voice of one disembodied coldly beckoned from the temple doorway. The shadow of the leper fell on the men.

"You again," the officer said. "Cheeky bugger, aren't you?"

Behind the men a stirring began. When they turned to see what the disturbance was, the decaying bodies began to rise.

THE JOURNAL OF ANDREA WILKINS

1798

January 17, 1798

As father feared, the winter monsoons have arrived before he could reach the mountain range to locate a favorable pass for future Company travel. The East India Company wants him to go through Nepal and into Tibet. These winds may be dry, but they are powerful and bitter cold in their frigid yowlings. There appears to be scant population in this area unless, of course, they are in hiding. The reputation of the British is not particularly good.

From what my father says, we are some two hundred miles short of our destination. One of the army regulars, a Sergeant Miles, agrees with his calculations.

It seems strange to know that I will be celebrating my seventeenth birthday so far from home. Feeling the edge of these winds makes me long for the warm hearth left behind in London.

I must close for now as mother is calling me to dinner.

January 19, 1798

We moved our camp because of the wear on our tents by the persistently strong monsoons. Sergeant Miles located a small village called Pasha about five miles south through a pass that cuts the effect of the winds. The place is built into a recessed hillside and consists mainly of clustered huts. The hill deflects the wind making the area, although still cold, rather calm. The people here look as desolate as the surroundings. However, they do not seem afraid or in awe of us.

There is one man who looks to be the leader of the village. He is not as gaunt as the rest of the people and is muscular and tall. His skin is dark and his eyes are an exotic brown. He has talked through an interpreter to my father, and I am certain he is responsible for arranging the large square living area for my parents and me to be housed in.

Toward evening he came to our door and spoke, through an interpreter, to Father again. From what I overheard, he was assigning a few men to help us get settled. Before bed, I asked my mother the man's name. She eyed me suspiciously and said, "Your father calls him Dayal, but to you, Andrea, even though he seems to hold a position of importance, he is only another dirty native, whatever veneer of respectability he has. Remember that." She, like all mothers, suspects sexual innuendoes when their daughter asks about a man. In this case, dear diary, she may be right, for he is indeed a handsome fellow, and before he left earlier this evening, he cast a dark glance to me that made my legs feel as if they were made of rubber.

I have tired now and feel a little off. Our supplies of dried beef and fruits are nearly exhausted so we accepted a local meal tonight. It was horrid, consisting of a lumpy gruel spiced to conceal its true taste and smell. Although I cannot get Dayal's longing stare out of my mind, my stomach is becoming more wretched by the minute. Besides that, as can usually be expected to occur at the most inopportune time, I feel my monthly cycle approaching as well. So, I will say goodnight, dear diary.

January 20, 1798

I am still not well. I have slept most of the day and plan to stay in bed. Mother has checked on me off and on. She says I have no fever and that it is probably a gastric disturbance I should soon overcome. She says she has been sick herself, but not to the extreme that I have. She tells me that my father is in no way ill. He is his usual stout burly self and is planning to leave soon with an expedition party that Dayal has arranged. We are to remain behind in Dayal's care. Also, from my mother's suggestion I am certain, some of the army regulars will stay with us. By the tone of her voice, it is clear that mother does not trust Dayal or his people.

I am fatigued and will stop for now.

January 22, 1798

I slept yesterday away and missed my entry. It was worth it as I feel much better today.

Father left. I seem to remember him coming to my room to say goodbye, but it is more like a dream than reality. I find it odd he should have left without knowing if I was well or not. I suppose mother must have reassured him, but I am still a bit perturbed as he will miss my birthday tomorrow. I realize I cannot expect the party I would have had in London, but it would have been nice for father to be here.

Dayal has sent us some servants. They are two young girls and the older man who serves as Dayal's interpreter.

As I am writing this, I feel the familiar cramps of monthly pain. I was right about the nearness of my cycle. At least it is not as bad as the gastritis I suffered. I just wish it could have waited until after my birthday.

January 23, 1798

Today I am seventeen years old.

My mother arranged with Dayal for a few village children to attend a small party. I've noticed that she is much more irritable with father gone. They are hardly ever apart from one another.

The party was held in the center of the house. There was a local type of pastry present that resembled a cake. Mother located a few candles to place on it. There was also a bland pudding. I found neither tasty, but my younger guests were beside themselves to have such a treat. After awhile, Dayal and the interpreter arrived and sent the children away. They sat with mother and me and had tea. Dayal spoke to the interpreter. "He wishes you a most happy day," the older man said to me. Dayal spoke again, and this time the interpreter said to my mother, "He wishes also to tell you, Madam, that your beauty shines truly through your daughter's eyes." I thought mother would choke on her tea, but she managed a pleasant smile and thanked him, telling him how much we appreciated his hospitality and protection while her husband was away. She would never be rude to someone she had to trust, no matter how suspicious she was of them. That is why she allowed me to accept the gift Dayal gave to me. It would have been an insult otherwise.

My breath escaped as Dayal placed the necklace around my neck. The jewels in it were heavy. I knew they must have been precious and probably some type of family heirloom. With as much composure as possible, I thanked him. He then made an amazing gesture; he took my hand and kissed it. I didn't know if it would be mother or me who fainted first. Thank goodness we both maintained our poise.

After Dayal left and the party things had been cleaned and put away, my mother took me to my room and sat me down on the bed. "No matter what you think you feel, young lady, this man means nothing to you. Why, he is at least twenty years your senior." When I protested, she cut me off. "Get him out of your head, Andrea. Remember, he is just a native. As far as that piece of jewelry he gave you, well, I'll leave that for your father to deal with. I could not very well refuse his gift and insult him. Your father trusts this man, although I can't fathom why, so we must be careful not to offend. I just hope your father is aware of the predicament he has put me in. Why, if I didn't know better, I'd believe this Dayal person was courting you. Imagine that, a savage foreigner courting a proper British woman. How absurd!"

She told me goodnight and was so flustered she forgot to take the necklace. After she was gone, I held it in front of me. It was so beautiful and extraordinary. The light from the candles by my bed reflected through its red and green stones, throwing shadows like restless painted ghosts on the walls. I held it close to my breast and vowed no one would ever take it from me. Surely I will dream of Dayal tonight.

January 24, 1798

Was what happened last night only a dream, or did Dayal really come to me?

I had put my nightclothes on and dozed with the necklace safe on my neck. The force of the wind may be depleted by the hillside, but some gusts manage to steal through. One of those errant breezes was playfully knocking on the sides and roof of the house last night. Its mischievous dance awakened me.

It was late. The candle at my bedside had burned half way down. The lacy curtain that covered the doorway to my bedroom was moving as if caught in a breeze. Since the doors are secured at night, there was no way this could happen unless someone had entered the house.

Like a phantom, Dayal stood by the curtain. I should have been afraid, but I was not. I felt instead a chill of expectation as he moved slowly through the split in the curtain. He was wearing a long white robe, opened down the front. He wore nothing beneath it. His beautiful sienna skin glistened in the candlelight as he moved to me, his face set without expression. I did not speak. Dayal dropped the robe from his shoulders and sat next to me. He smelled of incense, sweet and dark. Placing his hands beneath my shoulders, he pulled me up, his movements deliberate, but tender. I wrapped my arms around his neck. His hands moved behind me, loosening the tie that held my gown. He slipped it from my shoulders and free of my body. For a few moments we embraced, content at the touch from each other's skin. Then, he started kissing me, my lips, my breasts, and the soft skin of my abdomen. A low moan settled in my throat. On hearing it, Dayal gently spread my legs and lay between them. I wrapped myself around him and pulled him towards me. There was a sharp pain followed by a warm sensation. It was terrible and it was wonderful, so primitive. Part of me wished to cry in pleasure whilst another part of my essence wanted to vanish.

When the moment was finished, he lay by my side until sunrise. Without speaking, he got up, put on his robe and left as silently as he had entered. It felt surreal. Had this actually happened or was it only a wishful dream? The soreness I felt answered my doubts. Dayal is now my lover.

January 25, 1798

Dayal did not come to me last night. I will be patient. I know he will come again to my bed.

Mother has been brooding about the house. She seems distracted. She said she has grown weary of staying in the house and arranged for the servant girls to take us on an outing so we can explore the geography of the area. Much to my surprise and delight, Dayal and his interpreter joined us as well.

Although clear and sunny, the weather had remained cold so we dressed accordingly. Dayal wore a heavy white smock with baggy trousers. Mother and I donned fur-lined coats and hats. The interpreter's garb seemed a bit light for my taste, but he didn't appear uncomfortable and turned down our offer of a coat as if insulted.

Dayal's attitude toward me was only cordial, betraying no other emotion. I thought that wise even though I yearned for a secret glance or touch as he took us around the village. Through the interpreter, Dayal pointed out homes of the oldest residents. I asked the interpreter where he had learned to speak English. He said that Dayal's brother, who had been educated in England, taught him. When I asked where the brother was, he said 'gone' and then abruptly left me to point out something to my mother.

After seeing the village, we walked over a hill and down into a small ravine which ended in a circular flat area surrounded by cliffs. At its center were the ruins of an ancient temple. Pillars which had crumbled into ragged fragments formed a ring around a central stone alter. Stairs descended from it into the earth. Intricate carvings decorated the altar and stairway. They were obscene, but I did manage to get a good look at them before mother skirted me away. Men and women in various sexual positions leered from the stone. Those that weren't engaged in sex exposed their genitalia. On the neck of each person was a carapaced insect. I was about to ask the interpreter about the strange bug when mother pulled me away. I told her I wanted to go down the steps to see what was below. Before she could stop me, I headed down the stairs. Dayal rushed in front of me and held up his hands to stop my progress. He rattled something to the interpreter who said, "It is not for you to go down there, Lady. It is not for foreign eyes." I admit I was agitated by Dayal's actions, but there was a wildness in his look that made me stop and walk back up.

When we returned home and Dayal and the interpreter left us, mother told me she thought it rude and tasteless for Dayal to have shown us the carvings and just as inappropriate to have stopped me from going down the steps. What could we care about his ungodly religion anyway?

I was put off by the incident, but, as the evening progressed, I cooled down. When mother came to say goodnight, she looked lonely. I knew she missed my father.

I will stop for now and sleep, hoping that Dayal will come to me once again.

January 28, 1798

The last few days have been a blur, enshrouded in the passion that Dayal has brought to me.

He came on the night of my last entry and on each of the following nights. The scenario is always the same: I awake in the early morning hours to find him standing at my door. He enters, disrobes himself and me, and then proceeds with new and wonderful ways of lovemaking. It is as if the temple carvings have come to life in my bed.

Since my period is nearing its end, I wonder if he will continue to visit my bed if the threat of pregnancy exists.

Mother acts even stranger than before. I don't believe she has any notion of what goes on between Dayal and me. The fact that she sleeps through the night like a dead soul may be due to alcohol or even drugs. One night I awoke earlier than usual and heard voices coming from the living room. I got up to investigate and saw mother and the interpreter, whose name I discovered is Sanjay, talking. They were speaking softly so I could not catch their conversation. They had teacups in their hands. I noticed mother sipped at hers while I never saw Sanjay drink any of his. At one point, mother set her cup down and placed a hand to her head as if to swoon. Sanjay helped her up and to her bedroom then came back and took the cups away for cleaning. I wonder if Dayal is having her drugged so he can come and go unnoticed.

One point of interest, dear diary, is disturbing. I have not seen any of the soldiers father left behind. Being young, perhaps they have women of their own in the village or maybe they have become neglectful of their duties. I'm certain father would tan their hides if he knew about their behavior.

I will close for now.

January 29, 1798

Mother has informed me why the soldiers are gone.

Sanjay gave her some information about a rumor spreading from village to village. A group of bandits with a distinctly murderous leader are raiding in the southeast and could possibly come across my father's expedition. This group of raiders is made up of Deceivers, meaning they were part of a larger group known as Thuggees who worship Kali the goddess of plagues, destruction, and violent death. These Thugs are especially feared because of their habit of garroting victims before stealing their possessions. Sanjay explained to my mother that the leader had a singular dislike for the British, especially those connected with the East India Company. Evidently the man blamed the death of his family on the Company. Before that time, the leader had been very helpful to the British government.

At the urging of Dayal, my mother had the remaining soldiers sent to join my father in case trouble should arrive. "Let me tell you, Andrea," she said, "I was uneasy about the whole affair, but what choice did I have? Had it not been for the medicine Sanjay has given me for my late night tea, I'm certain I would have suffered the vapors."

Whatever drug had been administered to Mother served my nights with Dayal as well, but now I cannot help a feeling of dread in regard to father's expedition. I can only pray, dear diary, he will return to us unharmed.

January 31, 1798

Almost two days have passed and I have not seen Dayal or Sanjay. Perhaps the fact that my cycle is finished has kept Dayal from my body, but I do not understand why he has avoided mother and me altogether, and Sanjay never missed a day of checking in on us. The situation is odd, made stranger by the sudden snowstorm that has bested the natural geographic protection of the village. The winds howl a ghastly wail, day and night. Ice and snow pepper the roof and walls of the house in a continual staccato rapping.

The serving girls still see to our daily food and cleaning needs. They seem to look at me differently, as if they know of my sexual liaisons with Dayal. Just now and again I will catch a flash of jealous anger from their eyes. Could it be they are Dayal's concubines? That I have taken him away from their beds? If so, will I be able to trust them, or am I becoming suspicious due to the isolation in this storm?

Melancholy does have the better of me, and mother's progressively distracted state only makes my loneliness more intense. Maybe Dayal has not come because of the storm. If that is the reason, it is an odd one indeed. I do not understand how passion could be so easily tempered.

I will close for now, dear diary, but I doubt sleep will come tonight. Besides my longing for Dayal, there is my father's continued absence to dwell on. Not to mention this horrid storm. If demons exist, they are full of hunger and seek entrance to our home on this icy night.

February 2, 1798

Last night I had a disturbing dream.

I was back in England standing by a small pond adjacent to our house. Father and I have been fishing there many times. Surrounded by trees and wildflowers, it is a place of quiet contemplation for me as well. In my dream, the trees are still, not one leaf disturbed by wind. The pond, however, is in turmoil with rolling waves that boil above the surface. A solitary figure occupies a small boat. I move closer and see it is Dayal who is dressed in formal affair: a top hat and tails grace his upper body. Strangely, he wears the same baggy trousers he had on the day he showed Mother and me around the village. He holds a long fishing pole and struggles to land his catch from the turbulent waters. The pole is bent to the extreme, attesting to a large creature on the hook below the surface. Dayal senses my presence. He turns, tips his hat, and smiles grotesquely. With his free hand, he reaches in the water and pulls out his catch. A human head dangles on the end of the line. Wet hair is plastered to the sides of the face. Its swollen eyes bulge. The nose and ears have been eaten away. Attached to its cheeks are clumps of the insects I saw in the carvings at the ruined temple. The mouth opens to speak. Thick dark gore rushes from it. It is my father's head. "So good of you to come, my dear," Dayal says in a sharp British accent. "Your father has told me so much about you." Dayal then laughs a high piercing cackle as he swings the grinning head back and forth like a hideous pendulum.

I awoke to the screaming of the wind. The day only worsened.

Although only one of the servant girls has come of late, she has managed adequate meals for us. Mother consumes hers like a ravished wolf, never conversing between her hurried bites. The general gloom has killed my appetite. I can only pick at my food.

Before the girl left tonight, she tried to communicate with me. Her actions seemed desperate, but I could make no sense of them. She finally gave up, shrugged, and left.

Dayal and Sanjay have still not shown themselves. Perhaps they have left the village to search for my father and his party. I need to make an effort to lift Mother's and my own spirits. This custom of being trapped by my depression must cease no matter what nightmares I suffer in dreams to come.

February 6, 1798

Dear diary the world has turned to ashes. Whether this will be my last entry lies in the hands of a bandit.

The day after my wretched dream, I was awakened by my mother's screams. Somehow a young soldier from my father's expedition, a Sergeant Miles, had managed to make it back to the village despite being seriously wounded. Mother had answered his knocking. I found him lying on his back with my shocked mother kneeling beside him. A gaping wound extended down the whole right side of his chest. Dark blood bubbled from the torn tissue. A pale figure near death, he tried to speak through the pink foam on his lips but could only rasp unintelligibly. He must have traveled in great pain to warn us. "We must get our things together and leave immediately," Mother screeched hysterically. As I tried to calm her, the sergeant let out a gasp, then convulsed violently and died leaving his eyes wide and empty. Mother clasped her hands to her face. "Oh, lord. Oh, my lord," she whispered. I managed to calm her enough to be able to go out and look for help.

The winds had abated. A cover of thick gray clouds accumulated above. The contrast of dark sky and thin light brought a picture of desolation. No living being stirred. The village looked deserted.

I moved from door to door, but no one answered my knocks. I became frantic and pounded wildly on the doors. Still, there was no response. I sat in front of one of the homes, placed my head in my hands and wept. As darkness approached, I knew we must plan our next action. Should we stay in hopes that father would arrive, or leave, placing ourselves in jeopardy because of ignorance of the terrain? We certainly could go nowhere that night. To travel in darkness would only amplify our danger.

When I returned to our house, Mother was sitting in a chair, staring blankly ahead. I tried to talk to her but even a sharp slap could not bring back her senses. I tired and slumped in a chair. I looked at the sergeant's body and thought how sad it was that one so young should die so far from home.

How capricious life is. A few nights ago I experienced pleasure with my strange lover, felt warm and protected, fulfilled as never before. Now, cold despair held me. I sensed that I might fade away and vanish into the air of hopelessness around me.

My father, Dayal, and Sanjay arrived on horseback the next morning.

I spent a sleepless night concerned with the disposal of the corpse in our house. When I finally managed to doze, the sound of approaching horses awakened me.

I opened the front door and saw three riders coming into the village. The horses exhibited a confused erratic gate. At first, I couldn't make out who the riders were, but then I recognized my father's coat. I ran toward them, rejoicing at our rescue.

As I came closer to the horses, I realized something was very wrong. They milled in front of Dayal's house, whinnying and jerking their bridles. Their riders sat rigid with rigor mortis. My father, Dayal, and Sanjay had been tied to wooden poles. Each had been strangled. A large black bruise ringed their necks. Their eyes had been cut out, leaving sockets filled with clotted blood that dried in dark red tears streaming down the sides of their faces.

I stood transfixed as the horses, frightened by their ghastly burdens, moved about in nervous agitation. I sensed someone stood behind me and turned to find my mother. "James," she said irritably, "you come down this instant. Why, the very idea of leaving us here in the care of savages. I think we should pack up and leave immediately. Do you hear me, James? I said immediately!" She continued to babble, moving back and forth around the horse my father's body was on. She turned and looked directly at me and said in a high-pitched squeal, "We must get some tea, Andrea. All your father needs is a little tea to make him right as rain. You'll see, right as rain." She collapsed at my feet. The sound of her fall caused the horses to bolt away toward the pass where we had walked with Dayal and Sanjay only a few days before.

I managed to guide mother back to house. I sat her down then dragged the sergeant's reeking body outside. I had no idea where to find a shovel, so I could not give the boy a decent burial. In truth, I don't know if I would have had the strength necessary to dig a grave. Now without father or fellow countrymen, I felt defeated. I went into the house, walked past my mother, and fell exhausted into bed. All hope had ridden away with the dead men.

My dreams were rambling things, a frightening ride into the abyss. I felt my body struggling for consciousness, but my mind refused to leave the safety of sleep. I was literally pulled from my slumber by the strong arms of a man who stood beside me. He was dressed in heavy canvas clothing. A small turban was strapped tightly around his head. He yanked me up and stared coldly at me. A string of incomprehensible words flew from his mouth. I was still in a daze, and my surprised stare only irritated him further. He grabbed and shook me. I heard my mother sobbing from another room. I shot up, startling the man holding me, and I broke free. I rushed toward the sound of mother's voice. In the living room were other men dressed the same as the one in my bedroom who caught up to me, grabbed me from behind and screamed in my ear.

Two of the men held mother down. I yelled at them to release her. Mother, upon hearing me, looked up and started screaming. We struggled to break free. Our captors found our resistance amusing. They laughed at us.

One of the men approached me. By his superior dress and the silence that transpired, I knew he was the leader. Standing taller than the others, his presence reminded me of Dayal's stature. One look at his face was all I needed. He could have, indeed, been a relative of Dayal.

The room was quiet except for a pitiful sob from my mother. The man before me issued an order, and my mother was gagged. The leader turned back to me. Small patches of scars dotted his granite face. His eyes were full of hate. He removed a kerchief from his pocket and gagged me as well. He spoke English with a heavy accent and said, "Gags and death are the only way to quiet a screeching British bitch!" He then put his face close to mine and whispered, "Watch what we do to British bitches in heat."

He barked another order, and the man directly in front of my mother disrobed. The odor of his unclean body filled the room with stench. The men holding my mother spread her legs as the naked savage tore her undergarments away. My mother's eyes widened, and her struggles intensified. The leader snatched me from the other man's hold, forcing me close to mother so I would have to witness each horrible detail of the rape.

The ravager spit on his hands and stabbed himself into Mother. She pitched her body spasmodically as the man grabbed her shoulders and thrust himself deeper, grinding and grunting like a pig. He ripped her blouse away and bit her breasts and nipples as he climaxed. Blood ran in slow streams from her torn skin.

Each of the men then took their turn in raping her. All, except their leader. I tried to lower my head away from the horrors, but my captor jerked it up and pulled my eyes open. After they were through with her, my mother lay still. Her eyes open, her expression blank. Had it not been for the soft rising of her breast, I would have thought her already dead. She was a discarded torn doll covered with the men's sweat, her breasts and body bleeding from the inflicted bites of passion. The leader issued another command, and two of the men lifted her upper body from the floor. Her head flopped forward for a moment, then, she raised it and looked at me. "And this is what we do to all bastard British," the leader spat in my ear. One of the men approached Mother from behind. He held a thickly knotted rope. I uttered a stifled scream through my gag as he looped it around her neck and pulled back with killing force. Her hands grasped in desperation at the rope around her throat. The strangled air trapped in her throat rasped as she twitched in a dance of death. At that moment, her hair strewn wildly about her face, I witnessed the primal craving for life. Only raw animal instinct remained and struggled violently for the air needed to stay alive. Finally, she fell forward, limp, a swollen purple tongue protruding from her mouth, her eyes fixed and void. The assailant took the rope from her neck and pushed her body away.

I felt myself fainting. The leader shook me and screamed to keep me awake. He pushed my shaking form back toward the bedroom. I was thrown on the bed, and there I resigned to let him have his way in the hope of pleasing him enough not to be killed immediately. He stood looking at me for a few unbearable moments then reached out to grab me. I jumped back, but his intentions were only to remove my gag. I looked at him with as much hate and loathing as I could muster. He seemed only amused.

"I could use this gag to kill you," he said with cold malice.

"Go ahead then," I responded with pale conviction. "It seems easy for you to prevail over women as you did with my mother!" I tried to hold back the tears but one slid slowly down my cheek. He laughed and I lunged at him. "She was innocent you coward!" I screamed and beat at his chest with my fists. He shoved me back.

"You will not speak to me of innocence!" He roared, grabbing my wrists. "Not of innocence!" His tight grip remained then he relaxed. A slow composure embraced him. "My brother gave you something that must be returned. He was weak, and it was not his to give. Dayal was always tempted by the sweetness between a woman's legs. Even from one, whose people killed our parents."

This was the man Sanjay had spoken of? Dayal's brother who had attended school in England? "You are Dayal's brother?" I asked.

He held up his hand to silence me. "You will not," he demanded, "speak yet. Not until you are ready to return the necklace. Really, it has no value for you. How could my mother's necklace be anything more than a trinket to a spoiled child of the Company?"

The necklace. His mother's necklace. I was astonished. "You murdered your brother because of a necklace?"

He slapped me. My face stung but I realized he was not ready to kill me, not until I gave up the necklace.

"I will have it back," he growled then flipped me on my stomach. He reached under my skirt and pulled down my undergarments. He sodomized me. The pain was terrible. My breath left me with the humiliation and injury, only a strangled sob escaped my throat.

When he finished he said, "I will return, and you will gladly tell me. Yes, and you will beg me to kill you afterwards."

Then, he was gone. I was left torn and bleeding. I could only stare at the trunk against the wall where I had hidden the necklace from my mother in a small secret compartment.

February 10, 1798

The man who holds me captive is the bandit Vairaja.

For the past four days he has kept me confined to my room, allowing me out only to go to relieve myself. He has sodomized me repeatedly with no attempt at normal intercourse. He has been brutal and relentless in his search for the necklace, but I will not relinquish my only advantage.

On one occasion he ransacked my room, but the compartment in my trunk held its hidden treasure through all of his berserk rampaging.

He threw up his hands and left in a rage.

February 11, 1798

Last night there was a meeting in the living room. I could hear angry voices arguing. After a while there was silence. The acrid smell of smoke permeated the air. Vairaja must have been smoking a narcotic plant. When he came to my room, he was subdued, not annoyed. His eyes were puffy and dreamlike. He spoke in a whisper to me in his native tongue. It was as if Dayal had returned. He made love to me slowly, with care, and I loved him back. It was not a murderer who filled me; it was my lover's ghost, returning through his brother's drugged body.

When he finished, Vairaja fell into a deep sleep. I could have cut his throat. I curse myself for not doing so. Had I suffered so much to actually believe Dayal had returned in his hateful brother's body?

I got out of bed and walked into the living room then out the front door into the night. The guards must have smoked the same plant as no one attempted to stop me.

The air was still. The moon sat austere against a cold sky. In its brittle light, I saw the body of my mother on the ground. As I approached, I heard something scurry and saw flashes of red and yellow animal eyes, scavengers that growled lowly at my intrusion. I circled around then headed for the ravine at the edge of town.

Eventually I stood on the center slab of the ruined temple. Something the size of a large dog lay on the altar stone. When it became aware of my presence, it stood on all four legs and raised its head in a mournful howl. In a second it was gone, leaving me alone by the altar.

The carvings and broken stones were outlined by the moonlight. Each stark ray pointed to the steps Dayal had forbidden me to descend. At the bottom of the steps, direct moonlight illuminated a large door. I walked down to it. Like the crumbling walls of the temple, ornate carvings also adorned the door. I pulled on its large ring, but the door was stuck in place by years of neglect. I struggled to pull it open. Sweat broke out on my cold skin and I shuddered. Someone grabbed me from behind. I turned into the strange stare of Vairaja. His expression was a pale effigy of marble. Without speaking, he moved me aside and pulled at the door which, with reluctance, groaned open. As if from some long dead putrefying lungs, a rush of foul air covered us.

Vairaja went ahead of me. He entered the vault and faded into the darkness. He came back holding a lighted torch. He took my hand and led me into the vault. I was not afraid as I glided in a dream of mold and decay.

The walls were lined with torches. Vairaja lit each with his own. Their light filled the room with flickering shadows, the heavy smell of tar and the crackling of flames split the damp silence around us.

A great statue towered at the vault's center. The figure had long flowing hair and four arms. One hand held a sword and another a severed human head, while the other two hands seemed to beckon. Corpses dangled as earrings. A necklace of skulls hung from the neck. Its face was monstrous. Deep red stones were depressed into its eye sockets. The tongue lapped crimson from its mouth.

Vairaja bowed before the form. He whispered "Kali" again and again. In time he stood up, the last murmur of the name withdrawing in a ghostly echo. "She is great and terrible," he said. "She is Kali. She holds the head of Raktavija, the leader of a demon army." Vairaja turned to me, his eyes vacant as he continued, "Kali beheaded him in a fierce battle, but Raktavija had great power as well and each drop of his blood became hordes of devils. Still, Kali claimed victory. She swallowed all of the fiends, draining Raktavija of his blood. Kali then vomited their mass, forming a great gray stone. She covered it with a bubble of blood, trapping the demons inside."

Vairaja moved closer to me. I could feel his warm breath on my face. His eyes cleared. "But even Kali cannot save us from you damned British," he said flatly. "One of my scouts has brought news of a large group of British soldiers moving steadily toward us. They have superior weapons."

Vairaja turned back to the figure of Kali. "My father sent me to England. He wanted me to be educated there. He felt that our cultures should learn from one another and that we could exist peacefully and develop trade. But, he could not imagine the greed and malice of the British." He faced me once again. "Kali has come to me in a dream. She has instructed me to impregnate a British woman. She told me that the child will bring a terrible plague to the British and that I am to help the mother of this child release the demons of Raktavija in preparation of the savior's coming."

Now I knew why he made love to me. But to believe the madness of his dream only proved Vairaja's insanity. I was certain of this until he took my arm and led me behind the statue. A large square area had been cut from the base of the figure. A massive lump covered by a membrane resembling an insect cocoon sat in the recessed area. Vairaja removed a small curved dagger from his waistband and placed it in my hand. He then guided me to place the tip of the blade just beneath the casing, removing it as easily as one would uncover a sleeping child. Exposed was a pumpkin shaped object. Instead of a bright orange shell, the thing was a mixture of ugly grays like it was rotten. Whether it was a trick of the shadows or my imagination, the object undulated as if something struggled to break free from it.

Vairaja whispered in my ear, "You must be Pandora, opening her box of miseries. You must be the creator and destroyer Shiva from whom all is and continues to be." He moved my hand forward, slicing through the outer shell of the gourd shaped object. A cloud of smoke was expelled. The vault filled with thousands of tiny bodies, insects that covered me and Vairaja. They were the same creatures I had seen in the carvings only more infantile. Voracious from years of hunger they bit and tore my flesh. They drained my blood as they did Vairaja's.

Before collapsing, I saw broken rays of moonlight through the flowing mass as it pushed down the vault door with the might of its ancient hunger.

* * *

Whether today is actually the 11th of February I cannot substantiate. I dated my entry as a matter of chronology.

After passing into unconsciousness from the assault of the insects, I awakened in my bedroom. Bites covered my body. I had difficulty rising because of dizziness from blood loss. The creatures had not taken enough to kill me, but I was weakened. I don't think Vairaja, if he is still alive, would have possessed enough strength to bring me back to the house.

How did I get here? Have days passed unknown to me? Did I somehow manage through instinct to make my way home?

The effort of writing is exhausting.

I must rest.

February? 1798

I have no idea what day of the month it is. It may not even still be February.

I suffer from high fever and bouts of oblivion. I cannot comprehend the passing of time. I must have had seizures as my room is in total disarray. It is all I can do to pull myself from bed to write this.

I should be starving but all I feel is a strange thirst. Maybe I am a ghost, unaware of my own death.

I must stop because of fatigue once again.

. . . will no longer attempt to date these entries. There is no point.

I am dying, of that I have no doubt. I feel I have no connection with the physical world and that I am floating.

An animal's corpse lies in the middle of the room. It has a wretched marvelous stink.

It is difficult to concentrate. My brain is on fire and all light is painful. My throat is aching and parched but the thought of water is dreadful.

The sound of scraping feet resonates in the darkness. Groans of hunger are joined with my own. Vairaja appears through the blackness. His face is strained and pale. His touch icy. We kiss each other on the neck and taste the saltiness of our blood. I must drink for two. My belly swells.

. . . I no longer see the day. Only shadows bring comfort. The dead walk around me, their howls of hunger are ghastly. My child's wails are silent in the womb.

DR. GLENN RUSSELL, ROUND ROCK, TEXAS

1995

1

The small emergency clinic where I moonlight three days a week had been quiet since just after the witching hour. I dozed off in the front office.

All hell broke loose when the screaming woman came in.

The girl, of not more than sixteen years, had been rushed to the trauma room by the night nurse. When I walked in the room, I almost slipped in a large pool of the girl's blood. I could see there was probably more on the floor than in the child's body.

A young man of about the same age stood fidgeting in the corner of the room. While starting what treatment I could, I learned from him the girl was his sister. He said she had suffered a bad abortion, but, in my judgment, the hack that performed this brutality went way beyond bad.

The girl appeared to have been gutted, the fetus ripped away by a powerful force, leaving ragged tissue behind. She convulsed on the table making it difficult for me to stabilize her. I yelled at the nurse to get two IVs of Ringer's started immediately and to have the blood bank bring down four units of O negative, ASAP.

Before the nurse made it to the medication room, the girl's convulsions abruptly stilled. She reached one bloody hand to her mouth as if to catch the last escaping breath, and then she died.

It happened so quickly, before I could do anything to help. I turned to ask the brother some more questions, but he was gone. I went out of the room to find him. He must have panicked and bolted.

When I went back to the trauma room, the nurse was pale and shaking. The dead girl's eyes were open and fixed on the nurse. "After you left," the nurse said in a whisper, "she moved her eyes."

"Just an involuntary reaction," I said with a shiver as I walked over and closed them. I never got used to the tricks a dead body can play.

I heard the outer doors opening and hoped that the brother had returned, but it was not the boy, just another trauma case. A worker at a metal plant had a significant laceration of his right hand. While I attended to the man, I told the nurse to notify the police about the girl's death. The injury to the hand would require surgery, so I called the clinic operator and advised her to alert the surgeon on call. By the time he got there, the police and the coroner had arrived.

They went through their routine: What happened? Did it appear that foul play (no shit!) had occurred? What did the brother look like? Had I seen him before? Would I recognize him again? Their questioning went on for the better part of an hour.

They thanked me and advised that since the girl appeared to have been murdered the body would be sent to Dallas for an autopsy. They also said they would need me to come downtown to look at some mug shots.

I went to the police station just after my shift ended, sorted through what seemed a never-ending array of pictures but could not identify the dead girl's brother. Again I was thanked and told that I would be contacted if needed.

They never called me back. A few months rolled by and I assumed they must have come to their own conclusions. Oddly, I never saw the incident mentioned in the paper. I might have missed it since I tend to be half asleep when I read the news. I suppose it might have been mentioned on television, but I haven't owned one of those idiot boxes since my divorce.

Events in the emergency room continued in their fickle manner. No case I saw after that night was as gruesome, and the affair was eventually diluted in the jumble of cuts and bruises that came my way for treatment.

2

Before I made my way to Round Rock, I was a partner in a small general practice clinic just outside of Dallas, Texas. The practice was thriving, and all seemed well until my wife, Janice, became restless.

She got into aerobics. She also got into her instructor as well. Turns out they were doing exercises everywhere but the gym. The day I caught them in the garage, on a weight bench of all things, I actually thought I had walked into the neighbor's by mistake and was about to apologize when I noticed Janice looking up from under the dripping instructor and of all the things to say she just smiled and asked, "Home early, dear?"

I had not seen this coming. I was in such a state of shock that she managed to file on me before I knew what happened. Papers were thrown in front of me to sign. They might as well have been written in hieroglyphics. After the storm of lawyers and courts, I found myself sitting alone in an empty house, with only a half-eaten can of cat food for company. Seems Janice had taken her pussy with her.

My parents were consoling, but of no help. They were in that time of life where the realization of old age and all the things that go downhill with it stared at them from the mirror each day.

My work habits suffered. I couldn't get out of my depression. One of my colleagues at the clinic became concerned enough to suggest I talk with a friend of his who was doing some work in the Austin area. I think it was a kind hint that I find somewhere else to practice.

So I took the nudge before something embarrassing occurred. After all, the relationship with my fellows had been a good one. No sense in burning bridges. The more I thought about it, a change to a different area, and one a good distance away from Janice, seemed like a good idea.

I accepted a position at a satellite clinic near Austin between Georgetown and Round Rock. This was convenient as it allowed me the opportunity to fill my hours with moonlighting at the various hospitals and emergency rooms in the area.

I decided to rent an old farmhouse just east off interstate 35, a major highway that snaked through Texas. There were some scant acres of land involved, but the owner was more interested in renting the house. We came to the understanding that if the land eventually sold, the house would go with it and I would have to find somewhere else to live.

The house was an aging structure; a kind of Gothic ranch style affair. It was built on a grand scale, with high ceilings, a spacious living room, two bedrooms, and a large bathroom. These dominated the small kitchen, but that was fine; I wouldn't be cooking much or entertaining guests. I just wanted to work and stay isolated.

One of the striking features of the house was the ornately carved porch railings, windows and roof trims. It reminded me of a gingerbread house with a sinister atmosphere as if from a Grimm fairy tale. Other than the need of a little paint and some minor repairs, the home was in decent condition.

The land around the house was another story. Spreading out beyond a fenced yard and gravel drive, the ghosts of former crops, weeds, vines, and wild Bermuda grass populated the few acres that remained. It was dry and desolate and just the seclusion I needed.

After the first year of living and working in my new location, the medical community selected me to be part of a group assigned to inspect clinics that offered abortions. I advised the committee that Obstetrics and Gynecology were not my strongest areas, but they explained I would be involved in judging whether or not the proper counseling and waiting periods were being observed by the clinics.

These inspections started as autumn descended on the Lone Star state. The days were brisk with the smells of fall. The nights were chilly with the promise of colder days to come.

3

The committee decided to give us ten clinics each. The first nine I inspected were diligent in their methods. I could find nothing wrong in their procedures, and I discovered no documented incidents in their records.

By the time I got my last assignment, the better part of September had drifted away.

Located off a state county road, the Branson Medical Complex seemed a bit out of place. I suppose the rapid growth of Austin and its surrounding communities would soon bring a more suburban atmosphere to the clinic, but approaching it down Pond Springs Cemetery Road bestowed a certain gloom to the spot. A sort of "The Munsters Go To Medical School" impression. However, as it was my last clinic, I drew near with more relief than dread.

Sure enough, there were no creaking door hinges, howling wolves, or squeaking bats. Instead the clinic was a clean, well organized place. The staff was friendly and cooperative. They appeared to adhere to OCEA guidelines and legal restrictions.

When I completed my assessment, one of the nurses directed me to an empty exam room where I could fill out a preliminary report to which the chief physician, a Dr. Lockley, was entitled. It was late in the day and the majority of the staff had departed.

The nurse returned and informed me that Dr. Lockley had left earlier for a hospital consult in Austin. She said that his assistant would be in shortly to pick up the preliminary report. Soon a man close to my age came in, introduced himself as Dr. Kraig, took the report from me and left with the promise he would give it to Dr. Lockley first thing in the morning.

As I was about to leave, the janitor came in to clean the room. He spoke then quickly averted his face. I didn't think much of it at the time, but on the drive home I couldn't get what little of his profile I had seen out of my head. I was certain I recognized him and just couldn't put my finger on from where.

The next day I received an early call from Dr. Lockley. I had failed to cover an item dealing with counseling offered to a patient seeking an abortion in my report. He asked if I could stop by after my clinic hours and clear it up. Although I didn't relish making the drive back to the dreary locale, I knew he would not discuss the issue on the phone because of patient privacy rules so I agreed to come by later that afternoon.

I arrived just after three o'clock. Except for two cars, the parking lot was deserted. Lockley's secretary, a striking Latino woman who looked to be in her early twenties, greeted me. She explained that the clinic closed at noon that day, but the doctor usually stayed over to catch up on dictation and other paper work. She led me to Lockley's office and smiled as she opened his door. I could only imagine her glance was more than cordial. I should be so lucky.

Lockley sat behind his desk. He stood when I entered and offered his hand. A tall gaunt man he looked no more than fifty years old. His hair was blonde and trimmed. His appearance was neat.

"Sorry for the inconvenience, Dr. Russell," he said, releasing my hand.

"No trouble at all," I answered. "Now what point did you need covered on my report?"

His office door opened and the janitor I thought I had recognized from the day before entered.

"Is this the man, James?" Lockley asked.

The young man nodded.

"Thank you, James," Lockley continued, "you can go now."

I knew then where I had seen the man before. That night, the night the young woman came into the emergency room butchered from an attempted abortion, he was the one who brought her and then disappeared.

"I'm afraid we have a delicate situation to resolve, Dr. Russell." Lockley sat down and gestured for me to do the same.

"I've seen that man before," I said. "The police were trying to locate him. His sister died in the emergency room when I was on duty."

"He remembered you. That is why I asked you to come in."

"So this has nothing to do with my report?"

"No."

"I'm confused. What was the outcome of the police investigation involving this James?"

Lockley advised me that James had told him about our brief encounter yesterday and that the young man was concerned I would alert the police if I remembered the night his sister died.

"His sister's death was an unfortunate event," Lockley observed in an odd, almost distracted, tone. "She was scheduled for her abortion here. James had arranged it since he knew and worked with us. But the girl's lover found out and went into a rage at what she was going to do. He cut the fetus out of her. He said anyone who didn't want his child should not live. I believe he was quite deranged and psychotic."

"So her lover was arrested?"

Lockley sighed, "James panicked. He never should have brought his sister to the hospital that night."

I was mystified. "I don't understand, doctor. What has this to do with me? Do the police need another statement?"

Lockley poured a glass of water for himself then offered one to me which I refused.

"This girl's lover," he said after a drink, "comes from a powerful family in Austin. They have strong political and economic connections."

"But surely not that influential."

"I'm afraid you're a bit naïve in regard to what can be done when a family has the amount of clout this one does. This isn't fiction or some movie, Dr. Russell. Even you can appreciate what leaders of governments and cities can accomplish and what they can arrange."

I suppose I was naïve to a point. My ex-wife's activities made an argument for that. I knew what presidents and dictators could do, that genocide exists in places we are unfamiliar with, that money is misappropriated, and all the other dark dealings in the world, but I had witnessed the death of that poor girl. How could nothing be done? I felt my anger rise.

"Just who are these people, these pricks who are above the law?" I said with a noticeable edge.

Lockley frowned, "Well, I cannot name names, Dr. Russell. I don't think prick is quite appropriate, however." He looked directly at me, like I was being scolded. "Let's just say they have whatever it takes to cover up any scandal."

"So their son just goes about his daily business now?"

"Not exactly. They had him admitted to a psychiatric facility where he could receive help," Lockley answered, looking very pleased.

"This is incredible. What about the girl's family?"

"James was all she had," Lockley said. "Because of some past criminal activities he had been charged with, James felt he should not press the issue."

Lockley directed his last statement to me. To make sure I understood he added, "I realize it is a lot to ask, Dr. Russell, but I wonder if I might rely on your professional discretion. The family I mentioned is willing to help your future career. Besides, any attempt to right this matter is, I assure you, futile."

This time I gave him a cold smile. "How do you know I haven't already tried to right the matter?"

He laughed softly. "Because they haven't contacted me."

"If you're in bed with them, whoever they are, they must be doing some favor for you. The same type of favor they will do for me, right?"

"Well, we do have some research projects here at the clinic. Some of these projects would ordinarily be difficult to fund. So, yes, I have had some mutual dealings with said individuals." Lockley then further explained, "Before the girl's untimely death though."

"This is unbelievable," I almost shouted as I stood. "And no, you will not be able to depend on my professional courtesy. I will report this to the police. I can't imagine a person of your training simply dismissing this."

Lockley shrugged and made a gesture to the door, dismissing me with a wave. "Well, if you must, you must."

I answered that indeed I must and headed toward the door. I felt a sharp sting. I don't remember touching the doorknob.

4

I was in and out of consciousness for some time. I experienced hallucinatory dream states. In them I felt restrained.

One dream was particularly disturbing: I was at my home in Richardson, Texas. The room was dark except for the receding rays of twilight filtering through the window blinds. There was only one piece of furniture in the room—the kitchen table. My ex-wife sat there. Her head and face were as I remembered, but her lower body was that of a bloated cat. She gazed at me while she licked the remaining morsels from an open can of cat food and purred with a rasp as her tail flipped against a table leg.

It was enough to awaken me.

I was strapped to an examining table. The room was dark, the door to the adjoining office open. Lockley talked to his secretary there. He somehow sensed I had come around.

"Well, Maria," he said, "it seems Dr. Russell is awake."

I raised my head and saw him standing in the doorway silhouetted in the light behind him. He flicked on the light to the room where I lay. It took a moment for me to adjust my eyes. By the time I could see plainly, Lockley stood beside me.

Still dazed from the drug that had been injected, I asked, "What exactly do you want?"

Lockley smiled. "Nothing now that we have you, Dr. Russell."

"You know I will be missed. I was to moonlight in the emergency room tonight, not to mention my daily duties at the clinic."

"We have some people filling in for you, Dr. Russell, colleagues that owe us a favor, those who work with us. You see, you'll not be missed at all."

I felt too drained to fight, but I knew it was my only hope.

"Listen, you fucker!" I hissed. "Untie me. I mean right now!"

Lockley grinned down at me.

"Do you have shit in your ears, asshole?" I tried to scream. "I said untie me. Right fucking now!"

I struggled as Lockley bent down, "No need to be insulting," he said, his face next to mine.

Lockley grabbed my head and wrenched it to the right. Then, he bit me. His teeth tore into my neck. I could hear him chewing and slurping my blood like a wild dog. I was left breathless by an intense orgasm followed by a sinking sensation. Just before I passed out, I heard a voice plead with him, "Stop. Stop before you . . . !"

* * *

I awoke to a strange bubbling noise. The pain in my head and neck was excruciating. I was no longer restrained and could move my arms and legs. I stirred slowly as any attempt to reposition myself resulted in more pain.

I had been placed, ironically enough, in a blood donor chair. Through nausea I raised my head. Around me was a large laboratory. Lined against the walls were rows of aquarium tanks. It was the constant murmur of their water pumps I had heard before. The dim light in the room came from the bulbs inside the tanks. And there was something else in them.

I thought my eyes were playing tricks on me. In the semi-darkness it appeared that each tank held two to three developing human embryos.

"Your eyes do not deceive you, Dr. Russell." Lockley's voice came from the darkness. "What you see is very real." He walked out of the shadows and stood in front of one of the tanks. "Don't they look delicious?" he asked, tapping on the glass and pointing like a gourmet peering at a prospective lobster.

A strange urge rushed through me. For a dreadful instant, they did look luscious, so much so that I drooled.

My body shook and a flood of repulsion swept over me as I realized I wanted to eat those things in the tanks. I tried to speak but my throat was sore and swollen. I touched it with my hand and felt the gash surrounded by puffy tissue from the bite. I managed to whisper, "What is happening to me?"

Lockley turned from the tank and smiled, the light from the aquarium reflecting on his slightly prominent canines. He knew I had seen his teeth. "That's right," he said, his smile fading.

I tried to respond but a strong spasm seized my larynx. The agony of it was so intense I thought I would pass out again. I lay my head back and fought the spinning motion of vertigo.

"It would be better for you to remain silent," Lockley said. "The swelling in your throat is from the virus I introduced into your system. It is a cousin to the Rabies strain but not a killer. In fact, it is more of a resurrector."

Virus? Rabies? What had this bastard done to me?

He approached and I made an attempt to turn my head away from him. He grabbed my face before I could, forcing me to look directly into his.

"You've been here for three days. That might be hard to believe, but it is a fact," he said and released his hold. Too exhausted and ill to resist I could only gaze at him. He seemed pleased at my weakened state and actually patted my hand. "A captive audience," he almost laughed. "How nice."

Lockley moved to the tanks and stood with his back to me. He clasped his hands in contemplation behind him. "I spared you for two reasons," he said. "One is Maria. It's not love in the sense you understand it, but you will learn soon enough what she desires. The other is something I sensed when I was drinking from you." He turned and licked his lips. "By the way, your blood was exquisite. It has been ages since I have feasted on the blood of such a healthy young male as you, Dr. Russell."

His words made my body tingle with pain. I had the perverse notion I wanted him to drink from me again. The sounds in the room became exaggerated. His voice and the bubbling tanks assaulted my eardrums. When I opened my eyes, the dim room light had turned into a blinding sun. All my sensations—smell, touch, hearing, sight, and taste—were exaggerated. I thrashed in the chair and my body shook violently. Calm descended when I stopped breathing. My diaphragm would not move. My lungs screamed for air.

I was dying.

I could feel what urine and feces remained in my body soil my underwear. I sensed myself fading away with Lockley's voice.

Then, oblivion swallowed me.

5

When I awoke, I was in my bed at home.

I felt wretched. Every muscle screamed with protest when I moved. My mouth was dry and raw. My head hurt beyond reason.

The sun was just setting, and a purple twilight extended pastel fingers through the partially opened bedroom blinds.

I had been stripped of my clothing. My body was hot and clammy. I craved water to soothe the dryness in my throat. Gingerly, I got out of bed and made my way toward the bathroom. As I passed the dresser mirror, I gasped at the reflection confronting me.

My hair had grown in length and was a mass of tangles. When I reached to touch it, I saw long fingernails that curled like animal claws.

To avoid scratching my skin, I carefully parted the hair away from my face and was relieved to find my features haggard but unchanged. I thought it odd that I had no beard. With the abundance of hair on my head, I had expected to find a grisly face. The smoothness made it appear as if I had just shaved.

I then did what anyone would reflexively do when looking in the mirror—I smiled. My upper canines were missing. What remained in their place were black gaping holes. I moved my tongue over and around the empty sockets and felt protrusions of new teeth working their way in. The tips were sharp and rigid. The moment I touched them the gums around the developing teeth began to ache.

A parched throat, still mad for a drink of water, moved me away from the mirror toward the bathroom. I felt unusually light as I walked. Examining my body, I found the paunch around my waist had disappeared. Indeed, all the body muscles were tight against me like I possessed no residual fat.

Just as I was about to walk through the bathroom door, I slipped on something wet and sticky. A horrid stench made my stomach roll and my eyes water.

To the side of the door was a silhouette of something on the floor. I flicked on the bathroom light to see through the falling gloom of evening. The decaying body of a large pig lay on the floor in front of me. The animal's body was ravaged with bite marks. Around the room were piles of dried feces and crystallized splotches of urine the pig had expelled trying to escape.

Fighting the odor, I moved closer for a better look at the carcass. I turned the head toward me and was met with a glassy condemning stare from the wide eyes. As I ran my fingers around the neck, I felt something stuck under the bloated skin and removed what looked like two thorny objects. When I examined them closer, a feeling of despair and revulsion overwhelmed me.

They were not thorns.

They were my missing teeth.

I just made it to the toilet before vomiting a large mass of clotted blood. Dizziness struck me. I hugged the toilet afraid I would fly into space. As swiftly as it had arrived, the spinning sensation abated, and, like a dog, I consumed the blood I had vomited.

It was a reflex action. No thought of the repulsive act occurred to me. My body needed nourishment and could not afford to have the undigested mass flushed away.

When I had finished, I scrambled back to the bedroom. The stink was no longer abhorrent. It was enticing and luxurious. I fell on the corpse and gorged myself. Rotten juices and tissue gas exploded into my searching mouth. My lips and chin were sticky with gore. I tore and ate until I lay swollen by the dead animal. Then, I slipped into a sated dreamless sleep.

* * *

I awakened to the sound of someone whispering my name.

When I opened my eyes, I was back in bed and Lockley's secretary, Maria, sat beside me. She ran her fingers gently through my matted hair.

"We'll need to trim this and get you cleaned up," she said softly.

I stared at her, not certain if she were real or only a phantom.

Her skin was dark brown and her hair black, nesting in a pool on each side of her neck. Her deep chocolate eyes regarded me with consideration.

I felt grimy and smelled appalling. I was not presentable for a woman's company.

She held out her hand. "You will be weak, Glenn. I will help you."

It had been so long since I had been addressed by my first name that it echoed with a strange displacement through my head.

"No, please. I think I can manage, I . . . ."

She sensed my shame and placed a finger on my lips to hush me.

She helped me out of bed and led me to the bathroom. My legs shook as she sat me on the closed toilet lid then drew my bath water.

Looking out the door, I noticed the body of the pig had been removed. Only a dark stain remained as proof that it had been there at all.

"What happened to the animal's body?" I asked.

Maria smiled. "No need to be ashamed of your actions, Glenn. All of Dr. Lockley's clan went through the same thing in one way or another. As for the body of the pig, it was removed and incinerated."

"Then you are . . . ?"

"Yes, I am," she answered while pouring bath salts into the steamy water.

"What are we?"

"Dr. Lockley will tell you what you need to know. He takes care of all his children."

She finished preparing my bath. "We'll let the salts sit for a while," she said then walked to the bedroom. Returning with a pair of scissors and nail clippers she added, "Let's get you trimmed up first. You'll find this has to be done more often than you're used to."

Maria stood behind me and started to cut my hair. I watched small tangled clumps fall silently to the floor. The bathroom fogged over from the hot water. It was like being in a sauna, but I was far from relaxed. I felt leaden, limp, and a little nauseous from the clammy heat.

When she finished with my hair and nails, Maria took my hand and helped me into the tub. I felt better as soon as the water touched my body.

Standing in front of me, Maria pulled her dress over her head. She was naked beneath. Her body glistened from the steam. Her breasts were full and firm, the nipples dark and erect. She slipped effortlessly into the tub, the dark mass of her pubic hair disappearing below the line of bubbles in the water.

Where passion should have stirred, I felt only emptiness. I lowered my head, embarrassed by my flaccid response. I sobbed like a disappointed child.

Maria glided behind me. She put her arms around my waist. Her body was like fire against my back. She spoke with reassurance. "This will pass. Your time will come."

"Why didn't he kill me and be done with it? If he was afraid I would cause trouble, why not eliminate me, not leave me in this pitiful state."

"He was going to but he sensed a ruthlessness in you." She began washing me with a sponge, letting the water squeezed from it flow down my body. "The transformation can never destroy all our humanity. If it did, we would be nothing more than mindless beasts." She moved her hands to my head, rubbing the soap into my scalp. "Only the savage hunger that comes when we have gone too long without feeding can overpower our human emotions. Even then we feel remorse after the act." She stopped for a moment then started to rinse the soap from my body. "But some have a genuine taste for killing. Dr. Lockley believes you are one of these. He told me that our race needs more like you—those who can overcome a conscience with rage. He thinks you will be a great leader, and that you will sire an even greater one."

I wanted to tell her how wrong Lockley was, but then I recalled how savagely I had fed on the carrion in my bedroom. Could Lockley sense the darkness in one's soul?

These thoughts brought even more exhaustion to my lethargic body. I felt no need to talk to her anymore and resigned myself to being bathed by the strange and lovely creature behind me.

After Maria had finished washing me, she got out of the tub, dried herself with a towel then helped me out and dried me off as well. She made no attempt to dress and remained naked as she led me back into the bedroom. She put me in a chair and I silently watched her replace the soiled bed linen with clean ones.

The bedroom windows were open slightly and a light breeze brought a pleasant nature to the evening air. Maria lay on the bed and covered herself with a single sheet. She motioned for me to come and lay beside her.

I sat on the edge of the bed and pulled the sheet away from her. I moved my fingers down her throat over her breasts and through the thatch of hair between her legs, but even her beauty could not inspire an erection. I was flooded with shame and turned away.

Maria placed her hands on my face and turned me toward her. "Look at me," she whispered then reached between her legs. She brought her fingers to my lips. "Taste me," she pleaded.

I ran my tongue over the saltiness of her. My nostrils burst with her smell. The same mindless hunger that forced me into a rage of feeding now drove me in sexual fury. We made love like savage animals, grunting and twisting our bodies together. Every nerve ending screamed with pleasure. I convulsed an eternity inside her, spilling what was left of me into the shadows of her womb.

When it was finished, she fell back and I lay beside her. We were covered with sweat and neither of us spoke for a long while. Finally, Maria got out of bed, dressed then turned to me. "Dr. Lockley will be here later to feed you," she said coolly. I wanted to say something, but the words stuck in my throat. "I'll see you at the clinic when you have recovered," she stated flatly then walked out the door.

I had been no more than a drone, ensuring the survival of the species.

I understood instinctively that I would never make love to Maria again, that this would be the last act of sex for me. Of the desires that drive us to live, only a hunger and thirst that begged to be satisfied remained for me.

6

Lockley arrived not long after Maria left. He carried two small packages wrapped in butcher's paper. Blood had soaked through them. As he handed them to me, Lockley licked the excess from his fingers.

I ripped them open. Drool clung to my lips.

"I'll let you eat in peace," he mused then added, "bon appetit!"

I never realized he was gone as I assaulted the slabs of raw meat, tearing and gulping the sweet congealed gore. It was much tastier than the rotten flesh of the pig. I stuffed my stomach until the food backed up into my throat, spilling down its corners in waves of tacky red. I fell into bed and slept like an engorged tick.

The days that followed were mixed with periods of euphoria followed by heavy fatigue that left me sick and ravenous. I had no desire to leave my home.

Lockley came daily with more portions of red, raw meat. I was soon eating more slowly, without the urgent need to consume. As the meals continued, I found I was full and satisfied but something still seemed to be missing.

One day Lockley did not come, nor did he show on the following day. By the time he arrived late in the evening on the third day, I was in a panic from lack of food. I had experienced the need to go out and hunt, but I still could not stand the thought of leaving the house.

When he walked in, he was not surprised at my wild appearance. In fact he seemed smug, like he had expected it. I approached him like a wild man, shaking from the need to eat. I gnashed my growing teeth at him; guttural growls came from my throat.

"I've brought you something," he said, "but you have to settle down if I'm to get her in the house without any trouble. I apologize for not coming the last few days. I had to be certain your appetite would be at its peak."

I calmed some then, knowing I was to be fed.

"You will need to straighten up your appearance a bit," he added, and by the time he returned, I had done as he asked.

The girl looked to be around eighteen. She was nonchalantly popping a wad of gum and regarded me with little interest. She wore a dirty lettered football jacket much too big for her, but I knew her going-steady days were long over. It was clear the girl had been hardened by life on the street.

Lockley whispered something to her. She shrugged and held out a hand for the fold of bills he passed to her. He then led her to the bedroom.

In a few moments, Lockley returned. He walked toward me with a big grin on his face. "I told her it was your first time," he giggled. "If she only knew."

I was in no shape to share his joke. All I could think of was the meat waiting for me.

When I walked in the room, the girl was slipping off her panties. She had already removed the rest. A pile of dirty clothes lay in a lump beside the bed. The girl was muscular with large breasts, her body thick with just a hint of cellulite on her thighs. She stretched on the bed and spread her legs to show what had been purchased for me. Her unwashed clothes and body spilled a sour fish tank stink into the air.

"Better come and get it, man," she offered.

Like a stalking beast, I moved toward her slowly. She eyed me suspiciously, as if to question my hesitation.

"Oh, that's right. You don't know what to do with it, do you?" she said and scooted across the bed, wrapping her legs around my thighs. She unzipped my pants and pulled them and my underwear down. She frowned. "Why are you so shriveled? You got to get some lead in it if you want to fuck, man." She took the pink wad of gum from her mouth and stuck it on the bed rail. "Maybe I can blow some life into it," she said and placed my limp member in her warm mouth, sucking like a greedy child on a nipple.

I pushed her away.

"Hey!" she exclaimed, looking at me with disgust and just a hint of fear.

Before she could utter another word, I was on her.

She struggled but even her toughness was no match for the power of my hunger. I sank my teeth into her throat and ripped it open. She gasped and wrapped her arms around me as if inviting death. The taste of living flesh and blood was maddening. I couldn't get enough. I slurped and smacked as the warm arterial stream filled my mouth. I moaned with pure pleasure.

The girl whispered, "Please don't stop," then she gasped and stiffened under me when she stopped breathing.

I kept drinking from her throat until there was nothing left. I was wild for the taste and started biting all over her body. In my rage I tore off her breasts and sucked what I could from them. With my nails I slit open her abdomen and fed, searching for any pooled blood in the vascular system. I removed her heart which was full of clotting blood and wolfed it down. I flipped her body and dug for the kidneys, eating them as well.

When I could devour no more, I fell forward on the ruined body and slept, bloated with my first kill.

I faded in and out of sleep. The effect of the live meal was puzzling. One moment I would be relaxed; the next I would wake unable to move as if paralyzed. At times I would see Lockley standing in the bedroom doorway. He looked amused.

When I finally did become awake and alert, I found I was still in bed with the girl's corpse. Her skin was mottled and reeking of decomposition.

Lockley appeared by the bed. "The time for your days of being spoiled has come to an end," he piped.

"How long have I been out?"

"A little over three days. Enough time for that creature next to you to ripen, don't you agree?" He then told me I was going with him to dispose of the body, but he wanted me to bathe the stench off first. "Feeding in this manner," he added, "is crude and messy, but necessary for a fledgling such as you."

When I got up, I was a bit shaky. I noticed my hair and nails were already growing back so after bathing I cut my nails and pulled my hair back in a ponytail. I could get it trimmed later.

After I got dressed, we put the body in a sheet, carried it out and placed it in the back of Lockley's black Suburban. We drove to Sam Bass Road, an area not far from my house, then past Old Town Cemetery. Not long after, Lockley turned down a road paralleling the cemetery. It wound for better than a mile before passing into a thick area of weedy growth and ancient Oak trees.

The path we followed was in the heart of a forested area. Trees on each side of the road had expanded over the path, forming a canopy that covered the way. It was near sunset, but the dense growth had put the place in early darkness. Lockley turned the headlights on as we moved through a pallid ground fog.

Eventually, we went down a slope that ended in front of a large mausoleum encircled by a rusty spiked fence about five feet tall. We got out of the car and removed the body, carrying it by the fence to a gate where Lockley opened a corroded lock. He pushed the gate open and then unlocked the door of the mausoleum as well. We carried the body into the structure. We were greeted with an odor of rot and mildew. The gloom was so thick that Lockley used a key ring flashlight to point the way to another door just across the stone floor. He asked me to open it.

On the other side of the door was a downward staircase illuminated by a row of low wattage bulbs on each side. As I turned to go back and help move the body, I became aware that my vision had adjusted to the darkness. I discovered two sepulchers rising from the middle of the room. Heaps of dried flowers littered the floor around them and they were enshrouded in a cocoon of spider webs.

As we carried the corpse toward the stairs I made out the dim letters of a name carved above the door—MORGAN.

At the bottom of the stairway was a large living and dining room. The living area contained a spacious red leather couch, coffee table, and a big screen projection television. The dining room had a table that could have seated twenty-five people with no problem.

"We need to carry the body to the kitchen area," Lockley instructed as he pushed through a pair of large swinging doors at the back of the dining room. The extensive kitchen on the other side had an array of assorted utensils and cutting instruments hanging from the ceiling. Several ovens, open pits, and grilles lined the walls. At the center was a generous food preparation island with a large square wooden cutting board. It was big enough for the girl's body.

Lockley removed two cleavers from the wall, handed one to me then pulled the sheet from the corpse. He told me to start at the head while he went to the ankles. I needed no further instruction. What he wanted me to do came quite naturally.

We cut the body into sections and, with the exception of the head, wrapped them in butcher paper and placed them in a large freezer. Lockley took me through a door at the back of the kitchen. This smaller area had a dirt floor. It smelled like a root cellar. He dug a hole and buried the girl's head. I had asked no questions on the drive over, and I asked none now. I knew in due time he would explain why he saved the head.

We washed our hands in the kitchen, went back up the stairs and left.

Lockley secured the mausoleum door and the front gate. We got in his car and drove away. On the drive back to my house, Lockley informed me I would start working at his clinic. I asked about my old job and he said it had been taken care of.

"But won't I be missed at the Georgetown clinic? And what about my emergency room duties?" I asked.

"Apathy is a great ally these days, Dr. Russell. Any excuse seems to be a good one. Besides, as I have previously pointed out, we have friends who can arrange anything for us."

Lockley said he would clarify my situation at a dinner party he was having this weekend. It occurred to me I had no idea what day of the week it was.

"It's Thursday," he said. "I will pick you up this Saturday for the dinner. You'll start at my clinic this coming Monday."

"I'm afraid my experience in OB GYN is limited," I said as he turned down the drive to my home.

He smiled a bit. "Don't concern yourself too much. Like everything else, after you've done the procedures time and time again, they become second nature."

After he left, I walked to my back door and entered the house. Someone had collected my mail and placed it in neat order on the kitchen table. The junk ads, bills, and one personal letter were separated from each other. The letter was from my mother. Her script had always been precise and lovely. Now it was a shaky scrawl. She said my dad was getting worse, not knowing who she was most of the time. Couldn't I come home and help them because she tended to misplace a day or two lately herself and . . . .

I didn't finish reading the letter. I dropped it in the trash without care or guilt.

If I had a parent now it was Lockley. I did not love or hate him; he was simply the source of my new life.

I went to the living room, turned on the light and watched television. I felt no hunger. After awhile, I turned the television and light off and stared into the darkness. There, without need for human companionship, I sat alone.

THE RECORD OF CHARLES VAIRAJA

1820

October 20, 1820

I have decided to write a record of the events leading up to my twenty-second year.

I must say I do not enjoy keeping diaries. For that reason I have no existing account of my life so far. As I have recently found my mother's journal, however, I feel that I must put my memories down. Research by my fellow scientists may find it helpful in the future.

My adolescence is vague. Assuming that my mother's records are correct, I was born in 1798 in Pasha, India. I have no recollection of the place or my parents.

I must have been no more than nine or ten when I was taken to England. That is the most concrete memory I have, so it will be the beginning of this account.

I remember being transported by coach to an orphanage. It was late fall and the trees' foliage had been replaced with an austere skeletal appearance, stark against the gray twilight of the English countryside.

I was not alone in the coach. A shadow sat next to me, holding my hand.

The coach was stuffy and smelled of tobacco and sweat. I recall being nauseated by the odor and the rough ride. I did not particularly enjoy sunlight, so the overcast day and coming night made the trip endurable. Being adverse to bright sunshine, my skin was a lighter brown than most Indian children, but there was no doubt of my heritage, nor could the blue eyes of my mother keep my British inheritance a secret. These physical traits made me pleasing to the eye but were a handicap in a society of

Britons. I would quickly come to understand what the term 'mixed breed' meant.

As the coach made a long winding turn, I looked out the window and caught sight of the distant silhouette of a large structure at the top of a hill. The closer we came, the more brutish the place appeared.

The orphanage and the ample grounds it stood in were surrounded by a tall stonewall. At the center of this barrier was a massive iron gate. The coachman got out, opened it then drove the coach to the front door of the building.

I remember how dark and immense the place was. Carved stone beasts adorned the roof and ledges. Its two stories culminated in numerous gabled windows. When my ghostly companion grasped the lion-head doorknocker and pounded, we were soon face to face with a tall stick-figure of a man. He was dressed in black except for an immaculate white shirt that reached out of the darkness. This gaunt figure held a lantern. Its light exaggerated the lines of his face. I saw that his left eye was partially covered with a webbed growth of skin.

As I continued to gape at the hideous face before me, my hand was released. Before I had a chance to understand what was happening, my companion walked away, deserting me on the steps of the orphanage. I made an attempt to follow, but a hand grasped my shoulder.

"Now, now, little one," the cadaverous sentry said, "come inside out of the cold and dark."

I heard the coach leaving. My stomach sank to my feet.

The man released his hold on me, replacing it with a reassuring pat. "You will fare well here. Just wait and see."

His name was Broom.

Many lamps hung from the hallway walls, but darkness was still prominent. The house appeared to be operating on meager funds. An orphanage for children of mixed races and those below the poverty line, it was isolated and, ironically, owned by the church. As I was to learn, the children within these walls were not given a proper education. Instead, they were hired slave labor. Later, I was to be shown a small cemetery behind the main house. Located on a sloping hill were graves without headstones, only a soft rise in the earth distinguished the resting places for its inhabitants.

Broom surprised me. He was the opposite of the ghastly countenance he presented. Kind and helpful he was a sort of 'dorm father and mother' to the children. I suspected he had been a resident here when he was a child and sympathized with us.

Other adults worked there, but the staff was limited and had little time or inclination to look upon us children as anything more than fixtures requiring care. We were lamps to be dusted or rugs to be cleaned.

A cook did pay more attention to me than most. She was Indian and had a girl not much younger than I, named Nara. She helped her mother and was never hired out of the orphanage. I sensed that the cook must have had another child, maybe a boy that I reminded her of. She once called me by a strange name and then realized her mistake. A pitiful gaze spread over her as if some painful memory long buried had surfaced, catching her by surprise.

The orphans were of various ages and heritage. None were pure blooded British children, of that I was certain. We were not segregated boys from girls, infants from adolescents. We shared a large room on the upper level furnished with cots that hugged the floor. A clear blessing was the fact that no child picked on or ridiculed another. We were allies sharing a common desperation.

After I had been there a few weeks, a hefty, formally dressed man came to the orphanage. Broom led him to the dormitory where we were just rising for the day. The man went from cot to cot until he had made his selection: three of the older girls, me, and another boy about my age.

We were washed, dressed and moved downstairs to the main room. It was early morning and the lamps were still burning. The man who stood in front of us was a large burly character. He looked out of place in his suit, like a bulldog dressed for the opera. His face was red, sweaty, and huge. Enormous mutton chop sideburns covered the sides of his face. When he removed his top hat to wipe away the moisture from his face and head with a handkerchief, his baldness was exposed. Only a small thin ring of hair encircled the sides of his head.

"This, children, is Mr. Grubbs," Broom announced. "He will be in need of your services for the weekend."

Before we left, Broom pulled me aside and whispered, "Watch your step with this one, laddie." Grubbs was ominous enough and Broom's warning only added to my terror of the man.

Looking back now, I know that Broom held power only with his words of warning. The orphanage patron left him no recourse to discourage a renter's choice, for that is all we were, rented items. Broom accepted Grubbs' money, but when Grubbs turned his head, I saw an expression of loathing on Broom's face.

Two coaches waited outside. One was splendid. The other one was a scarred heap. It was evident which one we would be taking. We stepped into the antique, squeaky rig and headed to our fate.

The three girls sat across from me and the other boy. They were older. They were not beautiful but neither were they unattractive. Their figures indicated blooming womanhood, the one in the center of the three being more mature in physique. My attention went to her as did my companion's.

Her skin tone revealed just a hint of darkness, but her other features were very British. Dirty blonde hair spilled in ringlets to her shoulders, her face was handsome with delicate lines and a nose that turned upward just slightly above a pair of full pink lips. There was the thin outline of a pale blue vein just above the pulse in her neck. The longer I gazed at her, the more my throat constricted. Had I tried to speak, no more than a squeak would have escaped.

My attention had not gone unnoticed. She smiled at me.

"That one fancies you, she does," my companion whispered.

After he spoke, I stared in surprise as the girl pulled her skirt up just a bit above the knee. She pretended she was adjusting her dress, but her action lasted too long to be anything other than a flirtation.

The coach came to an abrupt halt, jarring me from my fascination. She had been a wonderful distraction, taking my mind away from the uncomfortable and bumpy ride.

The girls got out first. I was about to follow my companion when the girl I had been eyeing came back into the coach and sat next to me. She grabbed my hand, placed it on her thigh and said in a low voice, "My name is Elizabeth. Come to my cot some night when the others are asleep and after Broom has made his first rounds." She then took my face in her hands and kissed me on the lips. "You are so beautiful," she said, staring with deep intent into my surprised eyes. "There are so many things I can teach a lovely boy like you."

Before she could say any more, Grubbs was rapping on the coach door. "All right you two, enough of your silliness. Let's get moving."

The girl jumped out and I followed. As I passed Grubbs, I caught the unpleasant odor of stale tobacco mixed with whatever he had eaten for breakfast. He winked at me, cutting his eyes toward Elizabeth. "Never too young," he said and shoved a meaty hand into my crotch, "or too small to learn a thing or two, eh, boy?"

I hurried to take my place behind the others, my face pale and warm, and my stomach acid and tight. The lewd sneering figure of Grubbs followed close behind.

We had arrived at a large country estate. Grubbs deposited us at the rear where the servant's quarters were located. We were given uniforms and instructed by the head butler as to our duties. There was a gathering that weekend to celebrate the owner's recent appointment to a government position. We were to serve food and drink to friends of the host.

The work was boring but easy. We glided through the next two days, merging in and around people who could buy or sell us, people who only noticed us if their glasses were empty or if they needed more hors d'oeuvres placed in their soft hands.

As gloomy as the orphanage was, I found myself eager to return there by Sunday. Grubbs informed us, however, that we would be required to help clean up that evening so we wouldn't be leaving until Monday morning.

While we were busy polishing the silverware, Grubbs came into the kitchen with two men. They were young, lean, and hawkish. They smoked small cigars that, unlike Grubbs' giant green monstrosities, had a wonderful aroma.

The affluent pair scrutinized us. They would stare at me for a while and then whisper something to Grubbs, who would shake his head or grin and shrug his shoulders. Every so often one of the two would giggle, look over, raise an eyebrow then murmur something else to Grubbs.

Eventually, the pair left. Grubbs approached the butler and spoke to him while pointing in our direction then exited the kitchen.

Once we had completed our chores, we went to the sleeping quarters. Before the lamps had been turned down, one of the housemaids came in and announced that the girls would be needed for some extra duties in the dining room. I sighed with relief while the girls groaned at the thought of even more work. I fell asleep soon after they left. When I awoke the next morning, the girls were still gone. They did not join the other boy and me for breakfast. It wasn't until Grubbs came and took us to the coach for the return trip to the orphanage that we saw them again. Their hair was mussed, their clothes tousled.

"Where have you been?" I asked.

The three glared at me. "Just don't you worry about it, boy," Elizabeth answered icily, "and kindly keep your mouth shut the rest of the ride."

However, I was young and naïve and tried to lift the girls' bad humor. The other two girls just turned away from me, but Elizabeth, before gazing vacantly out the window, offered an angry response. "Just be glad they didn't prefer petite male cherubs for their amusement."

I decided to keep quiet. It was the first of many lessons taught to me by the opposite sex.

I realized that Elizabeth's earlier invitation to me had become unwelcome. In fact, I never did search out her cot. She and one other girl died from an influenza epidemic that devastated the orphanage that winter. Had it not been for the tireless unselfish efforts of Bloom and the Indian woman, I'm certain more than two of us would have perished from the fever, diarrhea, and respiratory symptoms.

Since most of us were on the path to recovery, we were not allowed to attend the girls' burial. It would have been risky to expose us to the wintry elements. I recall Broom came to our room and told us he had offered a prayer in our behalf at the burial.

I had no sense of loss. It seemed none of the other children did either. There was only the reality of two empty cots. Caring was a luxury too much to ask of those who only sought survival.

Later that year, when the first portents of spring appeared, Broom took us to the orphanage graveyard. The most recent mounds were easy to separate from the older ones.

"We cannot afford stones," Broom told us, "and we decided long ago a wooden effigy would belittle those who rest here. Innocents need no names."

I always admired Broom and would like to have known more about him. He was dedicated to us, even though we were nothing more than gears and spokes of a machine dedicated to labor. Unlike those who hired out our services, Broom saw us as flesh and blood individuals. As much as he possibly could, Broom attempted to give comfort and love to us. We gladly accepted him as our guardian and respected the privacy he held for his past. To this day, I still don't know much about the man.

* * *

It was almost a year before Grubbs came back to the orphanage. I have to admit the jobs in between, mostly manual labor in local factories, had been much harder than the first one with Grubbs.

As before, he arrived in the early hours of morning. This time he chose only one child. It just happened to be me.

I was taken downstairs and forced to wait while Grubbs talked with Broom. The more they talked, the redder the patch of flesh became on Broom's eye. He argued heatedly with Grubbs. I thought they would come to blows, but in the end Broom took Grubbs' money and left the room without looking at me.

Again, there were two coaches. Grubbs didn't lower his status for even one child, so I rode alone. Without someone to talk to, the trip was long and uncomfortable.

The estate we reached was not half as large as the first one. Grubbs took me directly to the front door where we were greeted by a butler dressed in dandy attire not quite suited for his station. Grubbs said nothing, handed me over to the butler and told him to "be quick about it," then left in a rush. Evidently, the place did not agree with Grubbs, but it seemed nice enough to me, grand in fact. The residence was immaculate and smelled wonderful, like scented candles and perfume. As I was led to the servant's quarters, I saw that the ceilings were adorned with flamboyant chandeliers and the staircases intricately carved with floral designs.

I was moved to a small room with a tiny bed and tub for bathing. The butler retrieved a pile of clothing from the top of a dresser in the room's corner.

"I believe your name is Charles," he said in a nasal feminine voice.

"Yes," I answered, suppressing a smile at his comical accent.

"Well, Master Charles, please bathe then change to this attire. We will be dining in the 'Arabian Nights' this evening."

The costume I was given to wear imitated a sultan's clothes: baggy yellow trousers, a red blouse with puffy sleeves, a maroon turban, and crimson slippers curved to a point with brass jingle bells on their ends. It felt like great fun, so unlike the boring jobs I had done before. It was like getting ready for a masquerade party.

Downstairs two young men and an older woman sat at the dinner table. She could have been their mother or an older sister as there was a certain resemblance between the three. When I came in with the soup tray, I got a better look at them.

The three were wearing wigs. One man's was pink and the other, fatter man's was periwinkle. The woman's wig appeared out of place and unruly on her head. The more I examined her, the more I became convinced she was no woman at all. The shadow of a beard under heavy makeup and a large Adam's apple betrayed the older man's disguise.

"Well," the thinner of the young men pointed out, "I do believe our small Aladdin is quite taken with you, Henry."

The three giggled, and the older one turned to me. He wiped a napkin across his broad mouth, leaving a trail of lipstick on the linen. I stood right beside him. He put his face close to mine and pinched my cheeks with stubby fingers. His nails were painted pink.

"My, my," he smacked, "what beautiful big blue eyes you have, Aladdin."

Their fatter companion remarked with a leer, "Does he realize, our little Aladdin, that he can have three wishes by rubbing your magic lamp, Henry?"

"Oh, dear, oh my dear," Henry responded, "just the thought of that, Clive, brings hardness to my character."

They were having immense sport with me and laughed loudly. I blushed and had no clue as to why, but they soon became involved with each other and left me alone for the rest of the dinner. I picked up bits of their conversations: "But is that wise, dear?"; "Don't waste your time on that one. He's such a tight bitch, hardly worth your tears."; "I think a grand tour would be perfect this September. The house gets so stuffy that time of year."

I was aware of such men, those who preferred their own company to that of women. I was confused as to how I felt about them. I knew it was not natural, but wasn't certain if it was offensive or not. My blush was certainly different from the one Elizabeth had caused, but they did stir something in me, something unwholesome and frightening. A shiver moved down my spine just being near them.

After dinner, the butler directed me to my bed. I had just started to doze when I was wakened by someone shaking my arm. The butler had returned. He held a lamp that threw light on his face, a face covered with a ghoulish white cream. His lips were outlined with a red slash, making him look like a diabolical circus clown.

"This way, little boy," he whispered as he took me out the door and down the hall.

I was still drowsy and stumbled a bit. "Where are we going?" I asked.

"Quiet, boy" he hushed me. "We are going to the study for a moment."

Once there, I was aware of an unpleasant salty smell just under the aromatic crackling of the wood in the fireplace. I wore a thin nightgown and shivered. The butler moved me closer to the fire. The three men were in the room. The two young men lounged on a large couch. The older one sat in a spacious armchair. They were naked.

One of the men on the couch looked to be in good condition, with just a hint of fat hugging his waist. His companion, however, had a bloated belly and spindly arms and legs, making him resemble a tick full of blood. The old one in the chair was not fat but lacked muscle tone. His skin hung loosely, particularly around the nipples, giving them the appearance of odd and unattractive feminine breasts. He also had an abundance of hair that covered his chest and trailed over his shoulders.

"Mmmmm," the chubby one chortled, "wake up you two, dessert has arrived."

Evidently they had been drinking heavily. It took a moment before the other two were aware of my presence. They looked pleased and told the butler to "position the sweet meat."

I struggled, but could not prevent him from bending me over the arm of the couch. The thinner man knelt in front of me and grabbed my wrists, stretching my arms toward him in a tight grip. The butler seized my ankles and spread me like a wishbone. The arm of the couch dug into my stomach; my rear stuck up in a painful angle. The fat one and the older one were behind me. I could not tell which one ripped the nightshirt from my body. Something cold and greasy was rubbed in and around my rectum. My sphincter constricted. I begged them to stop as I felt myself being spread even wider. My pleas were silenced by an excruciating pain that ripped through my body. The last thing I saw before fainting was the grinning face of the man holding my arms.

I awoke next morning and was hardly able to move, but I made it to the piss pot where I wretched until empty. No one came to check on me. When my door was finally opened, Grubbs entered and hurried me to get dressed.

His eyes expressed no sympathy; there was only repulsion and loathing in them.

The ride back to the orphanage was agonizing. My backside screamed with each bump on the road. When we arrived, I got out and noticed a large stain of blood left behind on the seat. Grubbs remained in his coach. As I tentatively walked to the door, I glanced back and saw large clouds of his cigar smoke drift from the coach's window.

Broom came out and rushed me inside. They must have suspected something foul in respect to my job, as the woman cook was waiting and spirited me away to the bath area. I saw Broom dash angrily out the front door, but Grubbs must have already left as Broom returned shortly.

The cook undressed me in the bathroom. I did not protest. I was too tired and ill to care. Gently, she placed me on the floor and turned me on my side. She began cleaning my wound with cool water from a small bucket. She called for her daughter. I made no attempt to cover my nakedness. The girl stared at me with large brown eyes.

"Nara," the cook instructed, "heat some water for his bath."

The girl left to do as her mother had asked.

The cook was easy with me. She made no attempt at conversation. When she had finished bathing me, she led me to my cot where I fell into an exhausted sleep. Not even a dream disturbed me. I remained there a few days in and out of sleep with only a vague recollection of being taken to the toilet. Whoever guided me was more of a shadow than flesh and blood. When I finally felt better, I found myself in urgent need of a bowel movement. It never occurred to me just how much pain would be involved from the damage the three monsters had inflicted on me. I literally screamed in anguish when I defecated. Broom came in quickly. I was in tears. His expression on seeing me was a mixture of pity and guilt. He helped me back to my cot. After I was down, he looked at me with tears in his eyes and said, "I'm sorry." That was all. Whatever hold Grubbs or his connections possessed was strong enough to cause Broom's unwilling alliance with them. I knew Broom to be haunted by the things he was forced to comply with; they left furrows on his aging face.

The incident passed, but was not forgotten or forgiven. Two years went by and Grubbs never returned. I overheard Broom talking with the woman cook, whose name I now knew was Ranjana, one evening. He said there was a rumor Grubbs had been killed over a gambling debt. She replied, "Shiva can be swift in delivering retribution."

"Whoever it was," Broom added, "I heerd he slit old Grubbs' throat in a wide grin all right. I hope he died squealing like the rotten swine he was."

I always suspected Broom had done Grubbs in. Broom may not have been able to refuse the devil's demand, but he could have surprised Grubbs and rid himself of his unholy taskmaster. Whether my suspicions were justified or not, there was a strange light in Broom's good eye after Grubbs had disappeared.

* * *

Before I had time to realize it, I was fifteen.

The fact that I could read and write fluently in English was a welcome discovery to Broom. I had come across a book on agriculture by chance, as we were never given the opportunity to amuse ourselves with anything other than work. I found it on a shelf in the room where cleaning supplies were stored. It had been so long since I had read that I closed the door for privacy and settled on the floor to catch what light I could from under it. Broom opened the door and caught me.

"Why, see here, lad. Can you read?"

I told him I had been taught to read and write before I came to the orphanage. The person who instructed me was vague in my memory, but I did remember it was an older man of Indian heritage. Broom was ecstatic and said he would notify the people in charge of the orphanage. "You'll get some nice work from this," he winked.

He was right. Being literate procured easier, but more challenging, work for me. Although I was not paid, the jobs were preferable to the tedious manual labor usually given to us at the orphanage. There were many businesses, counting houses, libraries, schools, medical and law offices that put the literate lower class to work with research and copying duties. The orphanage would lend me out for weeks at a time. On occasion, the company using me would provide housing during my tenure, especially if it were located a great distance from the orphanage.

I never made friends during my employments, but sometimes there was a library available that offered a wealth of knowledge and escape for me when I wasn't working. The fiction books were entertaining enough, but I developed a keen interest for life sciences. My drive for wisdom in this area would one day help me acquire the position of lab assistant in the medical school at London University.

As I matured mentally, so I did physically as well. The cook's daughter, Nara, had blossomed into a young woman and became the object of my youthful desire. When I was in her presence, I could not suppress a warm blush, and though she never seemed aware of my admiration, I would catch a brief smile from her occasionally.

My seventeenth birthday was approaching when a law clerk arrived at the orphanage. The clerk announced, in a formal snobby voice, that he was employed by the prestigious firm of Bennington and Heartstone. Imagine the stir at the orphanage and my astonishment when I learned he had come to do business with me.

Broom came to the kitchen where I was supposed to be helping Ranjana with polishing the silver. In fact, I was shamelessly lusting after Nara. Broom informed me that I had a visitor. He was quite excited by the whole affair. I, on the other hand, was tentative and a bit frightened.

Broom led me to the little office he used for record keeping. Waiting there was a mousy man with a slight forward bend of posture who studied me over a pair of harshly lined rectangular spectacles. It was hard to guess the man's age, but he must have been in his late forties or early fifties as the slight patches of facial wrinkles and subtle streaks of gray in his hair implied.

"This is the boy, then?" he asked in a grating nasal tone that reminded me of chalk being squeaked across a slate.

"It is, sir," Broom answered.

"Then be seated, boy. I have news for you. News that is important to your heritage."

He explained that his employers saved the government time and money by searching through unsettled estate cases. These could result in inheritance or indebtedness depending on the circumstances.

"Would you please state your name," he continued.

"I only know my first," I said. "I am called Charles."

"Our field workers have discovered," he informed with a ferret grin, "that your full name is Charles Wilkins."

The clerk then read from a document. His inflection was flat and mechanical, more like dictation to a machine than to an individual. "There is strong evidence that your mother was Andrea Wilkins, the only child of James and Catherine Wilkins. Your father is unknown. Records indicate you were born in the latter part of October or early November 1798 in India. As I can see, there are strong physical characteristics you possess that lead me to believe your father was a man of Indian or mixed Indian blood.

"Your grandfather, James, worked for the East India Company. He searched for trade routes through the mountains leading into Tibet. His last station was in a small village called Pasha on the border of India and Nepal. From what we gather, that village is desolate today. Evidently a plague of some sort devastated the area when your grandparents lived there. If this is why they perished, we are not certain, but our sources are quite sure they are, in fact, deceased.

"After giving birth, your mother somehow made it back to England. She was moving toward London, where her parents had lived, when you were separated from her. An adoptive parent of sorts took you under his wing. I gather he is the individual who brought you to this very place. He had suffered economic ruin due to unwise speculations. That is the reason he sold you to the orphanage for a tidy sum. By law, I cannot reveal his identity, but I can inform you that he has since passed away, dissolving any claims to you he might have had.

"We were unable to locate your mother. Since the allotted period of time has passed for her to be declared legally dead, we are under the assumption she has met her maker."

I was almost hypnotized by this clerk's matter-of-fact monotone. The manner in which he said 'met her maker' caused me to feel as insignificant as the thin layer of dust on the desk before me.

"To continue," he said, "I will now explain the dispersion of your family's properties."

According to the clerk, my grandparents had owned a small town house in London and my grandfather had been in the process of purchasing a modest country home located by a small lake. Upon his and my grandmother's death, what properties they owned were dispersed to the East India Company to make up for the financial losses incurred by my grandfather's failure to find the trade routes. The Company paid off and released the servants employed by my grandparents.

Save one brother who had departed England for America some years before, there were no relatives to be held responsible for my grandfather's debts. My grandmother did have surviving relatives, an aunt and uncle, but they were senile and destitute. As for the brother in America, some attempt was made to locate him with no result. It was assumed he was part of the westward migration in the Americas and that trying to find him would be like looking for the proverbial 'needle in a haystack' and not worth the effort. So the Company claimed legal possession of my grandparent's assets. The town house was sold to a lady of independent means. The country estate brought a nice profit, but still not enough for the Company to retrieve their investments.

The Company's interest was renewed when they learned of my mother's movements back toward London. They anticipated she might be able to contribute to their monetary losses, but her disappearance and the fact that I was basically sold for labor to the orphanage deterred their notions of ever breaking even. The Company accepted the fact it would be impossible to recover the investments placed in my family with any expedience.

Finding me had been a stroke of luck. My guardian's financial problems were cross-referenced to my grandfather's obligations by one of the law firm's field workers. The trail ended with the orphanage and me. I was not to receive any monetary inheritance, but would be, by law, responsible for the money lost with incurred penalties of interest.

"However," the clerk informed me as he gathered his papers together,

"Bennington and Heartstone are not monsters. They expect you to make payments on your family's debt only after you have found gainful employment. I suggest, Master Charles, you are hasty in this enterprise as the interest will only grow the longer you wait. I have discussed this with the church and made arrangements that will allow you to search for such employ. Once you have gained a position, you will no longer be under their patronage here."

How ironic it was to be freed from the masters of the orphanage only to be placed under the thumb of Bennington and Heartstone. I would become my own man due to my grandfather's failure, not my own self-significance.

"In conclusion," the clerk continued, placing some documents in front of me, "I will now ask you to sign these papers stating that you understand the information I have given you." I hesitated for a moment and he said, "If you are unable to sign, Mr. Broom can offer his signature in your stead and I will witness."

I felt Broom place his hand on my shoulder. "The boy can read and write better than meself, sir. Go ahead, lad, sign the papers."

"I will sign," I said to the clerk.

"Fine," he answered and pointed out the spaces where I was to place my name.

After Broom had witnessed, the clerk removed another document from his folder. "There is one last item to deal with," he said. "We happened to receive a personal item of your mother's from India. It is a lady's travel trunk. Since we located the trunk after we were aware of your whereabouts, and since it was locked and securely sealed, we had no legal right to open it. It is, however, within Bennington and Heartstone's privileges to have a legal representative present when you break the seal. If there is anything of value in the trunk, Bennington and Heartstone possess the rights of possession of said items and the dispersal thereof." The clerk placed the paper on the desk. "So when the trunk arrives within the month, either I or Mr. Broom will be present when you open it." He placed his finger on the blank space. "Place one last signature here please."

I did not hesitate. For once, I had something to anticipate: a past I longed to discover.

The trunk arrived five weeks later.

It was a large piece. I was barely a head taller at five foot seven. The trunk, dark blue and bordered by brass fittings, must have been heavy as the two deliverymen struggled to get it up the front steps. As the clerk had stated, three padlocks sealed it.

The clerk could not attend, so it was in my favor that Broom would witness the contents of the trunk. I knew if there was anything of real value he would turn his head away and allow me to take possession of whatever I found inside. A locksmith came with the deliverymen and went swiftly about his job as soon as the trunk was placed in Broom's office. After he opened the locks, the man gave me a form to sign, then he and the deliverymen left, bidding Broom and myself a good day.

I stood there face to face with the only link I had to my past. I opened the partition, gradually separating the two halves. A sudden stream of stale air wafted over me. It did not smell of decomposition, only of musty toilet water and old clothes. Five sets of drawers were on each side. Besides a thin nightgown and one pair of ladies black shoes, the trunk was empty. The struggling men had delivered a heavy but almost empty trunk. I would discover nothing of my past here. The hopes I had entertained in regard to my mother's history were as pallid as the nightgown I held in my hands. I placed it on my face and inhaled, hoping I could breathe a trace of her essence into my lungs, but only the scent of a delicate phantom perfume lingered there.

After Broom witnessed me sign the document left by the clerk in respect to any valuables found, we moved the trunk to a storage room near the kitchen. I noticed Ranjana and Nara were preparing dinner. I took the nightgown and shoes to Ranjana. I told her that after they had been properly cleaned and aired she might be able to wear them. She held the nightgown against her and giggled at the fact I had presumed her large body would fit the petite gown. She made no attempt to try the tiny shoes either.

Ranjana held the gown next to Nara. The girl's slim developing body was perfect, if not a bit too small, for it. "Thank you, young Charles," Ranjana said. "Nara will grow into this and the shoes nicely."

At that moment, my lust for Nara was not the only feeling that overcame me. As I watched her turn, the gown clinging to her, she smiled with those full brown eyes, her lips slightly parted in expectation. My heart fluttered and plummeted to my stomach, and I realized I was hopelessly in love.

I often wondered if Broom and Ranjana were lovers. I knew that her husband had been killed in a tragic accident, so Broom had told me, and, on occasion, I would happen upon her and Broom in isolated areas of the orphanage. I never saw them embracing, but they did seem to be whispering confidences to each other. It would have been delightful had my theory been true. I had come to care about them very much.

Broom must have told Ranjana about my predicament with Bennington and Heartstone because she approached me with a suggestion one day. I was making a nuisance of myself in the kitchen, trying to spend as much time with Nara as I could when Ranjana said "There is a man I know, Charles, who might be of help to you. He lives in a section of London where Nara and I used to stay."

The man came from a similar background to mine except his mother was Indian and his father British. He had attained a high level of importance in the overseas trade market. His mixed blood may not have been necessarily acceptable in British society, but the familial passion his father gave to him was incentive enough for a push in the right direction. His parents had been killed in rebellion against the British Crown in India. Luckily he had been in England at the time, attending London University. After his parents' death, he inherited a large amount of property. The Empire put certain legal restrictions on the man due to his Indian heritage, but not enough to prevent him from flourishing in the lucrative business of trade.

Ranjana and her husband had operated a small shop for the man. They sold various herbs, spices, and incense there. Ranjana told me the shop was in a dangerous area of London, a place not safe for any color of skin, especially after dark, and that the trade was poor. The residents there, other than those of Indian blood, were more interested in Mother's Ruin than spices or herbs.

The man she spoke of was named Thomas Hampton—this proper British name made his contacts feel at ease—but was known in the district as Pavan. He had treated Nara and Ranjana with much kindness after her husbands' death. Pavan believed the responsibility of the business would prove too trying for Ranjana, so he arranged to have her employed at the orphanage where she and Nara could live in better conditions.

Ranjana was certain Pavan could help me find a solid position. After three months, I was called to the man's office in London for an interview. Broom arranged my carriage ride and sent me off in a state of excitement. I realized in gaining employment part of my wages would be garnished by Bennington and Heartstone, but I was in great hope of having a job I could call my own. I was not to be disappointed.

Due to my experience with bookkeeping, Pavan hired me to work in his home office. It was an honor for one as young as I to be given this responsibility. Pavan would turn out to be one of the kindest and most gentle people I would come to know. He would also be my benefactor. Due to his patronage, I would erase my grandfather's debt and attain the education I sought. Pavan was one of those individuals who moved with ease through life's obstacles and was always assisting those he judged in need. Although I would be in his presence on many occasions, Pavan would remain a mystery to me. He preferred to keep his personal life in the shadows. I hoped he would live to see me graduate from London University, but a frail heart did not allow him to survive that long.

My joy at finding a job overshadowed a fact I had failed to recognize: now that I was free of my responsibility to the orphanage, I would not be allowed to live there anymore. As it turned out, this fact would prove to be beneficial.

As I had suspected, Broom and Ranjana were involved romantically.

They could not marry and continue at the orphanage. Without the funds to leave, they had been forced to hide their deep and abiding affection for each other. When Pavan became aware of their plight, he made arrangements for Broom and Ranjana to become the proprietors of the shop she and her first husband had once operated in London. There was ample space in the rear of the store to accommodate Broom, Ranjana, Nara and myself.

I guessed that Ranjana was aware and approved of my attraction for Nara. She permitted me to share a room with Nara, which, of course, was modestly divided by a curtained partition, allowing familiarity without impropriety.

We were to be a family and although it was not the most desirable of locales, Pavan assured us that over the years he had gained enough influence to confirm our safety there. It was the first real home I had known.

I started work and quickly mastered the system used at Pavan's office. Ranjana and Broom were just as swift in starting up the shop again. The increase in Indian population over time marginally supported sales. Nara, as always, was a great help to them.

Another year sped by, a year that witnessed my yearning for the shadow dancing on the other side of that curtained partition. During that year, Nara and I became friends, confidants, and lovers.

If I thought a wealth of books had been available before, it was nothing in comparison to the volumes Pavan placed at my disposal. Realizing my desire for education, he had done all in his power to help me prepare for classes at London University.

Nara began to share my interests, sitting for hours at a time with me. She did not know how to read, but I could tell she wanted very much to learn. So I became a teacher as well as a pupil. At times, when I was showing her a word or reading aloud with her following the printed lines, Nara would slip her hand into mine and move very close to me. I held her and kissed her gently. We remained clinched all night sometimes, embraced as lovers but not yet intimate.

One Sunday, Broom and Ranjana went to the market for the day. They said they would return before nightfall. I was preparing for an entrance examination. Pavan, to the dismay of some faculty and board members, had arranged for me to take to be admitted as a first year university student there in London. Now, as I neared my seventeenth year, I had assimilated enough basic and advanced knowledge in a variety of subjects. Pavan and his associates were impressed enough with my scholastic endeavors to use their combined influence to acquire an appointment for me providing I passed the entrance exam. So with the shop empty, except for Nara, who always stayed very quiet when she realized I had serious studying to do, I had immersed myself in the preparatory questions provided by the university.

In the middle of a boring history passage, I heard the soft sound of water falling. I believed it to be a mild rain pattering on the shop windows. Then, I heard the hushed echo of Nara humming and realized she was bathing.

I set my studies aside and walked to the bedroom. Nara was naked and standing in the hip bath. She held a sponge to her chest and squeezed it, releasing beads of water that flowed over and around her firm breasts. From there the droplets glided over her flat belly and collected just above the dark bush of her pubic hair.

I stood, stunned by her beauty.

Nara turned to me. She made no attempt to cover herself, smiled and continued to bathe with the sponge. Without speaking, I undressed and stood next to her. We were close together; her head came only to the middle of my chest. We examined every unknown line of our bare flesh. I moved my palms over her nipples, feeling their dark erection as she placed her hands between my legs and knew the urgency of mine.

We made love all afternoon without the fear of discovery. Every passing moment was filled with the joy of discovery and the pleasure obtained through it. I knew that I could not breathe without her by my side, her heart in rhythm with my own.

Nara would become my wife, of that I had no doubt. Ranjana must have known this all along. She and Broom were joyful at the news.

We waited to wed until I had successfully passed the entrance exam. It was a modest wedding but elaborately catered by Pavan who would take no refusal. We postponed any honeymoon plans during my first year at the university and stayed in the shop at the insistence of Broom and Ranjana. They said we could live there until I had finished my studies and could find suitable employment.

So, as I started my first year of classes, the veil had been lifted from the education I had been denied as a child and the curtain removed separating me from my love.

With Pavan's help I had managed to erase my family's debt to Bennington and Heartstone and was free to concentrate on my studies. Nara still worked in the shop with her mother and Broom. I procured a part time position at the university. Because of my interest and achievement in the sciences, I was assigned the duties of laboratory assistant, responsible for organizing the weekly biology and anatomy laboratory attended by a high percentage of medical students.

As the year progressed, I felt at home in my responsibilities and the school. I even made some friends among the predominately white students. I am certain they were a bit shocked when looking at the blue eyes beaming from my brown face. But I was not the only oddity. London University also allowed women and the poor to study within its new status.

No matter what friendship I acquired, none were inclined to chance visiting me in the district where I lived. There, they would be the foreigner, the outsider in peril. I was happy in both of my worlds: the one with Nara and the other of education. I was paid for my services as laboratory assistant. It wasn't a great sum, but it made me feel like I was contributing to our lives and not a parasite living off Broom and Ranjana's kindness.

I started to work exclusively for the medical laboratory in my second year at the university. It was during this period I was requested to carry out a mission that was not legal. Such an act could get me and others into trouble and I wasn't exactly keen on doing it. However, I was still a man of dubious heritage to the professors in charge of the medical students and enough pressure was exerted to leave me little choice. I was too frightened not to cooperate.

The faculty was adamant in regard to the need for cadavers, as fresh as could be obtained, for study in the anatomy labs and just as adamant to ask no questions of the shadowy figures that supplied them. It was my job to pick up the 'packages'.

Being informed that this business had been operating for a number of years with no problems made me feel a bit better. Certainly a well endowed university could wield enough influence over political and law enforcement groups to cause certain heads to look the other way in regard to what the medical students needed. However, there was always the possibility of an incident, a fact that gave me pause when I was asked to pick up the merchandise. There were even rumors that some suppliers, when faced with a shortage of the recently deceased, would not think twice about creating their own stock by whatever means required.

It was one evening toward the end of my second fall semester that I was asked to go with a fellow lowly laboratory assistant to collect a package from The Bricklayer's Arms in Lambeth. This was not my first trip, but I felt no more secure for it, especially when I saw the destination was to a part of London considered even more dangerous than where I lived. My very British partner in crime refused to go and I could find no other volunteer to help me. I suppose I could have asked Broom, but he, Ranjana, and Nara knew nothing of my shady activities. If I even remotely involved them, they might be considered accessories.

So I went alone to Lambeth.

My carriage driving was limited, but I could foresee no problems unless the horse was spooked. It was the early part of November and the night air was crisp and chilly. Snow had been falling for the last few days, but a cold mist was all that hung in the air that night, creating a frosty halo around the streetlamps. The streets were empty due to the lateness of the hour and the uncomfortable conditions. As I approached my destination, The Bricklayer's Arms, the horse's hooves echoed sharply in the still cold.

The setting was eerie, made even more so by the decreasing number of street lamps. In time, I spied the pub's light through what was quickly turning into a freezing mist. As I halted the carriage in front of the entrance, I saw a figure standing in the shadows.

"Are you the university boy?" a gravely voice asked from the darkness.

"Yes," I answered through a fear-dried throat. "I am here to pick up the package."

The figure walked with a considerable limp to the opposite side of the carriage and got in, sitting beside me. There was sufficient light from the pub window for me to see my companion. He was a stout short man dressed in a heavy coat and top hat. In his gnarled hands, he clutched a long black cane with a knobby crest.

I hesitated for an instant and he turned toward me, exposing a scarred face. There was one particularly ragged area encircling his neck. His rough raspy voice bore evidence of the damage inflicted there.

"Well, drive on!" he commanded, eyeing me like I was an idiot.

The man moved closer as if to get a better look at me, allowing the light from the window to further illuminate his face. I stared in shock at a mangled nose almost completely sliced away. He resembled a pig that had somehow survived its own slaughter.

He noticed my reaction and laughed through his mangled lips, "Not pretty, no not pretty at all." He took the reigns from me and said, "It's not here, your package. We have to drive down to the end of the street. Even the Runners have second thoughts about visiting where we're headed."

We entered an area that was shrouded in heavy darkness. Our passage was surrealistic, the carriage like a ship skating on a sheet of black ice. Even the horse's steady plod was muffled by the frost heavy ground mist. The distant barking of some dogs was the only proof we were still in the city.

He halted the horse by a dilapidated loading dock. I heard the lapping swish of water. He stepped down and told me to stay put. In a moment, I heard the low sound of conversation then the scraping of something being dragged. I started at the surprising shift in weight when a large object was thrown in the carriage bed.

The man climbed back in and took the reigns in hand.

"Don't worry at my rough treatment," he said with a slight chuckle, "that one back there can't be damaged none."

We arrived back at the pub after what seemed an endless trip through the shadow lands of London.

"This is as far as I go," the man said and held out his hand. "Now, I'll have my fee, laddie."

I handed over a small pouch. I had no clue how much the university paid him, nor did I want to know. I considered ignorance to be in my favor should I ever be caught.

After I gave up the money, he slipped it inside his coat pocket and withdrew a large cigar. When he lit it, the flame illuminated him fully. It was all I could do to stifle a shriek. Grubbs had suffered dearly from his injuries. Broom had been told the truth about the man's wounds, but Grubbs was certainly still with us. As much as I loathed him, I was terrified and turned away to keep him from getting a long look at me.

"Well," he said through the cigar smoke, "nice doing business with you, laddie. Maybe we can do it again sometime."

I did not answer, only shuddered under my coat as I watched him limp into the gloom beyond the pub.

I returned to the university and unloaded the body. I was still shocked at seeing Grubbs. By the time I got home I was exhausted and trembling. Everyone was already bedded down, so I undressed quietly as not to wake Nara. She turned over when I slipped under the covers but just sighed softly before returning to her deep slumber.

My night was restless and plagued by the scarred image of Grubbs. I wasn't certain if I should tell Broom that he was still alive or not. It was unlikely their paths would cross, but because of the ill feelings between the two it seemed prudent to alert Broom. I had long suspected that Broom had been Grubbs' assailant. Just because he had not recognized me, after all I had grown from a boy to a man since my last encounter with Grubbs, did not assure he wouldn't know Broom, especially with the tell tale patch of webbed skin covering Broom's eye.

As it happened, Broom had known about Grubbs' reemergence for quite some time and had said nothing in order to prevent old bitter memories from afflicting me. Broom was upset and worried that I had put myself in jeopardy by picking up corpses for the medical school, but he was even more disturbed that I had crossed paths with Grubbs.

"I thought that filth was, if not dead, gone," Broom said. "It's lucky, it is, that he didn't know you. I imagine he'll stay close to that area of London to keep away from the law, but you ought to steer clear of that territory no matter what the university wishes."

I confided to Broom my speculation that he had been the one to inflict those wounds on Grubbs. Broom chuckled but did not affirm or deny my suspicion. The subject was dropped, but both Broom and I still kept a vigil out for Grubbs.

Not long after my confession to Broom about collecting cadavers for the university anatomy classes, he asked me to accompany him to a local Public House called Shaw's. "There's someone I would like you to meet. An acquaintance of mine from earlier days," he said. I usually finished my Friday lab early and saw no reason not to go. After all, I trusted Broom in all things, including my wife and my well being. When I arrived home, Broom told Ranjana and Nara not to keep supper for us then whisked me away. Both women eyed us, but made no complaint.

So I was on my first night out with the man who had looked after me for such a long time. I had never been to a pub as a patron and was not prepared for the cold stares from within. "Pay no attention, lad," Broom said as he placed a hand on my shoulder. "This is not like The Bricklayer's Arms. It's a clean family place." He was right; the patrons soon turned their attention from me and went back about their own business. After the initial shock of unwelcome glances, I found the place to be warm and inviting. There was the aromatic odor of tobacco laced within the pleasant smell of cooking meat. Indeed, the dressed body of a pig turned slowly on a spit inside the fireplace. The clink of mugs and glasses along with good-natured laughter added to the pleasant atmosphere of the place.

Broom directed me to a table in the far corner of the room. There sat a middle aged man dressed in simple clothes. A faded top hat and weathered coat hung above him. He was thin of build and seemed to be drifting in his own thoughts. A flagon of ale and a plate of picked over food sat in front of him. He held a long slender white pipe nonchalantly in his hand while a line of smoke drifted out of the corners of his mouth. His spell of relaxation was broken when he recognized Broom.

"Well glory be if it ain't Mr. Broom," he said cheerfully, put down his pipe and extended his hand. "And who's this young fellow then?" The man took a second glance at me. His brow creased. "A bit dark isn't he, Mr. Broom. Don't know as they'll serve him here," then to me as he gave me his hand, "No offense, young sir. No offense."

"None taken," I answered as Broom and I hung up our hats and coats and sat down across from the man. Once I had a better look at him, I saw his face was sunken and dreadfully pocked. His hair was dark and fell to his narrow shoulders.

"This is the young man I talked with you about. This is Charles Wilkins," Broom explained to the man.

A light danced in the man's green eyes. "The university boy?" he asked Broom who nodded. "You'll have to excuse me, I've had a bit to drink already but it's comin' back to me, what you asked when we crossed paths a few days past."

A plump woman wearing a short bonnet and apron came to the table and asked what our pleasure was. She glanced at me, then at the publican behind the bar. He shrugged and went on wiping down some glasses.

"Are you hungry, lad?" Broom asked. I had to admit I was. The tang of the cooking meat had set my stomach to rumbling. "Then we'll take of plate each of that pork along with potatoes and peas and two loaves," Broom said then added, "I'll have a pint for me and," he pointed to the man across from us, "this gentleman. I don't think the lad cares for spirits though."

"Not ale," I answered, "but I've had a glass of gin now and then during late nights at the lab."

Broom grinned. "Then a glass of gin for the young man," he said to the woman.

As the woman walked away, I saw the man staring at my face. "Lord but your eyes are as blue as the heavens, boy," he said, "and the name Wilkins, that's not no foreign native tag by God."

"His mother," Broom advised.

"Well, I'll just say," the man extended his hand to me again. "A pleasure it is to meet a fellow countryman, even if only half." I could feel my cheeks blushing but checked the anger. This man was not insulting me. He was only a bit coarse, so I took his hand. "The name is Stevens, young sir," he announced. "John Stevens, cabman at your service."

Our food arrived. As we ate, Broom and Stevens exchanged pleasantries. I was more concerned with curbing my hunger with the delicious pork and vegetables than in their conversation, but I gathered enough to understand they had met through Stevens' cab service.

After our plates were picked clean and removed from the table, Broom ordered another pint for him and Stevens, and another gin for me. I was beginning to warm up from the meal and the drink. I could see the ale was relaxing Broom, but Stevens, who had been drinking before our arrival, was beginning to get that sotted look around his eyes. It wasn't long until his lips were loose enough to tell me what Broom had asked him to. "Resurrection Men," he said softly, stumbling over the s.

"Resurrection Men?" I asked, apparently too loudly as Stevens put a finger to his lips.

"Shhh, lad," he whispered then looked around to see if anyone was listening. Of course by that time of the evening the patrons were mellowed out with food and drink and content to commune in their own groups. Satisfied no one was spying, Stevens continued. "I used to be in Edinburgh," he said, his speech thickening. "The cabby trade weren't all too profitable so I did a little extra work for the medical school. Like what Broom tells me you do on occasion." I glanced at Broom who directed my stare back to Stevens who leaned back and sighed, then took another healthy swallow from his mug. "I had no missus and no children," Stevens continued. "My parents, God rest em', had departed a while back so I was my own man and not necessarily particular about the work I took. Mind you I never did no actual 'resurrecting', and, being the God fearing person I was, it took a right chill to me the first time I saw a body digged up in the wee morning hours.

"The university's contact was the actual digger. He used a wooden spade so to be as quiet as he could. He never said much, just told me which graveyard to go to. It didn't take long for families to raise a voice over the harsh treatment of their recently departed. A lot of them grievin' kin would guard the grave, or hire someone to, until they knew the body would be corrupt enough and less desirable for anatomy classes.

"So we mostly transported deceased paupers or those dead who had no family or none with enough money to post a guard at the place of interment." Stevens picked up and repacked his pipe. He lit the bowl and turned it upside down as he drew the smoke. "But even a bright boy like you, young sir, understands the rule of supply and demand. There just weren't enough bodies." I saw a visible shudder cover Stevens. He shook his head. He turned those piercing green eyes to me. For what had been an inebriated man, Stevens' look was stone cold sober. "The university's resurrector man contacted me as usual, only his meeting place this time was a group of old, run down lodgings derelicts frequented. You know the type: drunks, the sick, and the wretchedly poor. Anyways, when we arrived there, the man motioned me out. 'Your cozy days are over,' he told me. 'I'll be needing a hand tonight'. Well, downright insulted I was and told him so. He threw back his head and laughed. He grabbed me by the collar and snarled. There weren't much light, but it was enough. All the trips I'd made with him I had never been this close to the man. I could see a long scar round' his neck. And his nose, God's mercy, was almost cut away."

The food that had set so warmly in my stomach now turned cold and hard. A beaded sweat broke out on my forehead. Stevens let wisps of smoke drift from his nostrils. "That's right, lad," Stevens said, aware of the pained expression my face. "It was your Grubbs, one and the same. He must have fled London when some assailant laid a heavy hand to him and there I was, clutched by the vile man hisself".

"Well, I was petrified of him and put up no fight. The Lord hates a coward but I was willing to be hated by a forgiving God rather than killed by a madman. He smiled at my weakness, released my collar and brushed off the place where his hold had been. 'Just follow me,' he ordered, 'and be quick about it. These sods take their liquor better than you think. They won't be out for long.'

"We had no lantern, but made our way through the place following candles set and lighted sparsely down the different passageways. Grubbs stopped outside one open door and motioned me to follow. A ruined bed lay in the corner of the meager room. On the bed, stretched out in disorder, was a body, breathing with difficulty. Grubbs lit two wall candles. The light shifted in the stale air and shadow danced along the walls. The body was that of a man. His age was a mystery, but he was certainly not an elderly one. His grizzled appearance hid his true years. Wet snores came in spasms. As I walked closer to the bed, the smell was horrid, like rotted meat and sour wine. 'Tie this round' his legs and hold em', Grubbs commanded. "What?" I asked still appalled by the smell and condition of the fellow human lying in that poor state before me. Grubbs grabbed my hands, placing a rope in them. 'Tie up his legs and hold 'em!' he growled.

"I did as he asked, but my hands trembled. Grubbs grabbed the man's arms and started to tie them as well when the fellow woke up. The man belched loudly and a grimace covered his face. 'What the devil?' the man on the bed mumbled and began struggling with Grubbs. 'Grab them legs!' Grubbs roared at me, but I was shocked and let go. The man flipped away from Grubbs and landed hard on the floor. He held up his hands to knock away Grubbs' effort to garb him. Grubbs actually slipped, falling face first to the floor. The poor derelict was trying to crawl away and out the door. He was cursing and whining. It was pitiful.

"Grubbs was only stunned. He righted himself and stood. A slow trail of blood slid down his cheek. 'Idiot,' Grubbs said to me. 'Now I got to work harder.' He knew I was useless and gave me no more orders. He approached the crawling man. 'Come here, you rummy,' he said and tossed the man over. The weak fluttering of the man's hands was useless against Grubbs. 'Please,' the man begged. 'Mercy. I never done no harm. It's just the drink, just the . . . .' Simultaneously, Grubbs fell on the man, pinning his flailing arms, then put his thick hands in a hold over the man's nose and mouth. The derelict thrashed about, his wailing muffled under the force of Grubbs' powerful hands. As I had tied his legs, the man had no chance to break away. I watched him die, choking for air, any air, even the air that had only moments before ran with difficulty through his drunken body.

"When it was over, I stood stunned and speechless. Grubbs got up. 'You can't damage the goods, you see.' He said, wiping sweat from his head. 'You have to catch them passed out from drink, tie them and smother them. Asphyxiation don't damage enough to make a difference for the university lab.'

"But what about the authorities?" I stupidly asked "And the university professors? This one will still be warm, no rigor will set in yet.

"Grubbs walked to me. There was dried blood on his face and lips from his earlier fall. He punched a finger into my chest. 'Don't worry about those things. And don't think of telling neither. You've picked up plenty of stiff ones, and you just stood and watched me dispatch this one. You're in it just as deep as me and don't you forget it.' Grubbs removed his finger and smiled the most menacing vile grin I've ever witnessed. 'And the university? The warmer the better and bettered paid for it.' He went back to the body and tied the arms together. 'Just you grab one end then,' he directed, 'unless you want to be the second package for the evening.'

"I helped him all right, I did. And he murdered two more that week, one of them a frail lass. And I ain't had a decent night's sleep since." Stevens set his pipe down and looked directly into my eyes. "If you want my advice, young sir, you'll separate yourself from that monster just like I did. When I left Edinburgh, I thought I'd seen the last of him. Imagine my horror when I talked to Mr. Broom and found out Grubbs was back in London. Now I live in terror Grubbs will run into me one day, enough terror that what little sleep I did manage is taken away." Stevens sighed and took a drink then said, "And even though I never ratted on him, Grubbs will see my sudden departure from our work arrangement as an insult. He'll think I treated him unfairly, he will." Stevens sat down his drained mug and looked me straight in the eye again. "Unless you stop this business, young sir, you just might find yourself rubbin' elbows with them resurrectors down at The Bricklayer's Arms, for that is surely their second home." Stevens stood and took down his hat and coat. Putting them on, he visibly shivered. "Bit nippy out," he said with distraction as he looked around the pub. He shook Broom's and my hand. "Good evening to you both," he said then added, "I think I'll be headed to Wales. Too small an area for Grubbs to bother with." He tipped his hat and left.

Broom and I sat in silence for awhile. "I just wanted you to know what you're really exposing yourself to, lad," Broom finally said.

What could I say other than he was right, but I also told him that refusing to continue this grisly business might bring about repercussions from the university, maybe costing me my status there. "And what about Grubbs?" I asked Broom. "What terrors might that monster inflict on me, on you, Ranjana, or Nara if I don't comply?"

Broom stood and took down our coats and hats. He handed me mine, placed his hand on my shoulder and said, "Then if you won't stop, please let me go with you."

"But then you'll be involved, and you know Grubbs will recognize you."

He winked and walked me toward the door. "I'm not worried about being involved, lad, only your safety concerns me." Then, we walked out of the warmth of the pub into the night's chill.

I was called upon very little in the following months as far as picking up bodies was concerned. Fortunately, what trips I made were nowhere near the area I went with Grubbs.

That summer, Nara and I had planned to take our postponed honeymoon, but I was asked to help at the university. Their summer session laboratory assistant had broken his leg in a cricket match and would not be able to set up labs for the medical students. Nara was disappointed, but did not dwell on it. She said she realized the importance of my university activities in regard to our future.

"Besides," she said with a laugh, "in a short while I'll have you to myself, to do with as I please." She did add that if the opportunity presented itself, she expected me to whisk her away on a romantic trip.

The summer crawled by. The lectures in the laboratory were longer and more tedious than the ones held during the academic autumn and spring semesters. Close to the end of the second summer semester I was called upon to obtain another body for anatomy studies. The pickup was to be in an area close to where I lived, putting me more at ease. That section of London was populated by a high percentage of Indian and mixed Indian blood.

I told Broom where I was going. As usual, he said he would come along.

After picking up the body, we headed back through the night. The location was vastly different from the dreary area where Grubbs had taken me. The aroma of food being prepared permeated the nighttime air. I could almost be certain by smell alone just what was being prepared and the spices used. People milled about taking no notice of us. Death and the remains it left behind were a familiar event in India. Disease and starvation had made these travelers to London accustomed to the bundle we carried in the carriage bed.

As we reached the last turn before the university, a figure came out of the shadows and grabbed the horse's bridle, surprising me and the animal. My first impulse was that the police had been tipped off and were in wait to catch us with the evidence resting stiffly in the carriage bed. I turned to Broom and told him to run. If anyone was to be arrested, I wanted it to be me and not my innocent friend.

When I looked at Broom's face, I knew something was dreadfully wrong. He appeared to be caught in the middle of a silent cry, his mouth open and twisted. A pointed blade exited just below his Adam's apple. A knife had been skillfully and silently driven through the back of Broom's neck.

Only a faint trickle of blood ran from the wound. Broom fell forward, and his head landed in my lap just as I felt a blade being pressed against my throat.

"No screaming, laddie," an all too familiar voice whispered in my ear. "Get down slowly. No heroics unless you want to join your companion."

As I climbed down, he followed me out of the carriage. "No need in a young university boy choking on his own blood now is there?" I shook my head 'no' and he continued, "I think you know who I am. We did business last fall, remember?" This time I nodded in agreement.

Grubbs' silent partner was busy removing the cadaver from the cart's bed. I was petrified at the prospect of my own demise and, at the same instant, filled with a black primordial hatred for Grubbs. Had I been larger and stronger I might have bested him and his accomplice. Instead, my frail weakness placed me in the position of a predator's embrace.

One thing in my favor was that Grubbs still gave no indication of recognizing me, or Broom for that matter. Had he attacked Broom face to face, Grubbs might have recalled the scar tissue covering my friend's eye.

Broom! Staring at his body the comprehension of his death hit me like a steel mallet. I struggled and Grubbs tightened his grip on my throat. "No need for that, laddie," he hissed.

I went limp, the warm rage lingering on my face matched by the hot tears streaming down it. "That's more like it," Grubbs said and lessened his hold on me, "now listen, laddie, there is a man at your university named Hobbs who will be in touch with you soon. He will tell you where to make future pick ups." His grip tightened again, "You will do business with no one else. Is that clear!" I swallowed convulsively against his hold on my throat and nodded in agreement. "Good," he clucked then added, "if you cross me, boy, I will see to it your death is slower and more painful than your friend's was." Grubbs struck the back of my head, sending me dazed to the ground. He turned me on my back and struggled with his bad leg to put all his weight on my waist, immobilizing me. My sight blurred. Grubbs' face looked huge and inhuman as he bent toward me. He spoke, his words a strange echo in the night air. "Just a slight sting, laddie. Something to bind our contract."

It was astonishing! He stabbed me just above my navel. The pain was so severe I was certain Grubbs had changed his mind about killing me. As he slid the blade away, I felt the warm flow of blood soak into my shirt. I passed out watching him walk away.

There were no police, no questions.

I'm not certain how I was transported to my home, but I imagine Grubbs' collaborator had a hand in it.

When I finally regained consciousness, I awakened to the sound of soft weeping.

I was in my room. Nara sat next to the bed and placed a cool cloth on my forehead. I tried to move but a sharp sting in my abdomen stopped me. A cold sweat broke over my body and I shivered.

"Stay still, Charles," Nara sighed, "you will start bleeding again if you stir too much." I saw her face was set with concern, but there were no tears in her eyes.

I lifted my head tentatively. Ranjana was in a chair across the room. She was the one sobbing. She must have drained her eyes, only trails of dried tears remained on her cheeks.

I looked at Nara and asked, "Is she . . . ?" Nara shushed me. "But I want . . . ." Nara placed her hand lightly on my lips and implored with her eyes for me to be silent.

I lay my head back on the pillow. Nara gave me a spoon of bitter tasting liquid.

"This is an herb that will calm you and ease the pain," she said.

I was in and out of awareness for what seemed a long time. At times I would wake and see Nara still sitting by the bed. Sometimes I would hallucinate and see Broom's face descend on me as the knife point burst through his throat.

When the drug wore off, I awakened and found Nara asleep in the chair next to me. Ranjana was standing behind her. She glanced at me and said, "They took his body," then repeated, "took his body." She turned and walked away on shaky legs from the room.

I knew what she meant. Broom's body had been sold to the university. The idea of a student cutting open my friend was so repugnant it caused me to shake and sob. Nara woke at my disturbance and held me until I could contain myself. She looked into my eyes and said, "Your wound was just under the skin, no muscle was injured. You must lie quietly for the tissue and vessels to heal properly."

"But, Broom's body!"

"A man brought you here. He told us Broom's corpse had been taken away. He said if we contacted the police or anyone else about the matter we would find ourselves on a dissection table as well."

"You must ask Pavan for help," I pleaded. "You must . . . ."

Nara cut me off. "No," she said. "He cannot be involved. What happened is over, finished. You will heal and go on just as mother and I will do. I'll not have you taken from me. Never!"

"Nara, the man responsible for this hurt me in the past. He has to be stopped. He . . . ."

Nara put her hand over my mouth. "I know what you have been involved with. The man who brought you here told me. If you expose him, you will expose yourself. There is too much sadness in this home already. Do not add to it." My eyes brimmed with fresh tears as she continued, "My mother's husband, our good friend and adoptive father, is dead. We cannot bring him back. You have come too far in your studies to seek a vengeance that will only lead to your ruin. I beg you to put this behind you, dear husband. For my sake, I beg you."

She hugged me and shed tears of her own. I knew she was right in what she asked of me, but to allow Grubbs' escape from his monstrous deeds without punishment was a horror in itself. I accepted the need for revenge, no matter what Nara wished.

I was up and around in less than a week. As Nara had said, the wound was superficial, inflicting more pain than damage. The university had been informed I would be absent due to a stomach ailment, but would return to set up the remainder of the summer labs shortly. After I had gone back to my duties at the university, I was contacted by the man Grubbs had mentioned. This man Hobbs resembled a ferret. He constantly wrung his hands together when he talked. When I had finished the first errand he sent me on, Hobbs offered me my end of the money. I refused it and he smiled, saying he would put it up for me. I told him not to bother, that I wished no further profit from the dead. "Well, when you change you mind, you know where to find me," he offered as he left me alone in the hall leading to the anatomy lab.

It was during this period my grades hit bottom. I was still passing, but not with the high marks my professors were accustomed to. When they questioned me, I told them my health had suffered that summer and I was easily fatigued.

I was approached by Hobbs fewer times than anticipated. It occurred to me I could lie about the pickups. I might tell Hobbs no one had showed up with the body, or that the police were in the area where I had been sent, making it too risky for all involved, but I never knew when Grubbs would appear on an assigned route. Occasionally, he might show up along the way, surprising me at a dark corner. Sometimes Grubbs would be waiting at the pick up point. He never said much other than to give me some added instruction, so I could not risk trying to cross him. How I prayed for the day when I would find the right moment to dispatch him for Broom's murder. I carried a scalpel purloined from the medical laboratory in my coat pocket. Nothing would have satisfied me more than cutting out Grubbs' heart and shoving it down his throat.

As much as I hated Grubbs, I was still a coward in his presence. There was more than one instance when I could have attempted to murder him, but fear of Grubbs always took precedence over my abhorrence of the man. I would return home trembling in disgust at my impotence. I was short tempered with Nara and had become as despondent and moody as Ranjana. Poor Nara, how alone she must have felt with her husband and mother moving like zombies throughout the house.

My final year at the university would be marked by two life-changing events: the death of Pavan, and the discovery of my mother's journal.

It had been impossible to keep the events surrounding Broom's death from Pavan. I'm certain he had tried to bring Grubbs to justice, but although Pavan had influence, he was still a man of color and limited to how much power he could wield. Whatever attempts he made to obtain justice for Broom or to get me released from my association with Grubbs failed. Being the kind and helpful soul he was I'm sure Pavan's disappointment at not being able to aid me contributed to his failing health. He died from heart disease at the beginning of my final spring term.

In his will, Pavan left the spice and herb shop to Ranjana. For Nara and me, he had purchased a small town house near the university. He guessed Nara would continue to help her mother at the shop, but it was his desire that Nara and I have a place of our own for the privacy a young couple yearns for.

Pavan also left a large sum of money to Ranjana, Nara, and me. Enough, in fact, that we could make the grand tour for a year after I graduated and still have ample funds to begin our life with on our return. Nara and I decided to stay with Ranjana until I finished my classes. This would allow time for Ranjana to get used to the idea of living alone so soon after her loss of Broom.

I did not finish with honors, but I graduated. It was a miracle I managed to complete my studies despite all that had happened in the last year.

It would have been naïve of me to assume the end of school would terminate my connection with Grubbs. Hobbs came to the shop one evening and informed me that, since I had more time on my hands after graduating, Grubbs would be increasing my duties in the body trade along with some other special jobs. I told Hobbs I had no intention of doing any further missions for Mr. Grubbs. I was angry and shook as I spoke to him, but Hobbs was unmoved and seemed amused at my outburst. "We'll see about that, boy," he offered cynically and left.

I realized any physical harm to me or my family would come from Grubbs, not Hobbs. Had it been Grubbs come a' calling to the shop, I'm confident my cowardly manner would have surfaced again.

After obtaining my degree, the university offered me a position as assistant teacher in charge of the science and medical labs. It would be my responsibility to hire the laboratory assistants and conduct lectures. I was pleased and frustrated at the same time, hesitant in accepting due to Grubbs' illicit connection with the anatomy labs.

Being unsure of what action to take, I decided to seek a place in Pavan's old firm after Nara and I moved. Since I had worked there previously, I felt the new owner might take me in.

Our leaving the shop appeared to have no effect on Ranjana. Since Broom's murder, she had turned into little more than a specter, haunting the shop rather than living there. Maybe she felt ill toward me. After all, I was a witness and could have turned Grubbs in to the authorities. Surely she appreciated the fact that had I done so, Grubbs would have arranged for her and Nara's death by whatever grisly design came to him. After we moved, I could not help but feel a stab of regret and guilt toward the woman who had given me a home over the last four years.

The town house Pavan had purchased for Nara and me was situated in a strong middle class section of London. The new neighbors appeared suspicious of our brown skin, but I knew this would pass in time. While we were moving our things in, those who had been scrutinizing us became bored and went back into their own homes. Twilight was stirring the warm air as I struggled up the steps with the last piece of furniture—my mother's trunk.

On more than one occasion, I had considered selling the large bulky case but could not go through with it. I suppose it still tied me to a strange past I desired to understand. Nara and I were exhausted physically and mentally from the move. I told her not to bother helping me with the trunk. She could get started unpacking inside. Had she been guiding me, I probably would not have missed the last step, lost my hold on the trunk and tumbled with it to the yard below.

Besides falling hard on my rear, I was not harmed. The trunk appeared undamaged with the exception of a notable rattle when Nara, who had come to my aid, helped me right it and move it into the house. When I opened it to see what had come undone, I was met with an ornate jeweled necklace and a worn leather bound journal. On closer inspection, I discovered a concealed drawer had sprung open during the fall down the steps, spilling its secret treasure into the body of the trunk. I picked up the necklace. It was cold and heavy. Its gems winked at me with red and green flashes as the room light played over and around them.

"It is so beautiful," Nara gasped as I held it against her.

I clasped it around her neck and beheld a princess of India before me, the thick golden frame of the necklace leaping out from the dark brown of her skin. I was overcome with passion and kissed her deeply. She returned my kiss with equal intensity as I began to remove our clothing. We made love with abandon. The movement of our flesh against each other was primal and the most exquisite sensation I had experienced.

Slaked, we lay naked in each other's arms, the sweat warm and clinging to our skin. I stood up and she smiled, the necklace rising up and down slowly on her chest as she breathed. I picked her up in my arms and carried her to the bedroom.

"I love you and only you," Nara whispered.

In the morning I felt wonderful, all my darkest moments were far away. Nara must have been in a similar mood as she hummed when bathing, something she had not done in a long while.

As I listened to her soft song, I remembered the journal that had fallen from the hidden drawer. I went to the front room of the house. The trunk was standing like a sentinel who had observed our lovemaking in silence. The journal was lying just in front of it.

For the rest of the day, Nara and I read and reread my mother's writings of the wonder and terror during her days in Pasha, India:

January 17, 1798

As father feared, the winter monsoons have arrived before he could reach the mountain range.

DR. GLENN RUSSELL, ROUND ROCK, TEXAS

1995

1

Peter Lockley is not my friend.

Being a fellow M.D., he is a colleague, and as a mentor, my teacher. Friendship is an emotion I do not desire. When I asked Peter just what I had become, he left me some of his extensive research on the virus. I am certain he kept some knowledge from me. No sense in giving too much away.

His group was extensive made up of doctors, lawyers, and C.E.Os. There were lower members, but not many. Most of the females, like Maria, were used for producing a child from the above select group to insure intelligent breeding. If we were anything, we were social insects, ironic in itself as studies suggested the virus was originally transmitted by an insect. The queen of our society was the infection, the king Peter, leaving us drones and the workers.

During the days after I was taken home from disposing of my last meal's body, I studied the research Peter had done over a period of more than fifty years. The virus resembled the rabies strain, but, unlike that killer, it used the human brain to build a better beast. The virus selected the most efficient attributes of the animal it infected, applying them for a tenacious ability to survive. Any warm-blooded mammal would do, but man turned out to be the best vehicle, the highest on the food chain so to speak.

What a wonder the organism was.

The infected individual experienced physiological and metabolic mutations. Increased myoglobin oxygen affinity ensured a rich supply of oxygen to tissues and organs even in a state of decreased air for breathing.

The increased myoglobin required more iron, fueling the hunger for blood and raw flesh. The heart, liver, kidneys, and lungs decreased in size due to their enhanced efficiency. Waste in the form of dried feces came in small amounts from a shrunken stomach and modified intestinal tract.

To protect this marvel of anatomy, the subcutaneous muscle tissue thickened by doubling and redoubling its striations, enough to keep a small caliber bullet from piercing it. Large caliber metal, unfortunately, could still kill as well as a good strong blade, a blow to the head, fire, and old age. The virus could not make the body immortal, but it certainly gave it extraordinary healing prowess and longevity.

The teeth. Ah, yes, the upper canines were replaced by a slightly larger and more slender pair of razor sharp weapons. The new teeth were serrated on the reverse side for ripping and tearing. These killing machines could slit a throat and shred an abdomen in a matter of seconds. The increased pounds per square inch pressure from the jaw muscles and strengthened bone fashioned a human version of a pit bull.

And I was one of these wonders now, a monster and a predator in a world of bleating prey.

It had been two days and I was feeling pangs of hunger. Tonight Peter would pick me up for a dinner at the mausoleum in the forested area behind Old Town Cemetery. There I would meet my colleagues; there my hunger would be slaked.

2

After we arrived at the tomb and descended its stairs, we were greeted by a small group consisting of twelve individuals. Among them were other doctors and nurses from Peter's clinic, some lawyers and businessmen, and a few young women including Maria.

We were served a stimulating drink of champagne mixed with blood. Soon after, we were seated at the dining table.

"Glenn," Peter informed the group, "will be working at the clinic soon."

"That's marvelous," a man sitting next to Peter said. "We always welcome an experienced pair of hands."

"As I told Peter," I explained, "I'm a bit rusty in the OB GYN procedures I performed during my residency." The cook entered and all heads turned from my conversation. He placed a large steaming tray of medium sized pies on individual plates by the table. The smell was maddening. It was all I could do to restrain myself from seizing the one placed in front of me.

Peter noticed my yearning. He stood and said, "Our newest member looks a bit anxious." He paused then looked in my eyes. "By all means,

Glenn, you may begin." This prompted the rest of the guests to dig their forks into the pies as well.

My appetite was out of control. I ignored the fork and tore open the crust with my greedy fingers. Inside the pie was a living human fetus. The crust had been baked then folded around it. The tiny body twitched like a larvae inside a cocoon. I felt no abhorrence, no repulsion. All that came to mind as I ripped the fetus apart, gorging and slurping bits from my bloody fingers, was the nursery rhyme 'Four and twenty blackbirds baked in a pie'. It was the most luscious meal I had experienced in my life.

Unlike my impetuous feeding, Peter was restrained. He sliced his meal into small pieces and ate slowly and methodically. "It's a lovely preparation," he said to me as I wiped my hands and mouth. "The pastry shell consists of remaining body parts from victims like the young girl you feasted on recently." Peter pointed to bits of crust with the tip of his fork. "The cook grinds the parts into a pulp, adds water and flour," he continued while pinching his fingertips in front of his lips, "and voila, a delightful crust to wrap the squirming mass in!"

Just as Peter made his speech, the cook reappeared with another tray and asked, "Seconds, anyone?"

After all were satisfied, the guests formed small separate groups around the room. Peter took me aside, asking me to accompany him for a stroll outside. As we left, I heard a television click on behind us. With the exception of the meal, it was no more than a normal night after a family dinner.

The evening was cool and crisp. An October breeze fashioned a weird chorus in the treetops. Although obscured by the heavy growth of oaks and vines, a bright moon bled a pale light that filtered through the limbs and bathed the area in a pallid radiance.

We walked down a path leading away from the mausoleum and soon came upon another burial crypt. The body of this vault had crumbled and stretched out in sections of scattered stones. The coffins at its center resembled a pair of ancient altars awaiting a sacrifice. Most of the fence around the fallen structure remained intact. There were sections of it here and there that had collapsed and been covered by vines that twisted serpentine around rusted bars. A set of cement benches stood not far from the base of the vault. Peter sat there and I joined him.

"I'm sure you noticed," Peter said, "the young victim you had prior to this night sustained your appetite much longer than usual."

"Yes. I felt no hunger until earlier today."

"The meal tonight," he said smiling "will hold you for close to two weeks. Amazing, isn't it, just how much nourishment fetal tissue can provide."

"How did you discover this?"

"Actually, it was my teacher, Dr. Andrew Morgan, who revealed it to me."

I recalled the name above the mausoleum door. "Is this the same Morgan I saw carved in the stone?"

"It is. He and another rest there," Peter sighed and continued. "Our relationship came about because of my father. I was not infected by the direct introduction of the virus into living tissue as you were. Mine was genetic, from my mother when she gave birth to me in London. She had not received the needed stimulus to be transformed, but the virus was present and passed to me. My father, however, was quite normal.

"I was sickly and given to bouts of melancholy as a child. My father, being the proper Englishman he was, considered my behavior strange and decided I needed some 'straightening' out. He thought it prudent for me to be placed in a private school where I could learn the attributes of becoming a man. I was eight when he enrolled me at the Stillwell Home, a very stark and starched boarding school. Some of the neighborhood children were familiar with the home's reputation and were more than happy to share it with me.

"Stillwell had once been an institution for religious training. It was said to be an unsavory place, with tales of debauchery, molestation and murder littering its dark history. Ghosts had been sighted apparently, their moans echoing in shadowy places. You can imagine just how chilled a pale lad of eight felt at the prospect of living there.

"But the place proved to be gloomy, not haunted. The only beasts around were the upper classmen who made life a living purgatory for us underlings. There was one particular boy, an oaf named Henry Hull, who delighted in persecuting me mentally and physically. His behavior was never checked by our instructors despite several complaints, and when I pleaded with my father during his visitations I was told to 'buck up and act like a man.' When I was ten, just before the Christmas break, Hull chided me about my paleness, saying I was a soft, impotent excuse for a Stillwell Man. He shoved me against a door and proceeded to pinch the soft flesh under my arm. It hurt badly. The more he grinned and inflicted pain, the madder I became. Although sickly, I had grown over the past two years. I had endured enough of Hull's turdish behavior and kneed him in the crotch with as much force as I could muster. He screamed and doubled over, slipping to the floor. I leapt on him and pounded his back with my clenched fists then clamped an earlobe between my teeth and ripped it away.

"Needless to say, the fellow was quite surprised by my fury. However, he did recover his ground and awarded me the beating of a lifetime. Before he could kill me, which I'm certain was his intention, Hull was pulled away by one of the school masters. The punishment given to us was banishment to our rooms for the remainder of the day, nothing more. Sitting on my bed, tears and mucous streaking my face, I became aware of a strange sweet taste in my mouth. It was Hull's blood. And that was the key, the impetus for activating the carrier gene. Cooked or heated blood did not work. It had to be fresh from the vessels. As a scientific point, Glenn, there is an extra molecule on the enzyme chain of amylase found in a carrier's saliva. This is passed on to offspring. It opens the door for the dormant virus to infect the host.

"My transformation was gradual. I became sick when eating prepared food. The headmaster of Stillwell was concerned and summoned my father, advising him to take me for medical evaluation which was not available at the school. Of course, father dismissed the idea. 'This will pass,' he told the headmaster. 'The boy's just faking it to get out of Stillwell. It's too tough here for his tender nature. Just like his mother in that respect.'

"I did not improve. Besides loss of appetite, being in bright light or around loud noises caused me physical agony. Due to my mother's persistent pleas, father did arrange for an appointment with a local doctor. This was Dr. Andrew Morgan. Fortune blessed me as he suffered from the same viral infection. He recognized the symptoms immediately. It was astronomical luck that I was taken to him. Any other doctor would have suspected rabies and given me up for dead. Andrew convinced my parents I was suffering from severe iron deficiency and should be hospitalized for a time. I believed his diagnosis as well, but he was soon to instruct me in the true nature of the disease. He treated me, he taught me, and he fed me.

"Mother was pacified by my quick recuperation. My father seemed at a loss as to what to do with me. He wasn't sure they would take me back at Stillwell, but Andrew had connections and saw to my reinstatement. He made arrangements with the headmaster to allow me to be excused for weekly exams at his office, checkups Andrew deemed necessary for my recovery. Soon after I went back to Stillwell, my mother became pregnant. She died in childbirth and within a year of mother's passing father was murdered by unknown assailants. After their estate was settled, there was very little left for me. After resolving their debts, Andrew adopted me. There was no resistance to this arrangement by any of my parent's surviving relations. In fact, besides a few people who had worked with my father, I saw or heard from no one after their death.

"When I completed my studies at Stillwell, I was accepted into medical school. It was during this period that Andrew made his discovery regarding the nourishment of fetal tissue in regard to our condition. After I graduated, I went into practice with Andrew in a small clinic much like the one I oversee now.

"I became obsessed with the origin of the virus. I grew cultures to study its chemical structure and characteristics but was unable to keep them viable long enough for use in live animal studies. One evening when I was working late in the laboratory, Andrew came in and asked that I come with him. 'I have someone I want you to meet,' he said. 'I believe you are ready now.'

"As well as I knew him, I realized it was no use to ask questions, so I put on my coat, extinguished the lights in the lab and walked into the cool London night with him. We eventually entered one of the poorer districts of London. I recognized the area well as many of my younger female patients in need of a helping hand came from there. Eventually, Andrew stopped at a shop that sold herbs and spices. He took a key from his pocket and opened the door. He motioned for me to follow. After he closed and locked the door behind him, Andrew led me past a long counter where the herbs were stored then through a doorway covered by beads. Once we entered, a strong smell of incense filled the air. The more we advanced, the hint of an underlying decay drifted through the incense. Passing through another beaded door, we entered a small room with only the dim light of a candle illuminating it. The scent of incense was overwhelming, but for all of its pungent nature it could not cover the stench from a cot in the far corner of the room.

"A figure rested there in the dim candlelight. Its features made hideous by the flickering bursts of shadows. It resembled a hairless monkey on the verge of mummification. It was about five feet in length and no more than skin and bones. It was naked and had a shriveled tan color as if dried parchment had been stretched tightly over the skeleton. The prominent features of the body were an oversized head and stomach. I moved closer and saw two dark areas and a stubby appendage in the pubic region, shadows of dried and useless genitalia. Large fingerlike projections of veins spread over the sides and bald top of the skull, giving one the impression of a grotesque egg with large knobby ears. As I bent to touch the skin, the thing's eyes flashed open, a painful moan escaped from its throat. It spread its lips, bearing sharp yellow canines.

"I was taken by surprise and jumped back, almost knocking Andrew down. He held me until our balance had been recovered then said softly, as if not to disturb the horror on the cot, 'He has gone beyond the limitations of human flesh and no longer recognizes one of his own kind.' As Andrew spoke, I stared in wonder as the thing struggled to get up. It hissed and rolled, glaring milk-blue eyes at me in frantic hunger.

"Andrew moved behind the bed and gently massaged its forehead. It continued to snap its jaws, but was unable to lift its head so Andrew was in no physical danger from the pitiful thing on the cot. Slowly, under the urging of Andrew's touch, the creature calmed to its comatose state. 'As I did for you, Peter, this one cared for me. Although emotions seem to dim with each new generation of our race, there are some of us who hold an attachment for an elder such as this.' Andrew turned and I caught the brief glint of a tear in his eye. 'You should have seen us years ago. We were such dandies on the town in our capes and top hats. Imagine the surprise of those we encountered when our real intentions were exposed.' Andrew caught himself, 'But I digress. Another story for another time, Peter.'

"A noise came from a darkened corner. Andrew held up his hand to advise me there was no need for alarm. An old woman stood from the shadows and walked toward us. She stared at me through rheumy eyes. 'It is all right, Nara,' Andrew explained. 'This is my associate, Peter Lockley.' She was reassured then and returned to the corner. Andrew followed her, whispered something then bent down behind her. When Andrew stood, he had an object cradled in his arms. 'She watches the store and the foundlings,' Andrew said as he came closer to me. I saw before I could ask what he meant by foundlings. A young boy of only four or five years of age lay languidly in Andrew's arms. The child was waxen, his eyes vacant from sedation by drugs. 'I can no longer feed this old one solid food,' Andrew explained. 'I tried the embryos, but he choked and spit up the material.' Andrew looked at the child he held, 'There are so many of these children roaming the streets in search of food their families cannot provide. No one seems to miss them.'

"I stared in fascination as Andrew placed the child by the wrinkled body on the cot. The old being's eyes flashed open when contact was made with the warm body. The thing's lips smacked wildly as the jaws snapped in search of prey. Andrew moved the boy's arm to the old one's mouth. There was an instant clamping and loud crack of the wrist bones. The child stirred for a moment as the pain rose above the sedative level then settled back into his former passive state. Living blood flowed into the creature. The eyes rolled back revealing a pleasure of white. The boy opened his eyes and looked directly at me, but it was a blank stare, as if I were transparent. Then, the child's gaze fixed in death. Andrew moved the body away and had to use force to free the wrist being sucked. The creature howled when its food was taken away.

"Andrew carried the body to the old woman. In the shadows I could see glimpses of her opening the abdominal cavity for her own meal. After the old one had settled down into a dazed slumber, Andrew and I left the shop, leaving the smell of human decay behind. When we arrived home, Andrew built a fire in the grate and asked that I sit with him awhile. 'His name is Vairaja,' Andrew said. 'His mother was English and his father was Indian from the town of Pasha. Vairaja was an instructor of mine in medical school. I will not go into the details of our history. It is his present condition I wish to talk with you about. I have noticed, dear boy, your struggles in researching the virus. That is why I took you to see Vairaja. What you seek is not imperative. Why the virus exists and where it originated will do nothing to help you control or understand it. Vairaja studied it for years. He was born to a carrier like you. As he believed me to be a highly intelligent subject, he infected me and used me as a living lab experiment. He believed he could learn why we seek out victims, why their blood could give us longevity, but he discovered nothing more than he already knew. Whether we are infected from birth or by contact, the course of our lives is dealt.

"I believe our virus developed early in human evolution. Previous forms had undoubtedly infected primates as well as other mammals. However, it was in man that the virus found its most suitable host due to superior brain function, anatomical complexities, and, inevitably, the human tendency towards aggressive behavior. But the flesh has limitations. No matter the modifications imposed on us by the virus, the body will eventually be weakened by age or illness into the pitiful thing you witnessed tonight.

"That should make us strive harder to understand it," I interrupted. Andrew shook his head. 'You are mistaken in that curiosity. There is only one purpose in the nature of the virus. I will give you an example.' Andrew came and sat next to me. 'Will you kill Vairaja for me, Peter?' he asked. The question shocked me. I stammered, shaken by the idea of killing one of our own. 'The humanity remaining in you, Peter, prevents such an act. When this virus has finally reduced us to the beast it desires, that is when its purpose will be fulfilled.'

"I realized he was right. The virus would be in a state of constant change until it obtained complete control. No matter what I could learn of its origin or traits, it would always be after the fact. I stopped my research then."

Peter ended his story. The night was moving into the early hours of morning. As we walked back to the mausoleum to join the others, I asked him what had happened to Vairaja. "He lies in the second stone coffin next to Andrew," he said. "Andrew brought his remains to America. Nara, Vairaja's wife, would not leave the shop in London. She stayed behind. I have no knowledge of what became of her."

A few guests remained in the dining room. They were watching an old black and white movie on television. We said our goodbyes and Peter took me home. Silence was our passenger and I reflected in it. Was the virus, like other organic life forms on earth, searching for the power of control, or was it the remaining human part of our existence that struggled to contain the purity of the organism's effort to survive? At the dinner party the guests had dressed in the appropriate human manner, had discussed sports, politics, money, and the prospect of gaining more of it. They were alien organisms dressed as human beings. They cherished every moment of the lie.

"I'll see you at the clinic tomorrow," Peter said as I got out of the car.

I told him I was looking forward to it. Then, I walked into my home, undressed and went to bed, experiencing the deepest carefree sleep of my life.

3

All begins with conception. Ideas, the universe . . . life.

Those of us who harbor the virus procreate as other mammals, but for us there is only one chance. After transformation the female carries one remaining egg. She will produce no more. The male holds enough semen for one final ejaculation. It must be given only to his kind. If he impregnates a normal woman, the pregnancy will develop as expected for a while then terminate in a calcified fetus. The virus will only allow creation of its own carriers. One child who may infect many.

I had been at the clinic for less than a week when Peter and Maria came into my office. Without saying a word, Peter took my hand and placed it on Maria's stomach. I had suspected I would rejoice. I had so wanted a child with Janice. Now, my hand softly resting on the tiny bulge of our developing child, I looked at Maria with a sense of completion. I realized this was the closest emotion to love I would ever feel again as my being sensed, in every cell, the presence of its new brother. This must have been what the original cell, swimming in the dark tidal pool of creation, felt as it stretched its membranes and divided.

As the weeks passed, Maria would stop by my office from time to time, but it was only to tell me of her progress. We expected nothing more of each other.

One Friday, as I was about to go home, Peter stopped in. He placed a bundle wrapped in newspaper on my desk. "I am entrusting these journals to your care, Glenn."

"In all honesty, Peter, I find little time for reading anymore."

"Trust me," he said, tapping his fingers on the top of the bundle, "these will intrigue you. They are the writings of Charles Vairaja and Andrew Morgan. You will find answers to questions you have yet to ask on these pages."

I thanked him, promising to care for the journals. Besides himself, I was the only one he had allowed access to the writings.

It was a long while before I did get to the history of my surrogate family tree.

A cold front blew in late one Saturday night. The temperature plunged rapidly in my house so I built a fire. Sitting there, listening to the wood crackle and the rising wind moan like a banshee in search of souls, I picked up the stack of journals. The aroma of aged leather and paper filled the air around me.

I took the top one from the stack and opened it. The first page was blank with the exception of the name Vairaja ornately printed in the center. As the cold night trudged toward dawn, I was transported to a strange country where the history of the virus was first recorded.

THE RECORD OF CHARLES VAIRAJA

1820

Reading my mother's accounts brought a feeling of homesickness to Nara and me. Although, she and I could only recall the coldness of our youth in England, our blood cried for its home in India. It was decided we would take our long delayed honeymoon trip there. Ranjana would accompany us. Perhaps leaving the country would put an end to Grubbs' harassments as well.

After arrangements were made and the tickets purchased, we closed the shop, secured our flat and started the passage for the place of our roots.

The ocean voyage was long and tedious. There is no need to elaborate on it save for two interesting circumstances.

First, there was a murder committed on ship.

I was out for a stroll one morning, trying to get my sea legs. Nara and Ranjana had no problem with the motion of the ship, but I fought nausea from the beginning of the voyage. As I moved around a corner, I came upon a crowd of people. There was a young girl, who looked no older than twenty, lying face up on the deck. One of her pale hands still gripped the bottom deck railing. Her mouth was open in the silent wail of the dead, her eyes fixed and empty. The dress she wore was tangled above twisted legs, revealing naked thighs. I bent to pull the dress down for the sake of decency. An older man with stern gray eyebrows and mustache said, "Better not move anything, old man." But I ignored him and pulled the unfortunate girl's dress over the exposed parts of her body. As I did this, I noticed a small blood trail on the inside of her left thigh.

When the ship's doctor and captain arrived, I, along with the rest of the curious, was dispersed. It was now in the hands of ship's authorities.

Turns out the girl's father, who had recently separated from his wife, followed them on board. He had been sexually abusing his daughter for a long time, the very reason his wife had left him and departed from England. In the heat of passion, the man had strangled his daughter as she resisted his advances. He was discovered hiding below deck. They said he blubbered like a child when taken away.

The event dampened my spirits with sporadic nightmares brought on by the victim's grisly appearance and, no doubt, the state of my stomach's bout with seasickness, but I was soon to improve because of music.

A large orchestra was on the voyage for bookings in India. Whether it was out of boredom or just the need to play, the group held performances for the passengers, and not only those in first class. All were welcome.

The evening that Nara, Ranjana, and I went to hear them, they were playing assorted symphonic sketches followed by various waltzes. I danced with my wife and her mother, spinning to the music. It never occurred to me that I had been seasick. Somehow the exaggerated movements of the waltz actually helped my condition rather than aggravating it. Several men asked Nara to dance and, to my pleasure, she declined. Ranjana, however, took every turn offered, and did so with wild abandon. The bubble of loneliness she had born for the touch of a man was punctured. Ranjana was still a desirable woman, and she caught the eye of more than one male that night.

However, this was the beginning of unfortunate events for her, my wife, and me. Whatever had cured her mourning for Broom also led Ranjana into depravity. After that evening of dancing, she would be away from our cabin most of the night, returning inebriated and unkempt in the early morning hours. We never questioned or chided her behavior. Nara and I assumed Ranjana was learning to enjoy life again. We had no idea she had been sleeping with as many men as she could.

I stood next to a group of young men one afternoon and was enjoying the fresh air and the sight of the waves moving along the ship when I caught snatches of their conversation. Through cigar smoke, I saw them and heard them bragging about their sexual exploits on the voyage. There was no denying Ranjana was being touted in their gossip. The things they said of her were lascivious. The multiple partners, the orgies, an appetite that could only be quenched by a final oblivion of alcohol consumption were but a few of the acts Ranjana committed. Could this be only her guilt, self-abuse, and loathing? Did she consider herself dead to any real love a man could offer?

I confided in Nara and we talked to Ranjana. We told her how much we loved her and how we did not want to see hurt or punishment come her way. She laughed at us. Her eyes were wild and mad as she hurled obscenities, especially at me. I had, after all, been the one with Broom when he was murdered. Maybe she held me accountable.

The conversation resulted in a deep melancholy between the three of us. My nausea returned and I would rarely leave the cabin. One night, long before Ranjana's usual return from her prowling, I declined Nara's request for a breath of air on the deck. She was annoyed with my reclusive behavior and was trying to lift my spirits, but I told her my stomach was in no shape for moving around. This irritated her even more and she left without saying a word, slamming the cabin door behind her.

It was a short time before I heard the door open softly. I looked up expecting a remorseful Nara to be there, but it was Ranjana who entered and closed the door.

She walked in front of me, staring into my eyes.

"Ranjana, is something wrong? Are you injured?" I asked.

Her clothes fell free before me; her naked body just inches away.

"Ranjana, please," I implored. "Please cover yourself."

Before I could object further, Ranjana touched her breast and slowly traced the outline of her nipples. "Don't you want me?" she asked. "I am older, but still firm. I can give you much pleasure."

The scent of her recent sexual activities was musky and stimulating. My face went red. It could have been my mother before me, seducing me. There was no way I could deny the stiffness under my thin nightshirt. She knew what was there and moved to straddle me.

I placed my hands on her to stop the act. In doing so, I brushed her breasts. "Please stop this, Ranjana," I whispered, but she did not and continued to move against my waning resistance. No matter what reserve I tried for, the simple nastiness of her performance was overpowering in its excitement.

My relationship to her as a son-in-law vanished as I cupped her breasts. At that moment, she was beautiful. Ranjana positioned herself on my lap. She was shorter than Nara but almost the same lean weight. Her breasts were larger than her daughter's, the circles around the nipples much darker. Other than the faint trace of cellulite scarring down her belly from childbirth, her skin was smooth to touch.

Nara and I had made love many times. Sometimes softly and slowly, building to a delicious climax. At other times passionately, grinding into a mutual goal of pain and pleasure. Ranjana and I did neither. We were animals entwined in a primal catharsis. We struggled in the shadows with our despairs. The night of my rape so long ago at the hands of those hideous monsters, the death of Broom—these events wailed and twisted in the mass of our taut straining muscles until a shared climax brought us back to reality.

Her thick black hair covering me, Ranjana lay forward and hugged my neck. We wept as our racing hearts slowed. There was no concern that Nara could discover us, there was only the fatigue and guilt, the rapture and the absurdity of the moment.

We had liaisons many more times on the voyage. Nara gave no indication that she knew. I loved my wife more than anyone; she was my life, my soul mate. Ranjana never ventured out for companionship as she had before the night of our coupling and Nara may have realized what was going on, but chose to accept it as a healing process for her mother. Her love for both of us may have overcome the vulgarness of our betrayal.

When at last we reached our destination, an electric current of excitement filled the cabin. Now India, the land of our ancestors, was open before us.

Our progress was slowed by a large crowd milling about the port of Calcutta. Once we reached the district train depot, I was able to book the closest route to Pasha. The clerk explained we could travel the remaining distance by coach or even walking between the small settlements along the way. All told, it took us the better part of the month to get to Pasha. We arrived in good shape. Nara and I experienced some mild dysentery along the way, but fortunately we had recovered by the time our journey ended.

I had expected dismal conditions in Pasha, much as the clerk from Bennington and Heartstone had described a few years ago. Instead of the deserted village he mentioned we discovered an active city comprised of many buildings and a thriving population. The trade route my grandfather had sought was now a reality with a constant flow of goods moving between India and China.

We found a nice hotel with a room large enough to accommodate the three of us. After settling in for a few days, we began to venture into the city. Using the city's official buildings and library, I searched for information that might lead me to where my mother had lived. Nara and Ranjana usually went their own way to tour Pasha and to shop. With my mother's journal as a reference, I tried to geographically locate the village where she stayed. It was, however, a difficult task. The city had grown so much over the years it was as if any remnant of the village had been obliterated. People were of no help either. The majority of those I questioned were too young to remember any such community. Most were children of families who had traveled north for opportunities in the emerging trade routes through the mountains.

I felt a sense of failure. Nara and Ranjana seemed happy enough, and seeing them lifted my moodiness somewhat. I loved them in different ways: Nara as my wife and partner, Ranjana as a lover and vessel for the shared miseries of our past. I was certain Nara knew of her mother's and my sexual acts as there were times she would conveniently leave us alone, offering the excuse she needed to walk by herself for a while. Whatever mother and daughter shared with one another, jealousy was not one of them.

As I have less and less time for continuing this journal, I will stop for now and put all my efforts into locating where my mother and grandparents lived and died. I will make new entries when possible, but I have grown weary of writing and remembering. It appears I may never find the place I seek. Perhaps traveling here was a mistake after all.

Week of October 28th 1820

At last, hope has come my way. Earlier this week I ventured to a darker area of Pasha. Much like London, the poor and seedy characters of the city congregate in the shadow lands. It is a place I would hesitate to travel in after sunset.

During my daytime exploration I came across a small shop much like the one Ranjana and Nara kept back home. Spices and herbs were sold there. The owner looked very old and grizzled. One of his eyes had gone bad, leaving a milky center, but his other deep brown one still burned with intensity, especially when I told him of the area I was in search of. Although my use of the Indian dialect is quite limited, the aged one spoke rather good English and had no trouble conveying his information about the old village of Pasha which was actually about twenty kilometers northeast of the newer city. He said the place had been deserted many years ago because of a plague of some sort. Most of the population had perished from the pestilence there. I asked if he had heard of my family, the Wilkinses, or of locals named Dayal and Sanjay. He answered that these names were not familiar. When I asked about the bandit Vairaja who had brought death to my family there, a look of terror came over him. The old man shook his head. I heard him whisper 'Rakshasa' as he lowered his eyes from me. He would answer no more of my questions and became agitated.

I thanked him for the information and offered to buy something for his trouble, but he motioned for me to leave. "We are closing now," he said, almost pushing me out as he slammed and locked the door behind me. Evidently, Vairaja's cruel reputation had left an undying stain on the land.

The next day I arranged, with the aid of the hotel clerk, to hire someone to take me to the old village by carriage. I convinced Nara and Ranjana to stay behind as I realized it would be a long tiresome trip. I believe Ranjana would have come anyway had I asked her, but Nara had no desire to go. She had come across a few people who mentioned the area with dread, just as the old man at the shop had expressed. I asked her if she knew what the word 'Rakshasa' represented, but she did not know. Ranjana said she recalled it from her childhood. It had been used in stories told to her and her sisters in the dark hours just before bedtime. She described how her father spoke about what happened to children who were bad and disrespectful, of creatures like the Rakshasa that would come after midnight to consume their blood and flesh if they did not behave during the day.

I was up early the next morning and met the carriage just before sunrise. The driver looked to be my age. He spoke little English, but between my poor Indian and instructions the hotel clerk had given him, we were off on the journey with no major problems. Once out of the city the land became dry and arid, deserted but for an occasional desolate thatched hut, none of which looked to have been occupied in a long while.

After several hours we came upon what could have been the remains of my mother's last home. The place was in an advanced state of decay. What meager dwellings remained had given in to time and the effects of the weather, bowing in their centers as if asking each other to dance. The driver stayed in the carriage as I walked around the site, going through what structures remained. Besides dust and fragments of furniture the only interesting items I came across were a few British army artifacts. No doubt these half buried remnants were once property of the men sent with my grandfather on his expedition so many years ago.

When I was satisfied I would find nothing of importance there, I decided to walk over the ridge and see if the temple ruins still existed. I tried to convey this to the guide, but he stared at me with a wild look and shook his head. He must have thought I wanted him to go with me. I pointed in the direction of the ridge and started to walk away when the man shouted at me and pointed to the sun. His gestures were enough to let me know he did not wish to stay in the place after sunset. I shook my head that I understood and went on my way. I would occasionally look back and find the fellow craning his head to keep up with my direction.

Once at the top of the ridge, the ravine lay below, and I knew for certain this was the place my mother had described in her journal.

Surrounded by the collapsed mounds of pillars that had long ago encircled it, the altar stone was still intact. The stairs that led to the underground temple were still there as well. I examined what was left of the above ground structures and found the carvings my mother had mentioned—the characters involved in carnal positions and the strange insect that seemed to feed on them. I had an idea what type of insect was in the carvings and made a mental note to obtain an entomology book to see if I was correct.

After my inspection of the carvings, I walked down the stairs to see if the temple door might be opened, but it was sealed tightly and I could not budge it. I became so involved in my efforts I missed the fact the light was fading. A shadow fell over the steps and I realized I had better get back to the carriage. The driver was so fearful of the place I was concerned he might leave without me.

As I hurried away, I heard a soft dragging sound behind me. I turned and caught the receding image of something moving behind the altar stone.

Despite my dismissing it as a curious animal of some sort, a slight chill raced up my spine.

By the time I made it back to where the carriage had been, the sun was dangerously close to setting. The driver had indeed already started on his way back to Pasha, and I had to run to catch up to him. I pulled myself up into the seat. The man was shaking and mumbling under his breath. He drove the horses much faster when leaving that bleak place than when approaching it.

After the long trip back and the dim lights of the city could be seen, the fellow relaxed and offered, I am sure, a prayer to his gods.

It was late when I entered our hotel room. Nara and Ranjana were already asleep in their beds. There was a covered plate and a decanter of water left for me on the nightstand. I had no appetite and only drank a glass of water before sliding under the sheets with Nara as quietly as possible.

Week of November 4, 1820

It has taken a few days to acquire the book on entomology I needed. I did find one volume in a bookstore that was very helpful. I am confident that the insect depicted in the stone carvings belongs to the Subfamily Triatominae, Family Reduviidae. The external anatomy is unmistakably the same. The sucking and feeding characteristics of the bug also match. The Reduviidae take blood from vertebrates, they are cosmopolitan in dispersion, active runners and good flyers commonly found in the nests or burrows of animals. They can also be household pests, feeding primarily on man. If the need arises, these bugs will resort to cannibalistic behavior to survive.

One fact especially peaked my interest: the Reduviidae are vectors of disease. My mother's description of the tiny bugs flowing from the punctured egg sac and the plague that followed fits well with the behavior of these insects. Due to the dark gray carapace and the fierce proboscis present on these creatures, I will dub them 'rhinoceros vampires'.

A fervor to return to the spot for more exploration filled me. I ask the desk clerk to hire the man to take me there again. He stopped me in the lobby the next day and said the man would not go back, no matter how much he was paid. I inquired if he could find someone else but, again, the answer was the same. The clerk explained that not only superstition was to blame; there were rumors of lepers inhabiting the area as well.

I decided to rent a carriage myself. I was certain I could purchase some tools to pry open the temple door. My conviction above all was to open that door.

I tried to convince Nara and Ranjana to come along, but Nara was still hesitant. However, as I had suspected, Ranjana was willing to accompany me. Whether it was to be alone with me or to discover more about her culture didn't matter. I would not have to go alone.

We left earlier than I had before. I wanted to get as much daylight time as possible. Except for a few comments about the landmarks passed during the ride, Ranjana and I spent the time in a comfortable silence. I did warn her about the rumors of lepers in the area. I was more concerned that such desperate men might rob or kill for money and food than I was of their disease.

The trip passed unremarkably. We saw no one before arriving at the derelict village, only a few dust devils whirled around us along the way.

We walked through the remains of the village for a while, but I still found nothing of importance. When we reached the temple, I pointed out the interesting carvings to Ranjana. She became nervous. "There is something wrong with this place," she said.

"Wrong? In what way?"

"It is a foul place." She shuddered then said, "I won't stay here. I will wait for you at the carriage."

"But what if someone comes? You could be hurt and I would never know. It is too far away."

"Then I will sit and wait just beyond this spot."

So I continued my investigation with her well within a safe distance. I spent the majority of the day trying to open that blasted door. I still had no luck. I knew it would be useless to ask Ranjana for help. Her fear of the temple was honest and visible in her face.

The day passed and we headed back early enough to reach the hotel before nightfall.

November 10, 1820

I must put this down before my fever strikes again. Each bout is worse than the one before. I do not know if I will survive the infection from those nightmarish creatures. Oh, how life can change in an instant. The terror of it all.

I returned to the site two days later. I was surprised that Ranjana wished to go again, but she volunteered without being asked. She said it would not be wise for me to go alone.

I brought along some extra tools to work on the temple door. It was hard work and for an instant I believed the door had budged slightly, but it was only wishful thinking as the ancient entrance held tight.

Ranjana called out that she was going to the carriage to bring back the lunch she had packed for us. I told her to wait for me.

By the time I caught my breath from laboring with the door and walked up the steps, Ranjana was only a small figure in the distance. I did not run but walked at a fast gait to catch up with her. I was concerned for her safety. That is why my guard was down when the thing crashed into me from behind.

I fell hard to the ground. My breath rushed out. As I struggled to breathe my assailant stood over me. It was clad in a white tunic filthy with dirt, sweat, and matted gore. All but the mouth and eyes were covered by strips wrapped about its head. This had to one of the lepers we were warned about.

A distant scream sent a shiver through me. Ranjana! Other lepers must have attacked her.

Enough air had returned to my lungs for an appeal to the creature above me. "There is no need to harm the woman. We will give you what food and money we have. We…" Before I could utter another sound, it fell on me, clamping its jaws tight on my neck. I fought like a wild man. Its grip was inhuman. I could not break it. Even when teeth ripped into my throat, I was unable to free myself. Then, just as abruptly as it had attacked, the thing released its grip and stood up, staring with what could only be described as surprise and loathing. It spat out a mass of congealing blood then rubbed a sleeve across its mouth as if wiping away a foul taste. The stench surrounding the thing was revolting, and when it lifted its arm, I caught a brief glimpse of ragged skin covered with putrefying sores. My stomach convulsed and I turned, lifting myself to my knees, retching on the earth below. Then, I was struck on the head with a force strong enough to render me unconscious.

I came around and found I had been propped against one of the carriage's wheels. I was still in a daze. It took a moment for the scene before me to come into focus.

Ranjana lay about twenty feet away. She had been stripped of her clothing. Her body was being ravaged by four creatures similar to my attacker. They were drinking her blood and eating her flesh. One clung to her neck, sucking with a low moan. The other three gashed her skin. They tore and chewed, pulling muscle tissue and gristle free.

I screamed and the one drinking from her neck looked up quickly. It was then I noticed Ranjana's head had been severed. It stared with empty sockets just above the ragged stump of her neck. The thing had devoured her eyes as well. The abhorrent realization of what had been done to her brought an even louder wail of shock from my throat. The one who ceased its feeding hopped toward me like a bloated toad. I could not fight off my vertigo and stand, so I back peddled away from it. There was no way I could escape before the creature had clenched my right ankle in its jaws. The pain was dreadful, and, before fainting again, I heard my ankle bone snap like a dry twig.

I awakened in one of the decaying structures left in the village. Twilight gave little help to my vision. Gradually, as my eyes adjusted to the dimness, I saw the four lepers squatting around me.

"Do you know what you are?" a voice asked from the shadows in perfect English. The fifth leper, the one who had assaulted me, moved out of the gloom. He knelt beside me. "There is no need to fear me. I did taste you," he smiled, revealing sharp canines.

"Are you a Rakshasa?" I asked.

His eyes never left me as a dry cynical laugh came from deep in his throat.

"Are you?" he asked with amusement.

"Me? Like you disgusting monsters?" I answered with revulsion. "You who cannibalize? Your disease has affected your brain. You are insane!"

He reached out and grabbed my face. My skin crawled at his touch. The stink of his rotting body and putrid breath was enough to cause my stomach to roll. He squeezed my face and I tried to pull his hands away, only to have his flesh slide off.

He spat at me, spewing drops of saliva into my eyes. "We will see!" he said angrily. "We will see the measure of your disgust!"

The monster released me and walked outside and away from the structure. He returned shortly. A young adult male dressed in tattered clothes stood beside him. It was apparent the man was on the verge of collapse from God only knew what terrors he had suffered.

I tried to rise so I could help him, but two of the other lepers pushed hard on my shoulders to prevent me. The look in the man's eyes was pitiful. "My wife," he rasped as if breathing was excruciating. The mere effort of speech sent him falling to his knees.

"Wife?" the leper who evidently was the leader asked mockingly. He patted the poor man on the head. "You needn't concern yourself with her." The leper then addressed me. "We were keeping this one for a warm communion cup," he said as the other lepers moaned displeasure at losing their prey, "but since you intruded and have such high esteem of your morals, I think he will serve another purpose altogether."

He shouted an order to the others. They dragged me outside and pinned me against the ground. A half moon was just rising. In my resistance to get free, I turned my head and saw, not far away, a mangled body lying in the moonlight. No doubt the unfortunate wife of the captured man had fallen prey to these monsters. As Ranjana's had been, this victim's head had been ripped away too.

"Please stop this," I pleaded.

He stood above me, holding the man, who offered no resistance, roughly by the collar.

"Still a pompous British ass," he said and barked another command. My mouth was pried open. "Now, become what you are. Repulse thyself!"

Under the watchful moon, he sliced the man's throat with his nails. The blood rushed from his carotid in a rapid gout, spattering me. He placed the flow directly over my mouth. I spat and tried not to swallow, but the rushing blood filled my mouth quickly. My gulp was an involuntary act to survive asphyxiation. The hot mass moved thickly to my stomach. It was sweet fire, the living tissue that filled me. My concern for the victim vanished. I sucked and tore hungrily at the throat placed on my lips.

The cup was soon empty and ripped away. The monster tossed the body aside like an old used rag. The other lepers released me and fell on the corpse. They fought like dogs over raw meat. The man's head was torn away and kicked carelessly to join the sightless stare of his wife's. I rolled over and heaved. Syrupy clotted blood flooded from my nose and mouth. I curled into a fetal ball.

"Now you will know. Now you will thirst." Dry laughter split the night engulfing me. "Now it begins!"

* * *

How Nara managed to convince someone to help her is beyond me. Her beauty, money, whatever she managed, was what saved me. I have no recollection of being delivered to the hotel room, but here I am. Nara is out in search of a doctor to help. Between my bouts of fever and unconsciousness, she explained she hired two men deemed trustworthy by the hotel clerk to go and search for me and her mother.

Ranjana's body was never discovered. The state it was in made this a blessing. I hear Nara sobbing sometimes. I'm sure she wonders what has become of her mother. I don't think I can ever tell her the truth.

My wounds are healed. There is no scarring and no trace that I was ever injured. All that remains is this terrible fever.

How many days now? I am rarely alert. Nara is my deliverer.

I have awakened in the dead of night. I am covered with sweat. My fever has vanished.

I am so hungry. I must lie down next to Nara again. She smells wonderful, intoxicating.

I will take just a little, my love. Just a little.

DR. GLENN RUSSELL, ROUND ROCK, TEXAS

1995—1996

1

When I was a child, funerals terrified me.

Having my grandfather's body on display in our home certainly brought about that terror along with hideous nightmares. However, as I grew older the fear went away. I was instructed in the formality of attending interments for family or acquaintances and how to be a proper lad with all the solemnity due the occasion.

Now, funerals have about as much impact on me as paint drying, even if it is my parents that will be lowered into their place of eternal rest.

The Denton, Texas police contacted me about their deaths. The investigation unmasked the criminal to be a gas jet left open on the stove. In my parent's state, any explanation was possible. Anything from absent mindedness to a wish for an end made perfect sense to me.

I opted for a graveside service. Not many came, just old friends and a few distant relatives who still lived in the area. The Methodist minister was nice and assured me their souls were happily residing in heaven and so on and so on. Oh, the things I could have told him, shown him. It was quite a temptation.

I stayed over one night so I could contact an estate salesman and real estate agent. I instructed both all would be placed in their capable hands and told them to send me a check for my part, minus their commission of course.

On the way out of town I stopped at a gas station to fill up. There was greasy spoon next door where I went to get a cup of ice water for the road (we just need a little water between feedings). When I sat at the counter and placed my order, the waitress took a second look. She dropped her pad and pencil, came around the counter and startled me with a hug. It had been so long since I had seen her and so much had happened to me over the last year I didn't recognize her.

"What's the matter, Glenn?" she whispered in my ear as she crushed her breasts next to me. "Don't you know your own wife?"

It was my ex-wife, Janice.

She was very happy to see me, but I bristled at her touch. She couldn't quit questioning me: What was I doing? Where did I live? And the most important one, had I remarried?

I gave scant information other than the fact I was practicing in Austin. Janice, however, couldn't tell me enough about herself. The aerobics instructor had dropped her after she suffered a miscarriage. She married again but divorced soon after. She offered that last tidbit with a sly grin as she placed her hand on my thigh.

Anger rushed through me. I bolted from the seat and gave her the coldest hateful stare I could gather. Had we not been in a public place, I would have bared my fangs at her. That would have shut her up in a millisecond.

"Maybe I'll look you up sometime," she laughed as I headed toward the door.

"Don't bother," I answered flatly on my way out.

What a bitch! All I could think about on the drive home was the smug sweaty smile she wore the day I caught her screwing in our garage. If we are creatures without emotion, what would Peter call this? There is still something left after the virus claims us, even if others believe there is not.

Returning to work the following day, it was evident there was something wrong with me. Peter asked if I was all right and I shrugged my mood off to the annoying funeral arrangements I had been through.

The urge to tear open Janice's throat eventually faded and I settled back into my routine of working and going to the dinners to slake my hunger. Maria was beginning to show. It wouldn't be long until another member would be welcomed into our clan.

The routine of this existence continued. Then, something unexpected happened to me. I became ill. This was not supposed to occur. The virus's main concern is with keeping us healthy to ensure its survival.

It was late fall when the symptoms started. I began to oversleep. Innocuous enough in itself, but the periods began to stretch. In the beginning it was just a short time, like an hour. Then it progressed to two, four, and six. Peter questioned me. I told him I didn't feel ill, just tired. When I missed a whole day, he became concerned enough to get me in for an examination.

"What worries me, Glenn, is that you missed your feedings," Peter said.

He was right. "But I'm not hungry," I answered.

The drumming of a cold November rain on the office windows brought a chill to me.

"I've witnessed illness in our kind on only three other occasions." Peter stood by the window. The rivulets of water cast shadows on his face. It was as though his reflection was melting and reforming.

"And what happened to them?"

"One did not survive and one lived on in a weakened state."

I was covered in two blankets but still shivered. "I thought we didn't 'pass'. I thought our bodies eventually wore out over time. What could cause this?"

"Honestly, Glenn, I don't know. There have only been these isolated cases that I am familiar with and not enough information to compile any research data. There were a large number of atypical lymphocytes present in the blood smears I studied. This indicates an immune response of some type, like a transplanted organ rejection."

"Why so late?"

"I wish I knew. It varied."

"You said there were three. What happened to the third one? Did the person survive? Do I have a chance?"

Peter walked away from the window and sat across from me. "I know I was correct in my judgment of your strength. I cannot believe this has happened to you."

"The third, Peter. Tell me."

"He sleeps by his own volition. He is there above us as we feast. He slumbers with the one who did not survive the illness that seems to be affecting you. His name rests above the door to our gathering place."

"Morgan?"

"Yes, it is my old mentor Andrew who lies in an unbreakable coma by self starvation."

"This is just great, Peter! Just fucking great! I was supposed to be your wonder boy of the future. What future is there in death or eternal, living sleep?"

Peter flushed. "There is no need to be obscene." He glared at me. "There is no need to use that . . . that word!"

"What word? What are you talking about? I might be dying and you're worried about a word?"

"That foul 'F' word you and your generation drop so often. It is inappropriate for our kind. It is obscene and out of place."

"You have to be joking, Peter. To know what we do and how we survive, how can you judge that word to be obscene?"

"What do you know of obscenity? Real obscenity. I will tell you what obscenity is, it sleeps in that vault with Andrew. How can you be so indecent with your speech, so flippant with your words when the real profanity is the fact we are not truly immortal?"

I stopped shaking and felt flushed. "Why, Peter, I believe you are afraid of dying. Is that it? Are you afraid?"

He sighed and turned back toward the window. "Life is nothing more than pleasure or pain. How can I fear that which I have not experienced?"

"Are you certain this is what's happening to me?"

"One can never be sure, but your blood smear presented the same group of abnormal lymphocytes."

"Then what is to become of me?"

"You will gradually fall into a comatose state. Maria and I will do what we can to help and protect you during that time. Just because no one has completely survived this illness doesn't mean I will stop looking for an answer."

"And if I cannot awaken?"

"Then I will place you next to Andrew and support your offspring's talents as I would have yours."

"Better to cut my head off and end it. How can you be sure there is no awareness in oblivion? Can you imagine the torture and pain of knowing only darkness forever?"

Peter stood and walked back to the window. "If I could imagine that, my friend," he said tonelessly, "I would not have made you, only fed on you until you died"

2

My waltz with death lasted until early May.

When I was in junior high, I had an appendectomy. During anesthesia there was this wonderful void. When they woke me in the recovery room, it felt as if I had just lost track of time for a moment and not the couple of hours the operation had required. If this is what death is like, there was no reason to fear it. The lack of consciousness may be oblivion, but the absence of awareness is a kind lover. So it was with my illness.

Before slipping into that void, the last image I saw was Maria, her stomach swollen with our child, pulling the bed covers over my dimming eyes. The next thing I knew I was waking up. At first my surroundings were a mass of blurs coming in and out of focus. Finally, my sight adjusted and I found I was still in my bed at home. The sunshine from the open windows, sounds of birds and humming insects, and the soft fragrance of blooming plants revealed I had slept with winter and awakened in spring.

My physical state was a mess. I strained to move muscles whose tone was lost over the months. I was constricted in the fetal position. Through agonizing slowness, I tried to stretch myself. After what seemed hours, I managed to straighten out my arms and legs. It took much longer to right my curved back. If my throat had not been so dry, the screams I expressed would have been ghastly to hear. Eventually, I lay on my back with my arms at my side and legs straight. My body was reduced to skin and bones. Its skin was tissue white, clinging to a protruding skeleton. Dark branches of veins spread out just below the surface. There were a few ugly bruises on the back of my hands. Peter must have administered intravenous therapy during my sleep. I imagine my head was out of proportion with my body, like that of a baby bird. Just like that hungry fledgling, the first thing I did when Peter returned to the nest was to open my mouth to be fed. I wonder if Christ was that famished when he rose from the tomb.

Peter fed me a paste rich in blood and fetal tissue. He told me he had used an I.V. therapy of fertilized human eggs diluted in normal saline during my comatose state. The paste he gave me now was a mixture of fertilized eggs and placental blood, a caviar for monsters.

The healing power of this concoction was extraordinary. I was up on shaky legs in a matter of days. Maria came on occasion to bathe me and keep the house cleaned. Being in the bath with her, surrounded by steam, brought back the memory of our sexual encounter, but it was only that, just a memory.

My strength recovered to the point where Peter could take me to the dinners again. I was asked many questions about my malady but had few answers other than the treatment Peter followed. When we left and passed by the stone coffins a chill gripped me. I realized that, had I not awakened, I have would have joined the boarders in their endless sleep.

Thinking of Andrew and Vairaja brought the journals to mind. Once Peter had taken me home, I decided to continue reading these histories of our race and how they came to cross the ocean to America.

THE RECORD OF CHARLES VAIRAJA

1821 AND 1831

April 1821

The mirror does not reflect what lives in a heart or sleeps in a soul.

The same face stares back at me unless I smile. The new weapons of my trade rest in that grin. I am a killer, a hunter. I am an eater of human flesh, a drinker of human blood. A monster dressed in the skin of a man.

I have dealt the same fate to Nara and she revels in it. Ferocity has made a merciless killer of her.

We have been back in London now for almost six months. I opted to give up my town house and stay with Nara in the spice shop she and her mother had operated. The poorer district is much easier to hunt in.

The university reinstated me to my former position. Scientific curiosity keeps me well after the classes have finished. I have a wealth of equipment and tools to investigate what lives in my blood. Was it the bite from the leper, the tasting of the living blood, or the influence of both? Using chemical and immunological research, perhaps the answer and a treatment can be found.

One evening my work in the laboratory was disturbed. Strange that I should have forgotten them.

I had finished plating a new culture of infected rat tissue injected with my blood when I heard the door to the laboratory open. Soft footsteps followed. As I was in the microbe plating cubicle, I had the advantage of being able to see whoever it was before they could detect me. The gas jets had been dimmed, making sight even more difficult for the intruder.

I remained calm and still. Something collided with one of the dissecting tables and let out a chain of curses. "All right, now," announced a quivering voice, "I know you're in here, boy. Might as well come out and face me." Could it be? Was that Hobbs' nervous voice I heard?

Indeed, it was that ferret of a man straining to see in the weak light. Since being infected, old acquaintances had not been something I dwelt on, but witnessing this stick figure stumble around produced a distinct sense of hate in me.

"I'm here," I said, amused by the bobbing motion of his head in search of my location.

"A mutual friend is very happy you have returned, boy," Hobbs said still trying to find me. "He's willing to forget the fact you left without so much as a goodbye and is ready to pick up where you left off. In fact, he demands it."

I had crept along the opposite wall and stood just behind him. "Well, here I am," I whispered just behind his ear. He nearly jumped out of his skin.

As he turned to face me, Hobbs squinted, trying to get a good look at me. The effect of the disease had made me quite pale. There, in the faint glow of the gas lamps lining the walls, I must have resembled a ghastly phantom. I made it a point to smile, just briefly revealing my sharp canines. Hobbs actually gasped and backed away.

"You startled me, boy." His rodent eyes widened in terror.

"What is it you want from me?" I asked and moved closer.

Hobbs kept backing up and ran into one of the tables again. "Grubbs," he said nervously, "Mr. Grubbs wants your assistance once again . . . a pickup . . . he needs you to make a pickup for him."

I placed my hand on his shoulder. The man squeaked a sharp cry of fear. "Certainly," I answered with condescension "but I want you both to meet me when I finish the job, preferably at the end of the block near the university entrance. You should know the place, Grubbs met me there once. You were hiding in the shadows."

I released him and a wave of relief covered his face. With a trembling hand, Hobbs gave me a piece of paper with the address of the pickup. I stepped aside and allowed him to pass. When he reached the door, the distance between us must have brought a certain amount of courage to him.

"I'll make no promises, boy. I'll . . . ."

I was upon him quickly. Dispelling any notion he would ever be safe from me, I held his face in the vice grip of my hands. "Listen, you toad," I hissed, "this business of moving bodies is risky. Too many are curiously fresh, raising concern and an added element of jeopardy to the job." I squeezed harder. Hobbs' eyes were bugged in fear. "Just see to it that you and Grubbs are where I asked you to be when I'm finished," I continued, pushing in his cheeks with each syllable. "I want to come to a new arrangement, one of greater profit for the danger of exposure to the authorities."

I let go of his face. "Certainly, boy," he stuttered as he hurried away from the lab and down the hall. His voice faded into the darkness, "Anything you say, anything at all."

Control was never easy after being infected. I would feed and destroy the victim's body. There was no remorse, no other purpose than to eat. The evening Hobbs had made his surprise visit, I held food in my hands and let it go even though I hungered. It was controlled vengeance that replaced the need to nourish. I owed these two black hearted bastards a repayment of pain and death in the exact spot where Broom had been murdered. Of course, I would require Nara's assistance.

I knew Grubbs well enough to suspect he would pay me a visit the night before I was to get the body. I warned Nara of this and gave strict instructions that Grubbs was not to be harmed. Then, I shared my plan with her.

Grubbs did not disappoint me. He appeared from the shadows in front of the spice shop the night before I was to do the chore for him. I was just across the street, patiently waiting in the gloom of obscurity.

It was a little more than an hour when he left, puffed up like a partridge. Since he was in one piece, I knew Nara had done as I asked. She shared how easily the scum yielded to her seduction. Grubbs, she confided, acted the bully as usual, swearing he would teach her laddie a lesson about demands, but she convinced him she was just as loathsome as he was and asked for his help in her betrayal of me. Nara told Grubbs I had become useless and boring and that she wished to use me for as much personal gain as she could. As she disrobed in front of Grubbs, Nara added she could offer many things beyond mere profit.

Grubbs took the bait, but not without a barb of his own. After he had finished with her, he laughed and said he would consider the proposal. In fact, he added, she might be able to give favors to some well bred chaps he knew. They would pay top dollar for some sweet Indian meat.

Sweet Indian meat! What a loathsome being Grubbs was. I knew it had taken all of Nara's will not to gut him and force him to watch as she did. It didn't bother me that Grubbs had sex with her. That subject had faded after my transformation. In Nara there was always an urgent need for the raw passion of it, but I felt empty there. Nara had wanted more than anything to get pregnant. Even though I tried to give her that wish, she never conceived. No child had come from our couplings before I was infected, nor had Ranjana been impregnated by me. I must have been sterile even before the contagion. It was an irony then that Nara's desire to procreate was intensified while mine zeroed.

Nara was starved after her encounter with Grubbs so we went hunting.

We fed well. Nara was more violent than usual. It was remarkable what she could do to a human body that should have been more powerful than her own.

The following evening it was time to complete our plan.

Nara lay hidden under a tarp in the carriage bed as I went to make the pick up. After I reached my destination, another seedy area near the river, I placed the corpse in the back and drove away. Stopping before I arrived at the prearranged meeting place, I told Nara to come out, then rolled the body on top of her.

In a short while we were there. Grubbs stood just to the side of the streetlamp. His shadow reached across the street to just in front of my carriage. He was dressed in his usual top hat and cape. Leaning on his cane, he and his shadow resembled a seven legged spider, limping toward a victim trapped in its web, as he crossed toward me. I noticed a silhouette remained behind. Hobbs was not brave enough to approach.

"Well, well, what have we here?" Grubbs said. I could see a sneer under the shadow of his hat as he patted the cane against the palm of his hand. "Did you wish to speak to me, laddie? Is there something on your mind?" He inched closer as he spoke until he was standing just below me.

"I feel it's time for some new agreement," I said. "As I told Hobbs, this body collecting business is becoming dangerous and . . . ." Grubbs pulled me down, grasping my coat lapels tightly. I offered no resistance. He must have been cocksure of his power over me, especially since he believed Nara was now in his control as well.

"Why, it's more pay you want, is it?" he spat at me. "And after you snuck out of the country! That wasn't loyal of you, was it laddie?"

Grubbs berating of me gave Hobbs more self-assurance. He walked over to join in. Then, a deep moan rose from the carriage bed. Grubbs cut his eyes away from me. "What's this then?" he asked, looking in the direction of the sound. "Better have a peek, old chap," he ordered Hobbs. "Let's see what kind of package the lad brought us."

Hobbs complied, but it was evident he didn't want to. "I told you," I interjected. "Some of the bodies are too fresh. Stupid fools must not have finished this one off properly."

Between listening to me and bending to inspect the carriage bed, Hobbs' attention was divided just enough to make the impact of a leaping body more effective.

Nara threw the dead body at Hobbs who screamed, falling under the weight of the corpse. Grubbs was startled at the action and turned away giving me the chance to spin him around and bite off what remained of his nose. A look of surprise spread over his bleeding face. As Grubbs opened his mouth to scream, I bit out his tongue and spat it back at him. He jerked wildly, choking on the gush of blood in his mouth. He swung his cane at me, but it was a pathetic gesture made by a man who realizes he is about to die.

As Nara straddled the stunned Hobbs, I pushed Grubbs to the ground. "Well, old boy," I snarled into his ear, "looks like there will be two extra cadavers for the dissecting tables tomorrow." I clamped my teeth onto his ear and tore it away as slowly as I could. I turned and saw Nara was feeding on Hobbs. She was digging into the soft flesh of his stomach. Hobbs squealed in terror as he witnessed himself being eaten alive.

I turned Grubbs over on his back. Huge bubbles of blood formed then popped in crimson on his lips. Above them, dark clots had plugged his open nasal cavity. Grubbs' eyes were wide and filled with hate. "Fearsome till the end, old boy," I said then tore open his shirt. I ripped through the skin and muscles of his chest with my nails. "This is for the night you took me to those monsters' home to be buggered! This is for your cowardly murder of Broom!" I gazed at his beating heart, looked back into Grubbs' face, smiled and bore my fangs as I put my hands around his heart and pulled until the tenacious vessels gave way. I hope the last image his dying stare caught was my gobbling down the thumping organ.

Nara was not finished. I saw her head bobbing as she dug for more food in the lifeless body of Hobbs. After she had satisfied her hunger and rage, we cut off the heads and disposed of the bodies by our usual method of incineration.

Nothing was mentioned about Hobbs' disappearance. He was not well received in the university anyway. Grubbs, of course, would not be missed. His competitors would the fill the gap quickly.

In time, Nara became pregnant. We knew it had to be the result of her night with Grubbs, but that did not matter, she was finally to have the child she so desperately desired. Although she almost carried to term, the pregnancy terminated in a calcified fetus. Nara's depression only made her more aggressive and frenzied in her kills. I fear this may bring unwanted attention. Death in this district is one matter, but mutilation is quite another.

I will dedicate my time to studying this new phenomenon of fetus calcification along with my ongoing studies of the disease living in our bodies. I hope that Nara will assist me.

January 1831

My applications for further studies have come through. I have shown my research on the infective agent to some colleagues, although they know nothing of my or Nara's infection. I have limited their exposure to my studies of lab animals only; they are fascinated with the agent's ability to physically change its hosts. I have convinced them that I should return to

India as I believe this is one of the fertile areas for studying the organism.

So now we will return to the place where I hope to gain further knowledge of the organism and my heritage.

February 1831

I will write no more after this record of our second trip to India. There is no point.

The voyage might have proven difficult in regard to our feeding, so I bottled some whole blood with packed red cells added. Although not as enticing as fresh blood, it served our purpose of anonymity.

We arrived in Pasha on January 23. The city had grown considerably over the last ten years in business as well as populace. The streets remained crowded for most of the day's twenty four hours.

The hotel we stayed in on our first trip was no longer there. We would not have gone there anyway due to past unpleasantries for us and the management. Instead, we booked rooms in a smaller establishment toward the edge of the city limits. This would make our trip to the ruins even shorter.

I rented a carriage and we headed out early the next morning. The old village had little left standing. The years and the weather had worn most of its structures into sporadic patches of rubble.

The temple, for the most part, was still intact, although I did notice gouges in some of the pillars along with worn areas on the carvings. The large door at the bottom of the stairs was no longer closed. It yawned an invitation for us to enter its dimness. There were a few torches remaining, but the tar on them was reaching the point of degradation. Still, we managed to obtain sufficient light to see our way around after lighting them.

The inner chamber looked as my mother had described. The statue of Kali was still present, and there, hanging around her neck, we would make a surprising find.

Ten years ago, when I had suffered through my transformation and infected Nara, neither of us had remembered the object left behind in our hotel room. Nara had insisted on bringing it on the first trip, but the disease had made us impervious to its memory. The beautiful necklace found in my mother's trunk hung around the neck of Kali.

"It belonged to my mother." The voice came from a figure standing at the entrance. The body blocked out most of the light from the overcast January sky.

The figure advanced toward us. "What do you mean?" I asked as Nara circled behind the visitor to guard off any attack that might come.

"The necklace." The figure stood in front of the statue. "It was a family heirloom. My brother carelessly gave it to a young British woman he was bedding."

I felt a sudden chill. This man was speaking of my mother's affair with his brother. As he turned to face me, I recognized him as the leper who had assaulted me, the one who had forced me to drink the blood of that helpless man. His face was no longer covered and was in a state of advanced decomposition. The skin was red and raw. I could see the movement of maggots under the puffed areas. The smell of him was disgusting. One of his eyes was completely gone, leaving a wet empty socket staring blindly at the world.

"Why have you returned?" he asked then turned to look at Nara behind him. "Why have you brought her? Isn't there enough food for you in England, or must the British part of your soul still seek to cause my people pain?"

"Who are you?"

"I am Vairaja." When he spoke, there were rustling sounds in the dark corners of the vault.

"Then, you are my father."

He stared vacantly for a moment then said, "It is possible. I have always believed it was my brother, Dayal, who impregnated your mother. He was thoughtless and stupid when it came to young women, especially those with fair skin and blue eyes." Vairaja sat down wearily on the stone border surrounding the statue. "Since you are like us," he spread his arms and the rustling movements ceased, "I must assume my single drugged intercourse with your mother could be responsible for you."

"What was here? Is this where you were both infected?"

He smiled a wretched grin and black ooze rolled down the sides of his mouth. "My father had placed the little savages here a long time ago. He knew of the plague they carried and that it could wipe out an entire village. Had the bugs been mature, none of us would have survived after I guided your mother's hand to slice open the egg sac."

"Why did you do this? If you hated the British, why risk the lives of your own people?"

"News of a great British force had been brought to me by courier. I knew they possessed superior weapons and numbers. I knew we would be hunted down and killed. Kali came to me in a dream and told me to loose the plague."

"But . . . ."

Vairaja held up his rotting hand to silence me. "All of these things are past. You still have not told me the purpose for your return."

"I wish to study the disease, to learn more about what holds me and my wife."

"Do not ask why," he laughed, "it is of no consequence. You see before you proof of the life it gives. I have leprosy, but it will not kill me. It cannot harm the plague that animates my decaying body."

"But there is so much to learn. I need samples to study."

Vairaja got up and turned to go. "For some reason your mother had the urge to return to England after you were born. I lost track of her then. I only suspected who you were ten years ago when our paths crossed. But, let me explain, I care nothing for you." When he reached the door he turned and said, "Be what the sickness has made of you. Accept it. Most of all, go back to England. There is nothing left here for you." He passed through the door, came back and added, "And leave the necklace where it rests. You know that this is the right thing to do."

Then, he was gone.

Vairaja was right about the necklace, was right about all he told me. There was nothing left for me discover. I could find no evidence of the insect vector in the area. The species most probably still existed, but I could find no trace of it here.

What a strange reunion to have with one's father. There, in the silent vault, the shades of centuries surrounding us, we had been no more than passing creatures of a common new race. A race whose priorities did not include fellowship or family, only the desire to feed and live.

One thing I knew for certain, he wished me no harm. Whatever this illness entwined in our tissues was, it recognized its brothers and would not inflict willful injury or death upon them.

By the time we made it back to the hotel room, Nara was starving. She went out to hunt, but I stayed behind in a curious sate of uncertainty. My past—the orphanage, Broom, Ranjana, Nara and the monster Grubbs; the first trip to India influenced by my mother's diary and the fatal encounter there that had altered the course of my life; the bizarre meeting with my father—all these events coursed through my brain, mixing and coalescing. One would not stand separate from another. They only existed as a mass.

It was like trying to touch without touching, feel without feeling, to love without the ability to love. My ghostly memories were of no more use than phantom limbs to an amputee. They made themselves painfully known but served no purpose.

Vairaja was correct. There was no reason for Nara and I to remain in India. I would be able to discover nothing here that I could not find out in England. Tomorrow I will book a passage back home to London, only this time I will register in my proper name: Charles Vairaja Wilkins.

DR. GLENN RUSSELL, ROUND ROCK, TEXAS

1996

1

On the twenty fifth of June, Maria delivered a healthy seven pound eight ounce boy.

My reaction to the birth was mixed.

At first, I felt a sense of pride. Standing by the bed while Maria cuddled our child had a familial impact on me. It was close to tenderness, something I had not experienced since being infected. However, this feeling diminished rapidly, and a sense of apathy replaced it.

The child resembled most babies: fat with a wild patch of black hair on its head, blue eyes that squinted in the light and vocal chords chiming most of the time. I watched Maria's breast feedings and did not care for them. Her breast milk contained a small amount of blood, and that seemed repellent to me. The suckling infant, however, was delighted with his meals.

Peter pointed out an interesting development in regard to the child. His upper canines were already developing while the other teeth remained dormant. I thought this must have been painful for Maria, but she seemed to enjoy the small bites inflicted during feedings. She looked to be in more pleasure than pain.

After a few weeks, Peter held a small celebration for the newborn. He acted as proud as any grandparent might, enough so in fact that he invited one of his political connections and a representative from a pharmaceutical company. These guests were not like us and appeared a bit anxious, but there was no way they could refuse Peter's invitation. The fetal tissue we provided them brought stunning revenue their way. Wealthy individuals in progressive disease states would pay highly for any chance of a cure through direct implantation or stem cell research.

It was obvious Peter enjoyed wielding his power in front of customers just to let them know who was in charge. I had a mischievous urge to sneak up behind them and yell 'BOO!' just to see what would happen.

When the occasion was over and the relieved visitors had left, Peter pulled me away from the remaining people.

"Glenn, you should be more supportive of Maria and your son. You haven't even named him yet."

I told him I was in a state of mixed feelings. After all, he was the one who made me. Did he expect monsters to love each other?

He pointed a stern finger my way. "Not to love," he said, "to protect. Your son is now a part of this brood. Remember, we look out for one other, or have you forgotten your illness and just who cared for you?"

I suppose he had a point, but there was a distance I couldn't explain developing between me, Maria, and the child. I know that Peter sensed this. It was the first time I noticed a look of concern and fear in his eyes.

At least we finally decided on a name for the child. Although a cliché, Adam best fit the hope for the new generation Peter dreamed of.

2

Time moved on and I went back to my familiar drone-like state.

When Adam was close to a year old, an undesired phantom found its way into my office. It wasn't hard for her to find me. Just a few questions around town after I had settled my parents' affairs would provide the trail to my whereabouts.

I never checked a patient's name until I entered the examining room. Till then, it was just another appointment. Seeing my ex-wife sitting on the table in a hospital gown was quite a surprise. She hadn't even used an alias when she made the appointment.

I asked the nurse assisting me to leave. She gave a surprised look and I knew she would inform Peter something was up, but I didn't care, I was too angry to.

"What are doing here, Janice?" I asked flatly. "What are you up to?"

"Why, Glenn, I had no idea you worked here. I just moved to Austin and wanted to find a doctor for my yearly physical." She smiled and added, "You don't think I tracked you down, do you?"

"Look, Janice, I don't want to be around you or have any contact with you."

She got off the table, untied her gown and let it fall. She was still beautiful, still desirable. "That's not the vibes I got at the diner when you stopped by." She walked closer, her breasts lifted slightly with each breath.

"How about this contact," she whispered and placed my hands on her.

I was supposed to be beyond this. The virus should have removed sexual desire. I was not prepared for the emotions that strangled me as I gazed on Janice.

The memories of our high school dating flooded me. All the sweet nights of discovery in the car, the times we slipped into each other's room and made passionate love, the taste of yearning and the pain of it pounded in my brain.

Is our first love, the physical and spiritual one, so deeply rooted in the fabric of flesh even a force as powerful as the virus cannot subdue it?

I embraced her, filling myself with her scent. She whispered, "It will be better this time. Just wait and see." She poured kisses on my face and lips. "So much better, so much better."

Why had I stumbled into her embrace? Was the distance between my new family so great as to steer me back to my old one?

I told the receptionist I was taking the rest of the day off and asked Janice to follow me to my home. As I was about to get in my car, Peter approached.

"Leaving a bit early, aren't you Glenn?" he asked through my open window.

"Yes, I ran into an old college friend and wanted to show her around Austin. You know, she just moved here and I thought I could take her by some nice eating places and shopping areas, places she needs to know about."

Peter eyed Janice who was sitting in her car. "Did she have an appointment?" he asked.

"A routine GYN exam. She's not pregnant." Peter remained quiet. "It was just coincidence she happened to get her appointment here."

Peter scrutinized Janice again, then stuck his head inside my car. "Well, I suppose it can be a small world," he said as I turned on the ignition. "Just remember where your loyalties lie."

Peter removed his head from the open window and gave a reproachful stare as I drove away with Janice following.

"Quaint," Janice said as we walked in the house, "but, Glenn, I imagine you can afford something a little more uptown, can't you?"

Before I could respond, she informed me she was fatigued from the exasperating traffic and the trouble she had finding the clinic. She asked if she could use my bath to relax.

I showed her the tub and got some towels and soap for her. "Have any bubble bath?" she asked, undressing in front of me.

"I don't use it."

"Pity," she said and turned on the water faucets. "All those warm bubbles really get me going."

I turned to leave but she called me back. "Don't you want to scrub my back like you used to?"

It was just like our early days of marriage. I would wash her back while she bathed. This always excited me and we would make love right after she dried off.

This day was no different. I moved the soapy sponge over and down the curve of her back then passed it over her breasts. "Why don't you get the bed ready while I towel down," she whispered.

My blood was pulsing through me. I had not felt this kind of passion since my one night with Maria.

As I left the bathroom, I heard a car moving down the gravel driveway. I guessed it was Peter checking up on me. I opened the back door and saw Maria sitting in her car. She made no attempt to get out. She stared blankly at me, started her car and drove away.

"Who was that?" Janice stood behind me, her hair wet and loose on her shoulders, a towel was draped around her, clinging tightly to her naked body.

"Just someone turning around in the driveway," I answered. "Happens quite often around here."

She slipped her arms around my neck and whispered in my ear, "You can take me to bed now."

I carried her to the bedroom. We pulled back the bedspread and sheets, throwing them carelessly to the floor. Janice let the towel slip from her body as I undressed. We embraced as we lay down. She eyed my genitals with curiosity.

"Not up yet? I'll take care of that," she said and moved down.

I don't know what kind of miracle I had expected. The passion was only in my brain. My penis was flat and cold even with her attempts of arousal.

Janice straddled me. "Come on, baby," she moaned, "I want you in me."

I remained impotent. Janice grabbed my limp member and tried to move it into her, but it would not stay. Every time she worked it inside her, it slid out and landed with a wet plop on my stomach.

"Jesus, what's wrong with you, Glenn?" she asked, rolling off me and onto her back. She was hot and frustrated. "Here," she said and grabbed my hand, placing it between her legs. "Use your fingers. Use something!"

I tried. I really tried.

"That's it, baby," she groaned, breathing faster, grinding her hips. "Don't stop, I'm about to come!"

As close as she came she never got there, and I finally gave up.

We lay by one another in silence for a while. Then, Janice turned on her side, supported her chin in one hand and faced me. "Are you gay now?" she asked with sarcasm in her voice?"

"What?"

Her answer was smug and cruel. “You heard me, eunuch. Do you only drive down the Hershey highway?”

“Stop it. You don’t want to know the reason, believe me.” I got up and walked to window. The sun was hugging the horizon. Night was approaching.

“Hey, you!” she screamed. “Hey, butt fucker, I’m talking to you!”

I flushed with anger and spun around to face the woman who had once vowed undying love for me, who had promised she would be mine forever. I walked slowly toward the bed as she opened her legs, placed her fingers on her vagina and spread it.

“If you can’t use that worthless prick of yours,” she laughed, “try your tongue.”

There is a common thread running through all of us. It does not matter whether this connection is from the human spirit or an alien virus. It is the essence of our flesh and our blood and our bones. Before my transformation, my thread had been the love I held for Janice. It had sustained me through medical school and the trials of our early life together. In spite of the divorce and my fall into a world of monsters, it led me back here with her and had filled me with the hope of redemption and reconciliation.

Now, as I stared at the thing on my bed, the loathsome creature pulling herself open and snickering at me with contempt, I knew the thread had been cut. I saw the future as coldly as if I had stared down the sight of a rifle. If there was anything left of my old self, it perished then and there.

So I did as Janice asked. I approached her slowly. I crawled toward her from the foot of the bed like a dog. As I placed my head between her legs she stopped giggling and said, “Oooo, that’s more like it.”

When I started, she grabbed my head and pushed it harder against her and moaned. When I began to tear her apart with my teeth, she shrieked and tried to pull away, but I had already ripped deep inside her.

I shredded her from crotch to throat, then sat back and watched her convulse and bleed to death on the bed. What followed was the carnage of her body. I mutilated every part that had scorned and deserted me.

I did not feed on her. What I had done was for the pleasure of killing. It was the first time I had not feasted on a victim.

After my blood lust subsided, I bathed the gore from my body and got dressed. As I walked out, I saw the journals on the kitchen table. I retrieved them and went out to my car, knowing I would never return to the house again.

I pulled into the first cheap motel I could find. Through the night I would read the last of the written histories and wait for the dawn

THE JOURNAL OF ANDREW MORGAN

1848 AND 1938

August 1, 1848

This will be the first entry into the gift from my beloved Adrianna.

She said this journal was to keep my thoughts for her after I start medical studies at London University. I do not know if I can bear to be away from her for the years needed to complete my degree. I know there will be holiday breaks, but they will be short and, now that we have announced our plans to wed after I become a man of medicine, the idea of leaving her is even more agonizing.

What can I say about Adrianna?

She is everything to me. So lovely, so frail and all the more beautiful for that frailty. The childhood romance we kept over the years is like a dream. The great friendship of our families and their support of our plans to marry have only helped to strengthen the bond between us.

I should only be happy for what life has given me, but I fear leaving for school could cause the beginning of a strain on the solid structure of our relationship. Adrianna laughs when I tell her this. She says I am being sullen because we will be apart for awhile. "But don't worry so, my dear," she said, lightly squeezing my hand, "I will always be here for you."

If only we did not have to wait. If only we could marry and I could take her with me.

However, that is not to be. Both our parents say their wisdom is best, that in order for me to concentrate on my classes, solitude is the key. Although I trust and respect their advice, I still cannot help but suffer misgivings.

I will stop for now as these admissions have opened the door for melancholy. I want to show nothing but happiness around those I love in the few weeks remaining before I leave.

August 15, 1848

Next week will see me depart our reserved seaside town Gravesend for the teeming streets of London. Father has secured lodgings close to the university, but I will have to take a roommate for the sake of expenses.

It is a comfort that my parents, as well as Adrianna and hers, will accompany me on the trip. I have a going away gift for Adrianna that I intend to give her this evening. It is a spaniel puppy and will be perfect for her as she loves animals and is especially fond of dogs.

August 25, 1848

It has only been a day since my loved ones have left London. I already miss them.

The lodgings here are diminutive but adequate and should allow two to share the accommodations with little inconvenience.

My boarder has yet to arrive, so I have been able to choose the best spots for my belongings. "First come, first served" I always say.

I set up my desk by the window directly facing the street and a park area. I have always enjoyed the fading of day into twilight. This spot will serve me well.

Placing Adrianna's portrait on my desk, I am reminded of our goodbye at the train station. How wonderful it was to hold her, feeling her softness against me, smelling the faint scent of lavender clinging to the lace of her collar.

Being away from her will surely be the longest years of my life.

August 26, 1848

My fellow lodger arrived late this afternoon. Since he came alone, I felt obliged to help him move his possessions into our lodgings. He has a writing table rather than a desk. It was the heaviest of his meager items.

Thomas Brommel looks to be from a family of lower income. His mood is not made the better for it. He strikes me as oafish and unpleasant. I do not know if I will like him or not. He is rather fearsome in a strange sort of way.

I am tall and stout of stature, but Brommel is taller and more muscular in appearance. He says very little and tends to grunt more than speak. I cannot help believing that he is nothing more than a common laborer's son.

I hope he never reads this entry. I have the distinct impression he would give me a good thrashing if he did. If his sullen manner and apparent dumb wit are any indication of his scholarly abilities, I do not think I will have to concern myself with Mr. Brommel's presence for long.

God, I am only thankful that Adrianna was not exposed to this loutish brute of a man when she was here. Any creature as rough around the edges as Brommel has no place in the same room with my Adrianna.

August 30, 1848

I have mailed another letter to my love. I realize when classes begin two days from now there will be less time for personal correspondence. I only hope she will understand and continue to write as often as she can. I am sure I will need all the support she can offer, especially since I will have to deal with Brommel as well as concentrate on my studies.

I have discovered that Brommel has a taste for nightlife. In the short time he has been here he has gone out several nights, returning quite inebriated. On one occasion he brought a prostitute back with him. I protested this was not proper and that he shouldn't intrude on my privacy. After all, I was paying half the lease fees. Brommel laughed and pushed me aside, taking the woman down on his bed where he fumbled to undress her. Rather than see them rutting like animals, I left the flat and went for a walk in the cool night air.

It was late and I saw only a few shadows passing on the streets. The air was damp and foggy as it usually is at that hour. In my haste to leave Brommel and his playmate, I had grabbed a coat too light for the briskness outside and I shivered beneath it.

Eventually, I found myself close to the university's park area. I sat on a bench and cursed myself for being weak and not standing up to Brommel. These living arrangements were growing dimmer each day. I was determined to make my objections known to Brommel. If he had to have his tarts, he would have to do it elsewhere. I was not about to be run out of my own home anymore.

The cold and my burst of courage urged me off the bench. I walked back in the direction of my home when I heard a sharp short cry. It was difficult to judge where it had originated due to the elusive property of sound in the fog, but it seemed to come from behind me where a small clump of hedges were planted.

The cry came again and I was certain that it was from the hedges. I approached the area slowly and looked behind the hedgerow. Straining to see through the thickening fog and faint light from the street lamps, I noticed a dark shadow on the grass. I touched it. It was wet and sticky, smelling very much like blood.

Without warning, something leapt from the hedge and knocked me to the ground. When I righted myself, I caught a glimpse of a large form running away. It was hard to be certain, but it appeared it was moving on all fours, gripping something that bounced in its jaws.

Then, as quickly as it had emerged, it was gone, lost in the swirling fog.

It must have been an animal, perhaps a large dog that had caught a rabbit or rat. I do know that after seeing it, I had an instinctive urge to hurry home. The night and the fog, along with that pitiful cry from the hedges, had infected me with goose flesh.

My imagination took over. Anticipated footsteps and glittering eyes followed me with stealth on my brisk walk back home. My hands were shaking when I pushed the key into the front door lock.

"What's up, dearie?" A woman's voice startled me and I screamed out.

She screamed back and I held up my hand to assure her that all was right.

"Just a case of the heebie-jeebies," I told her. "I have too much on my mind lately. Enough to bring ghoulies out of the fog."

I asked her why she was still here and then heard Brommel's loud snoring. He was spread-eagled on the bed, his mouth wide open and drooling in a drunken stupor.

"Lover boy," she said, pointing at Brommel, "was too drunk to deliver."

She had been dressing and faced me in her frilly undergarments. I had imagined these women of the streets would be coarse of body and spirit, but this one had a luscious figure made tempting by the tight revealing chemise she wore. She was seductive in the low lamplight.

She caught my stare and asked, "Maybe you would like a round or two. You're a pretty one. I wouldn't mind it at all, I'm telling you."

The spell broke. "No," I answered, my voice had a slight tremble and a noticeable bulge cried out just below my belt.

"You sure, dearie?" she almost giggled, looking back and forth between the knot in my pants and the blush on my face.

I turned and groped with the lock. "No, I . . . please, you must go. You see I'm engaged. I . . . ."

She was putting on the remainder of her clothes when she noticed Adrianna's portrait on the desk. She lifted it and looked at it. I would have protested, but the woman showed no disdain. She gazed on Adrianna with curiosity before replacing the picture back on the desk.

I wonder what thoughts went through her mind. Under different circumstances, life may have given her a family and home like Adrianna's instead of the struggle of trying to survive on the streets.

I held the door open for her. As she passed me, she placed a warm hand on my face.

"It will be a long term for you at university," she said, smiling with a touch of kindness in her eyes. "If you get too lonely, just ask for Shannon. I think you'll be much better company than your roomy over there."

Before I could answer, the woman was out the door and consumed by the fog. A chill raced up my spine at the thought of anyone going out into the cold night where the animal I had seen must still be lurking in the shadows.

I went to bed trying to drown out the noisy snorting of Brommel and wishing to dream of Adrianna and home.

September 5, 1848

Hellish is the only appropriate word for my first days of school.

The initial assignments were overwhelming. I know it will take all of my dedication and convictions to get through this first term, but I am determined to be a successful physician and will give it my all.

I find it hard to understand why I need to take so many subjects I have already been exposed to. History and the arts are all well and good, but I would just as soon use efforts spent on those courses in my medical studies. Let Historians study history. As to arts, what physician worth his salt would have time for such eloquence?

Physical education is another matter. It is one of the few non-medical courses I don't object to. After all, one does need to let off steam now and again. Of the choices offered, I took fencing. We have not done any contact as yet, only getting a feel for the weight and balance of our foils. The instructor has also been guiding us through various stances and thrusting positions.

Besides giving me a healthy workout mentally and physically, fencing may provide some comic interest as well. Brommel has signed up for the course. He may be big and forceful, but I have yet to see the slightest hint of the graceful movement required for the execution of this sport.

I will give him some credit. He has been staying in nights since the beginning of the term. Maybe he is just as taxed as I am by the amount of material we have to cover and intends to make the necessary effort.

September 11, 1848

I have had no time to place a current entry, so I will do so now.

Brommel has already fallen fast asleep, a habit I find more appealing than his pre-school whoring and drinking. Although he still remains sullen and reclusive, Brommel shows a surprising intensity for his studies. Perhaps I have misjudged him

I must admit, although I am not fond of the fellow, I would like a little conversation now and then, even if it is nothing more than a pleasantry about the weather or, more applicably, a subject dealing with school. We are, as a matter of fact, in three common classes: anatomy, anatomy laboratory, and fencing. One would think Brommel could at least offer something on those courses.

Sometimes I feel I am sharing lodgings with a great ape that has been taught to speak a few words of English. Other than conveying a specific desire or need, Brommel remains silent to me. He is sheltered in his own universe of time and space.

I have had little time to make any friends. Maybe after the first weeks have settled into a routine, I will be able to engage some of those in my field of study. There is one professor, Prof. Charles Vairaja, who has made quite an impression on me by his fierce approach to anatomy. I know I will have to study intensely under such an instructor but will learn all the more for it.

I will close for now and try to pen a letter to Adrianna. I'm afraid I have fallen behind in my correspondence with her. I know, though, that she will understand.

September 20, 1848

There is to be a faculty dinner tonight.

Freshman who have caught the attention of their professors through industriousness and intelligence have been selected to attend. I was chosen but am unaware of who picked me. Although the affair might turn out to be a stuffy one, I dare not refuse to go. It is a rare and golden opportunity and one not to be wasted this early in one's university life.

Brommel, of course, was not invited. He may have a diligence toward studies, but his temperament in no way approaches proper British manners. An incident in fencing a few days ago confirms his disposition for sudden violence.

The class had been paired up. Mercifully I was not matched with Brommel for our first thrust and parry session. Even though we were novices, the instructor was going to keep a score of touches in the scoring zone. Brommel was so awkward that his partner was making multiple scores, enough in fact that most of the other students stopped to joke about how one could be so easily bested.

Brommel did not take the remarks around him well. Even through the mesh mask I could see his face was blood red and the veins on his forehead bulged to the point of explosion. His partner was carried away in a touching frenzy. Brommel stood helpless to the speedy thrusts scoring on his trunk.

"Touché! Touché! Touché!" his partner cried over and over. Had this been a real battle, Brommel would have been wounded enough times to kill twenty men.

I found the display quite comical until I realized what was about to occur. After all, one does not provoke a beast with dull arrows. Why our instructor did not stop the match is beyond me. Maybe he was just as mystified at Brommel's physical ineptness at fencing as the rest of us were. Whatever his reason, he waited too long to halt Brommel's energetic partner.

Brommel roared like a cornered animal. He threw his foil at the shocked smaller opponent and pounced on the poor fellow, pummeling him about the head and chest. I would have thought the mesh mask would offer some protection, but Brommel was strong enough to drive it into the face of his tormenter, causing a copious amount of blood to spurt freely.

It took the instructor and five of us students to pull Brommel off the man. It was one of the few occasions I heard Brommel utter anything beyond his noncommittal grunts. "You bloody bastards!" he shouted. "You right bloody buggering bastards! I'll teach you to laugh at me! I'll rip out your guts and eat them!" He continued cursing as he was led away from his partner who was passed out and bleeding on the floor.

It turned out that Brommel's unfortunate cohort suffered superficial wounds only, but his ego had been much more damaged. The fellow dropped out of fencing and signed up for rowing. Brommel was fortunate not to have been expelled. His punishment was to be removed from fencing and reassigned to boxing, a wise move on the instructor's part. I'm certain he realized that with good coaching Brommel's violence could be controlled enough to win many a match for the university.

I was frightened that Brommel might seek some sort of vindication on me. I had smirked at him along with the others, an act I should have performed with more diplomacy as I lived under the same roof as him. Until tonight, he had said nothing, remaining his usual somber self.

When Brommel saw me preparing for the evening dinner party, he glanced from the book he was reading and said with a sincere inflection of hurt, "You had no right to make sport of me, you know. I may be big and clumsy at some things, but that doesn't give you or anyone else the right to judge me as a stupid buffoon."

I was stunned that he could speak in such a well disposed manner. "Why, Brommel," I said, and before I could apologize he had risen from his chair, put on a heavy coat and opened the front door.

"Have a good evening, Andrew," he said, donning his hat. "I certainly intend to."

It was the first night he had been out since the beginning of term.

I must admit I felt horrid in my wrongful evaluation of Brommel. I suppose my social upbringing did tend to cause prejudgment of a person's character in an impetuous manner. Whatever caused Brommel's reclusive nature should not have prompted me to view him as a person of low class. I will most certainly strive to become his friend.

As the hour is getting on, I will close this entry and take my leave for the faculty reception.

One last note: Adrianna has written that she and my parents will be visiting at the beginning of November and staying a few days. This is wonderful news as the university has a harvest festival scheduled for the 2nd, and Adrianna and I do so love such affairs. I'm sure the time will pass quickly in expectation of seeing my dear one and my family again.

September 21, 1848

I think the wine has finally lost its hold on me. I hardly drink, but at the dinner last night you could not turn around without your glass being refilled.

The students were guided down a line for formal introduction. Once that was done and dinner finished, we were left to our own mingling. I discovered, to my surprise, my invitation had been sent by Prof. Charles Vairaja Wilkins, the professor I think highly of.

Prof. Vairaja, as he prefers to leave off the Wilkins, was present with his lovely wife. What a stunning couple they made. Prof. Vairaja trim and vibrant in his coat and tails and his wife glowing in a blue formal gown. Prof. Vairaja was slightly taller than she. Her skin tone was darker than his almost pale nature, making them that much more attractive and exotic.

"This, dear Nara, is the student I was telling you about." Prof. Vairaja said. "He's the one with a penchant for anatomy." He extended his hand to me. "It is good to see you here, Andrew. I have a matter to discuss with you."

After shaking his hand, his wife offered hers. "I am Nara," she said. "I think I have seen you somewhere before."

I told her I didn't think so and that if I had seen such a lovely woman as she, I would have remembered.

Prof. Vairaja laughed and patted my shoulder. "Why, Nara, either this chap is quite a diplomat or I will have to keep an eye on both of you this evening."

I was not trying to make points with my instructor. I was in earnest about Nara's beauty. She took one's breath away. It was impossible not to be aroused standing next to her. She smelled of exotic spices.

Prof. Vairaja chuckled at my distraction. "Well, enough of this admiration," he said. "I'd better spirit this young man away if I am to share my proposal with him, dear."

Nara took the cue and walked away, joining another group of students.

"I would like your help in my research laboratory," Prof. Vairaja said, moving me in the direction of the library entrance. We stopped there. A few students were deep in study at the desks. "I would like to hire you as an assistant. I'm afraid the pay is not substantial, but it should give you a little extra for concerts, plays, or whatever entertainment you desire. I would see that you received extra credit in my class, of course, especially if you aided me in the tissue research I am conducting."

There were rumors concerning Prof. Vairaja's research, and that the radical nature of his experiments was not looked on with favor by the university heads. However, whatever he had accomplished must have made enough of an impression to keep him funded. For him to offer me this opportunity was quite an honor, so I readily accepted.

"Very good, Andrew," Prof. Vairaja said and shook my hand again. "I knew you had a special talent for science from the first day of class. You have the light of discovery in your eyes."

I had never been as flattered as I was at that moment.

As we turned back to the gathering, Prof. Vairaja added, "I would like for you to have dinner with Nara and me after Sunday services this weekend. It would allow me time to give you a brief introduction to my research."

I accepted his invitation. I could think of no better way to spend a Sunday evening: learning of his research and, of course, being in the company of Nara.

As I close this entry, I feel ashamed. Perhaps it was the wine, or maybe my constitution is not as stoic as I believed because thoughts of my dearest Adrianna were obliterated at the reception. The only woman I thought of, in fact dreamed of last night, was Prof. Vairaja's wife, Nara. She must be a true siren to have removed the feelings from the one I love so.

September 28, 1848

It's hard to believe a week has passed since my last entry. So much has occurred, one being Brommel's attitude.

The evening after the faculty dinner I offered apologies for my behavior during the fencing fiasco. To my surprise, he readily accepted. He has now started to make bits of conversation with me, asking questions such as: "How was the gathering?" and "Would you mind glancing at my anatomy notes for a moment?" Even if this is just an attempt for short congenial conversation, it is well received. I feel as if a dark cloud is slowly leaving our lodgings.

In regard to Prof. Vairaja, I did indeed meet with him after mandatory Sunday services. I was surprised that his home was very near mine. He explained that he and Nara had moved back to it shortly after their return from a second visit to India over twenty years ago. He added that they still operated a small spice shop, which Nara ran. Even though the shop was located in a rough area of the city, they had owned it for many years and were not bothered by the locals who were quite familiar with them.

Prof. Vairaja's home was not much bigger than mine. Extra space normally available in the corners or on the walls was crammed with rows and stacks of books. The area was filled with the aroma of old paper and bindings.

Shortly after our arrival, Nara came in to say hello, then excused herself to continue with the dinner she was preparing as Prof. Vairaja and I made ourselves comfortable and talked.

I found it difficult to believe Prof. Vairaja had been at the university for some twenty-seven years. He should have appeared older, but, on the contrary, he looked to be no more than in his early thirties. I supposed that Nara must have been much younger, but he advised me she was only his junior by two years. I inquired as to their secrets for such a youthful appearance. He laughed slightly and said, "Nara and I were born in India. We came from a common district. Our genes seem to be delaying the aging process. Not stopping it, you understand, just impeding it. That, Andrew, is what my research involves." Then, he explained his theory.

He believed there was an organism responsible: a symbiotic rather than a pathogenic one. He had tried over the years to isolate this organism with media and tissue cultures. "I have come close," he continued, "but I cannot keep it viable for extended periods. That's why I want your aid. You see, Andrew, I have a strong belief in first impressions. I see your aptitude for science and don't believe in wasting any time tapping it. Do you agree?"

How could I not? At school not quite a month and I was being offered what others might not be given in a lifetime.

"I must warn you then," Prof. Vairaja said seriously, "some of my methods are considered unorthodox by members of the university staff. There are concerns that must be met with prudence, things that only you and I will know of. These must not be shared. Do you understand?"

I offered my hand and said, "You may depend on my discretion."

As he took my hand, Nara called us into the kitchen where she had set the table. Slices of roast beef, boiled potatoes, and pieces of melon, along with a large bowl of soup graced the table.

When Nara directed me to my seat, Prof. Vairaja excused himself for a moment. While we awaited his return, Nara reached across the table and placed her hand on mine.

"It is good that Charles has chosen a bright and attractive student to help him." She squeezed my hand lightly. "I hope you will be spending many hours with us here."

There was no mistaking her innuendo and no denying the thrill that grabbed my spine.

When Prof. Vairaja returned we had our meal, although I was the only one to eat any of the roast, potatoes, and melon. Prof. Vairaja and Nara dined only on the soup. He explained they had recently suffered from a stomach virus and did not wish to put solid food in their stomachs just yet. They offered me some of the soup but it was thin and pink, more of a broth and not to my liking.

During dinner it was hard to concentrate on the table conversations of my hosts. A predicament is eminent. I hope my love and devotion to Adrianna and my work relationship with Prof. Vairaja will help me avoid the great temptation Nara affords.

October 10, 1848

After reviewing my last entry, I realize how careful I must be in regard to Nara. When I am in her company, it is hard to control my attraction for her. At times I feel like an insect beckoned to taste the sweet nectar of a carnivorous plant.

Working with Prof. Vairaja has been a bit tiresome as he has only let me set up equipments in the laboratory. He explained that he wanted me to become acquainted with his work habits before sharing his research projects. He has, however, allowed me to work with some tissue cultures and review some of his notes on organism viability in vitro and in vivo. The studies appear fascinating. I recognized some of the organic formulas and growth charts he has recorded from my own studies. The extra time I am spending in Prof. Vairaja's laboratory will benefit me mentally and socially at the university, I am certain of it.

However, the most surprising event these past few weeks has not been my association with Prof. Vairaja, it has been Brommel.

I returned late from the lab one evening and found Brommel still up studying. I was tired and went directly to bed when the fellow started talking to me. He had been so mysterious and silent up until then that I wasn't about to miss a conversation with him, especially one that dealt with his past. So I pulled up a chair and listened intently to my curious fellow lodger's story of how he came here.

Brommel was from a small village named Laverstock near Salisbury. His father was a well respected blacksmith there and kept a thriving business which he intended to hand down to his three sons. Brommel was the youngest and the one most unsuited for his father's wishes. Large for his age and clumsy, Brommel appeared oafish and stupid when he was actually quite intelligent. No one in his family or the village took him seriously because of his size and trouble with coordination. So when Brommel announced he wanted to become a doctor, his ambition was met with ridicule rather than support. Even if they had approved, his father's prosperous business would still not have afforded the funds needed to attend the university.

For reasons unknown, the local minister became involved, it seemed he saw the potential in Brommel that had eluded others, including Brommel's school instructors. A fund was set up at the minister's church for a scholarship. Events started to improve for Brommel, and the education he desired seemed not out of reach after all. His family and fellow citizens began to treat him with a new found congeniality as well.

Then there was Alice.

Brommel had secured a job cleaning stables at a nearby estate. He intended to use what monies he acquired toward his college fund. As he was about to complete his duties one day, the owner's daughter rode in. Her name was Alice, and Brommel was quite taken with her striking good looks. Having been avoided by the fairer sex most of life, Brommel was surprised that this beauty actually struck up a conversation with him. Over the next few weeks it seemed a friendship was forming between the two and it wasn't long until Cupid shot an arrow into Brommel's heart. One afternoon he tried to kiss her and was rewarded with a slap and a good boxing of his ears. The girl had evidently just tried to be kind to the oaf cleaning her father's stables. She let Brommel know that she had no romantic feelings for a common worker as himself. In fact, she was engaged to the son of a neighbor who owned an estate that exceeded her father's holdings.

Brommel was crushed by the incident and intended to leave the job as soon as his contract had expired. Once, as he was about to finish the daily cleaning, Brommel heard the faint sound of laughter coming from the direction of the last stall at the end of the stable. He went to see who was there and came upon Alice and her fiancé. She was saddling her horse and telling her dandy companion about the incident with Brommel. "Imagine," she said chuckling, "that I would ever consider kissing a clod like that stable boy. I only conversed with him out of pity." Humored by the inane antics of a dumb boy, her fiancé joined in the giggling. "And of all things", Alice continued, "the clod actually believes he can become a physician."

Brommel stopped talking to me for a moment and placed his head in his hands. He confided that he had never been a violent individual. Even when others had made fun of his size and clumsiness, he had not been moved to aggression but rather felt himself somehow to blame for his appearance. To have Alice and her intended make sport of his genuine feelings toward her was the last straw. He fell on them both, screaming, hitting and lashing out all the years of frustration he had endured. "I was soaked in sweat and blood," Brommel said. "They must have struggled as I had a cut across my chest. It's a wonder I had not killed them." He had, however, delivered a hard enough blow to the fiancé's head to leave the fellow in a state of unconsciousness for a number of days. It was believed the young man would not survive and Brommel was thrown in jail. The families of Alice and her fiancé were quite ready to see Brommel swing from the gallows for his deed, and Brommel feared his own family would suffer financially for his act of rage.

Then, an odd thing occurred. Brommel's father came to visit him in jail and told Brommel that the man had recovered from his head wound and showed no mental damage. He also informed Brommel that the minister who had befriended him met with Alice and her family and her fiancé's family and had, by some miracle, convinced the injured parties to drop the charges against Brommel with the stipulation that Brommel was to leave for London University immediately and not be allowed to return home for even a family visit. Of course, Brommel's father agreed, asking the minister how on earth he had been able to pull it off. The minister replied, "Be still and count your blessings."

Brommel stood and said, "And that is why I am here, sharing this lodging with you, Andrew. After losing my temper in fencing class that day, I have made a constant effort to control myself. Staying clear of bars and the ladies has been a great help. I have been fortunate on two accounts now and do not wish to further tempt fate."

There exists an ease of living with Brommel now that makes life a more relaxed one. I truly believe that only good days are to follow for Brommel and myself.

October 21, 1848

My research duties with Prof. Vairaja have become more involved, so much so that between my own school studies and aiding him I have time for little else.

The organism that is the subject of his investigations is a peculiar one. In its growth habits and infestation of live tissue cultures it exhibits total domination of the host. Therein lays the fault: it consumes all and then dies trying to eat itself.

After I had set up the last student laboratory for the week, Prof. Vairaja asked me to accompany him to his other laboratory. He said I was ready to take the next step. He also added that if I had any doubts about his research, I could drop out of the project now because there would be no turning back after what I would witness.

Although the situation felt a little melodramatic, I agreed to go with him. I had come this far and there was no reason to quit now. After all, how bad could studying tissue cultures really be?

We traveled by carriage to an area of London where the setting sun was not generally welcomed by those who passed through. Even the few Runners who walked there did so quickly and with obvious apprehension.

Prof. Vairaja pointed out a small group of shops. As we continued to move down the darkening streets, he said this was where the spice shop Nara managed was located.

Eventually we came upon a waterfront area and stopped before a row of old warehouses. As we stepped out of the carriage, Prof. Vairaja said flatly, "This is where the university once acquired corpses for the medical school, an illegal and dangerous business to be sure."

We walked halfway down a row of wooden structures where Prof. Vairaja opened a large padlock. He slid back a door that screeched in resistance. The night air was damp and cold by the river. As he pulled wide the door to the building, my senses were assaulted by a dank fetid tropical heat. I covered my mouth and nose to keep out the stench of plant and animal decay. As he closed the door behind us, Prof. Vairaja said, "I must apologize for the rank odor, Andrew, but it is necessary to create a torrid atmosphere for the organism's optimal growth." He then handed me a white handkerchief that had been soaked in what smelled like eucalyptus oil. "Here, cover you face with this. It will help with the initial discomfort." It had a slight dizzying effect but did cut the disgusting odor.

Prof. Vairaja opened a second entrance that he advised led to his laboratory where the humidity was even more oppressive. The area was absolutely foggy with moisture. Straining to see through the mist, I made out cages arranged in a circular pattern close to the rear of the room. There was a faint rustling and an audible chorus of moans. Whatever inhabited those cages had been aroused by our entering the room.

"They smell us," Prof. Vairaja said with a slight sigh. "They're hungry."

He motioned for me to stand by him and pointed to some chains attached to a system of pulleys above us. "Help me pull these," he said.

As we pulled, a partition at the end of each chain started to open. A pair of turbine fans nestled in each began to turn, drawing the moist air up and out into the night. Once the room's visibility had cleared, Prof. Vairaja told me to pull the chains in the opposite direction to close the openings.

The room was lined with gas lamps that Prof. Vairaja lit. There were also rows of smudge pots he had placed in the area to generate the clammy heat. Once the room was illuminated by the lamps, I could see there were close to twenty animal cages present whose occupants were in frenzy, knocking against the side bars, squealing and grunting. I moved closer and saw wild eyes staring back at me. The creatures hissed and growled as I approached. They were baboons.

I was about to ask him how he had arranged to purchase them when the baboon nearest me slammed into the side of its cage. The heavy structure actually moved from the blow, catching me by surprise. I jumped back, startled by the quick movement.

Prof. Vairaja warned, "I wouldn't get too close, Andrew. They are caged, but still dangerous."

I stared at the creature. The face that gazed back was full of rage. The animal was disproportioned. Its head was larger than normal and had a swollen, diseased appearance while the body seemed shrunken with exaggerated musculature and prominent veins.

The baboon opened its mouth in a snarl revealing teeth, usually vicious enough, that were even larger than normal with sharp serrated edges. However, the most conspicuous feature of the animal was its eyes: wide, pleading, starving. There was something alien behind them.

Prof. Vairaja stood beside me. "If I opened the door to his cage, he would tear you apart and eat you," he said with a slight chill added to his voice.

"Why are these poor creatures in such a state?" I asked.

"Tissue cultures could not," he explained, "give me a clear picture of the organism's mode of infection, so I began to inoculate living beings, anything of a small nature like cats, dogs, and rodents that I could procure. The problem of survival still existed, as the host died before I could collect any useful data.

"Then I found a source that could provide larger mammals that better represented their human counterparts," he continued, pointing at the cages. "Baboons possess a similar anatomical structure and physiological balance to us. My research with them has yielded some interesting results."

The sound of a door being pulled opened echoed off the walls. Someone had entered the front of the warehouse.

"Don't be concerned," Prof. Vairaja assured me, "it is only Nara. I asked her to join us." Indeed, Nara walked into the room through the second doorway. She carried a small item wrapped in a blanket.

"Good evening, Andrew," she said as she removed the cover from what she held in her arms. A young chimpanzee emerged and immediately grasped Nara tightly around her neck.

"What you are about to witness, Andrew, might be a shock," Prof. Vairaja said, motioning for Nara to come to him. "Just bear in mind that your purpose is to learn, to understand why the organism I have isolated acts in the manner it does and how we can come to control its tendencies."

He asked me to help him lift a large empty animal pen that stood against the side wall. It was heavy and had enough area for a small child to move about easily inside. After setting it near the caged baboon I had been examining, Prof. Vairaja instructed Nara to join us. He opened the gate to the pen and told her to place the chimpanzee inside.

The chimp may have been young, but it was incredibly strong and had no intention of letting go its hold on Nara. With the smells and noises of the baboons thick in the room, the poor creature must have been petrified. Prof. Vairaja seemed to be no stranger to this situation. He seized the chimpanzee by the nape of its neck, pressing a nerve that would immobilize the animal briefly, then flung it inside the pen and closed the gate.

When the momentary paralysis left the chimpanzee, it started to screech and run wildly around the pen. It gripped the bars and looked directly at Nara. If ever a creature pleaded to be let out, it was that frightened chimpanzee.

Nara moved away and Prof. Vairaja pushed the pen against the baboon's cage. The effect on the chimpanzee was instantaneous. It ran to the opposite end of the pen. Cringing in the corner, I heard it utter a low cry like an infant who has exhausted itself weeping and can only manage a choked gasp. The chimpanzee's eyes were huge and gaped in the direction of the guttural growl growing in intensity from the cage in front of it.

Prof. Vairaja simultaneously lifted the front gates of the cage and the pen. A dark shape literally flew into the pen and crouched in the center.

The grotesque features of the baboon were intensified in the light of the room. Thick rivulets of drool oozed from its mouth as it moved stealthily toward the chimpanzee. A sour odor permeated the air when the chimp's bowels and bladder relaxed.

I had seen enough and turned to ask Prof. Vairaja to stop this exhibition. The intense stare on his and Nara's faces stopped me. They were enraptured by the scene unfolding in the pen.

Prof. Vairaja faced me, his eyes void of any pity.

"Watch," he said flatly and pointed at the stalking baboon. "Watch him."

The beast howled and leapt on the chimp, grabbing its neck with his jaws. As they rolled around the floor of the pen, the chimpanzee shrieked and struggled until the baboon started shaking it like a terrier would a rat. The chimp looked at us, its eyes briefly appealing before rolling back in submission as the baboon ripped open its throat.

Between the spurts of arterial blood, the baboon slurped and gorged. It was disgusting, and when the scarlet fountain ceased to flow, the monstrous baboon screamed in rage and tore the rest of the body apart as it fed. Flesh, organs, and bones were trapped and crushed by the baboon's powerful jaws.

I felt nauseous and moved to the sidewall of the room where I vomited. Someone grabbed my shoulder. I felt warm breath on my neck. A searching tongue pressed hotly against it. The sensation was repugnant and erotic. Giddiness came over me and the room seemed to be spinning down.

Nara whispered in my ear, "I'll come to you one night. Soon, one night soon." Then, she placed her hands under my arms and helped me stand.

Had I heard her correctly or was it just a fabrication from my swirling brain?

"Let me help you, Andrew," she said. "Charles should have realized just how strongly you would react to such a demonstration."

I saw Prof. Vairaja place something in the baboon's cage. Again he lifted the gate of it and the pen. Sniffing, the baboon raised its head and rushed into its cage. Prof. Vairaja quickly closed the gate behind it.

My legs steadied enough and I told Nara I could stand on my own. I looked into her eyes but saw no hint of the lascivious message either real or imagined. Due to the sensual attraction I felt for her, it would have been more than possible for me to create such a whispered delight only in my mind.

Prof. Vairaja glanced over and said, "This will not be the most terrible event Andrew will witness, Nara. You know that. He must be conditioned if he is to continue helping me with my research." He then looked directly at me. "Tell me now, Andrew, if you cannot handle something of this nature." He pointed to the gruesome remains in the pen. "I must be aware of your feelings. There will be no point in you continuing to aid me if you are unable to deal with this."

With bile still clinging to the back of my throat, with the wretched screams of the animals still rattling in my head, I realized my drive for knowledge would overcome my inexperience, a naiveté emergent from a sheltered life. A life made uncomplicated by my family's wealth. A life where I could ignore the poverty, disease, and despair that existed far away from my home and hearth, where the dark and violent nature of all things was excluded by the simple act of turning a key in a lock.

"Yes," I said, still a bit shaken, "you will be able to depend on me, Professor. The stuffiness of this room, the violent display . . . I was just overwhelmed. Have patience with me. I know I will learn to accept this side of your research."

Prof. Vairaja stood in front of me. His hands were bloody from whatever he had tempted the baboon back into the cage with. There was a strange hard gaze in Prof. Vairaja's eyes as if he were deciding whether to trust me or not. I felt an apprehension, a warning creep up my spine. Could he do violence to me? It seemed impossible. Prof. Vairaja was kind and gentle. The only intensity I had seen him display up to now was when he lectured or spoke to me of his research, but, for just a split second, I felt as the chimpanzee must have when staring into the eyes of its murderer.

Then, just as swiftly as it had appeared, the threatening mask vanished from Prof. Vairaja's features. "I think you speak the truth," he said. "I believe your quest for learning will prevail over what you once thought abhorrent. I have seen this in you from the beginning, Andrew."

After the night's events, I felt certain that Prof. Vairaja would involve me freely in his research on an organism that delays the aging process in human beings and could also create a violent and dispassionate disposition.

October 22, 1848

I find the source of the organism we study to be incredible.

That night at the warehouse, Nara left before us. As I helped Prof. Vairaja reposition the baboon's cage and clean up the mess in the pen, I asked him exactly where the agent for the infection originated. He responded that the tissue cultures had been inoculated with the blood of the infected animals he used and from his and Nara's blood.

I thought I had misunderstood him. He and Nara may have some genetic alteration that slowed their aging process, but I could not believe them infected by the same organism that produced a mindless killing host like the baboon. Nara and Prof. Vairaja seemed all too human to me.

But he assured me it was the truth and promised to offer concrete evidence in the coming weeks.

As we got in the carriage to leave, Prof. Vairaja commented, "To help you understand, to grasp what you were told tonight, reflect on what you have witnessed since your arrival at the university. Nara confided to me how she was familiar with you before I introduced you at the faculty dinner. She said she saw you walking alone one night. Do you remember, Andrew?"

I didn't recall, and it wasn't until I fell asleep that night and dreamed I was running from something in the fog that I remembered to what Prof. Vairaja had referred. It was the night I left the flat disgusted with Brommel's and his prostitute's behavior. Could Nara have been out at the same time? It was possible as their home was very near my own, but I certainly had not seen her.

Perhaps Prof. Vairaja had kept laboratory animals in his house and one escaped into the night. It might have been the thing I had heard in the hedges, the creature I imagined had followed behind me in the mist. Prof. Vairaja and Nara might have been searching for it in different directions. She could have seen me then and just not made her presence known.

Whatever happened that night in the fog, I couldn't stop the chill that grabbed me at the memory of it. If it had been an animal like the ones I observed in the warehouse, the being could have been stalking me before being recaptured by Nara or Prof. Vairaja. If this was the case, then providence has surely guided me to study with Prof. Vairaja.

October 30, 1848

I am anxiously awaiting the arrival of Adrianna and my parents.

I have spent the last few days in such intense study with my classes and the research with Prof. Vairaja that I am in need of a break. Prof. Vairaja agreed to let me out of the lab for a few days as long as I promised to introduce my fiancé and family to him at the harvest festival.

I invited Brommel to join us and he readily accepted. He has been in low spirits lately and my invitation looked to be just what he needed.

I will close this short entry as I must go to the railway station to meet my dears.

November 2, 1848

To be with Adrianna again was the moment I had anticipated since my arrival at the university.

When she and my parents disembarked from the train there were hugs all 'round, a few tears, and many questions. Of course I couldn't reveal much of my research duties with Prof. Vairaja, but what I did tell them of it and my other classes was taken with interest and pride at my early accomplishments.

When we got to my lodgings, I introduced them to Brommel who was the perfect gentleman. I was happy to find him so amiable with my parents, although he may have been a bit too taken with Adrianna.

My father had rented a small cottage on the opposite side of the university, but it wasn't that far from my lodgings. After Brommel and I helped them unpack and settle in, we discussed plans for attending the festival. It was decided we would give them ample opportunity to recover from their trip and return to take them to the festival late in the evening.

As agreed, we came to pick up my parents and Adrianna just at twilight. Before we arrived, Brommel commented on my good fortune to have such a beautiful and refined fiancé. I realized his past experience must have weighed heavily on him, so I assured him he too would find someone he could hold as dear as Adrianna one day.

Once all were dressed and ready, we walked up the sloping hill that led to the student hall. The night was perfect. A brisk brittle breeze danced under a full harvest moon. Wisps of clouds painted the graying twilight.

Students, faculty, and their families were gathered in the student hall. The place had been aptly decorated. Sections of straw had been tied and placed randomly among pumpkins. There was a long serving table filled with various offerings: roasted apples, pumpkin pies, glazed hams, and a variety of fruits and nuts were only a few of the items spread generously across it.

To wash these delights down, rum punch and apple cider were provided and served in warm cups or, for the heartier, large flagons. To complete the reverie, a group of fiddlers playing gigs and reels adorned the stage in the hall.

I had been introducing my family and fiancé to different students and professors when I spotted Prof. Vairaja and Nara watching some of the guests who were playing a game of Snap Apple.

"Ah, Andrew," Prof. Vairaja greeted as I approached them, "Nara and I were just observing the futile efforts to capture hanging apples without the use of one's hands." He then said to me, "I wonder what the Druid priests would think of such activity. It was, after all, their custom to offer blood sacrifices to the gods of harvest, not to snap for fruit with your teeth."

"I believe, Doctor," I answered with a smile, "that civilization has come a long way since those days of magic and nature worship."

Prof. Vairaja laughed softly. "What would we do without civilized man, Andrew? But I must disagree about magic. We still have a lot of that left in all of us."

Gazing upon Nara, I knew he was right. She could cast a spell on anyone.

I directed them toward Adrianna, who was dancing with Brommel, and my parents, strategically standing by a bowl of rum punch, a particular favorite of theirs.

When the dance finished, I introduced Prof. Vairaja and Nara.

It was a cordial enough scene. My parents had a slight blush in their cheeks from the alcohol. Brommel's and Adrianna's flush was not from spirits but rather from spirited dancing. I felt a tug of jealousy seeing them together. I had not intended to share Adrianna with anyone.

My father eyed the two 'foreigners' at my side with his accustomed proper British suspicion, but shook their hands readily enough. When Prof. Vairaja took my mother's and Adrianna's hands in succession, bowing and kissing the backs of them, I believed the women were going to swoon over his gallant gesture. Nara looked amused, especially with the attention from Brommel's eyes. He couldn't take them off her.

"It is unfortunate," Prof. Vairaja said, "that mistletoe is absent from these proceedings. It was a powerful talisman in the early harvest festivities."

My father, who was warming up under the influence of the rum punch, answered, "Bad luck, old man. It won't do to decorate with that berry and branch before Christmas."

Prof. Vairaja laughed, patting my father on the shoulder. "I was only referring to the fact I have no excuse to steal a kiss from these lovely ladies."

My mother and Adrianna giggled while my father coughed, unsure if he should be offended or complimented by what Prof. Vairaja had said.

Nara lured Brommel onto the dance floor and engaged in a lively gig with him. Prof. Vairaja offered his hand in invitation to Adrianna, taking her to the floor for a spin as well. That left me no choice but to ask my mother for a dance.

As we moved across the dance floor, spinning just out of reach of the couples who swirled by, I saw from the corner of my eye how relieved my father was not having to dance. He had found his comfort by the punch and cider bowls. I was certain in the morning his head would probably feel as large as one of the pumpkins in the hall that night.

Before the evening was over, I managed to dance my share with Adrianna. Between Brommel and Prof. Vairaja, I wasn't sure if I was going to have her company at all. I suppose they became aware of my slight irritation at their friendly advances and surrendered her to me.

The evening was a gala one. We left with Prof. Vairaja and Nara offering their pleasure at having met all, then walked down the slope combating a strong north wind that had arrived, bringing just the right atmosphere to the night. It rushed over and around us, howling in playful amusement as it sent hats rolling and hair flying in its path.

After Brommel and I escorted my parents and Adrianna back to their cottage, we headed home where Brommel lurched into bed and fell asleep immediately, aided by the spirits and dancing he had enjoyed. However, I was restless and found it difficult to relax. I suppose the wind, which was gusting by now, contributed to my insomnia as it banged against the windows and clattered over the rooftop.

The fire I had started when we first returned was dying, sending pops and crackles of sparks around it. The sound was soothing and I found myself drifting when I thought I heard the sound of pebbles hitting the front window. I rolled over and dismissed it as rain or sleet, but it returned, as if someone were tapping their nails against the pane of glass.

I got up to investigate and was startled by a face staring at me from the other side of the cold glass. It was overshadowed by the reflection of the dying fire, giving the countenance a necklace and halo of small flames. Then a hand was raised and its fingers tapped lightly on the window.

With relief I recognized it was Nara who beckoned from the cold night. She had a strange smile on her face. Her upper canines looked exaggerated through the glass. They were almost frightening.

An icy blast rushed into the room as I opened the door for her. Brommel stirred and frowned, but he was still deep in slumber and did not awaken.

"I am sorry to bother you, Andrew," Nara said, shaking from the cold as she stepped into the cottage. She was wearing a bathrobe, probably covering her nightclothes. She must have been in a hurry not to dress for the bitter conditions.

I looked at clock on the fireplace mantle and saw it was almost three a.m.

"What has happened? Is something wrong?" I asked.

She glanced at Brommel.

"It is all right," I assured her, "he will be out until morning."

"Charles needs your aid, Andrew."

"But what . . . ?"

"There is no time to explain. I must take you to the laboratory immediately."

I hastily got dressed and was in such a rush I forgot to leave Brommel a note. It occurred to me he would, more than likely, still be asleep by the time I returned so it really didn't matter.

As I closed the door behind us, I thought of something else I'd forgotten.

"Let me get you a decent coat to wear," I told her. "You are shaking from this cold."

Nara was already moving down the street. "Don't worry about me," she yelled back against the wind, "I'm fine. Now please hurry and follow."

I soon caught up to her. There was no rain or sleet as I had suspected earlier. Instead, the cold front had blown away the cloud cover. The sky was clear and glowing ghostly under the full moon as we sped down the street toward the university.

As we got closer to the student laboratory building, I felt relieved that we would soon be out of this bitter cold and inside where I could help Prof. Vairaja. Just before we reached the building, Nara stopped and leaned against a bench.

"Are you all right?" I asked her.

Our escaping breath formed frosty clouds. My face felt covered by a thin layer of ice. Nara turned toward me. She smiled fully, her face and teeth ghastly apparitions in the waxen moonlight. She let the robe fall from her body. She wore only a sheer white nightgown beneath it. The outline of her body pressed against its thin hold.

She moved to me, placed her arms around my neck and pulled her body against mine.

My objection was feeble. "What are you doing? Where is Prof. Vairaja?"

Nara placed a finger to my lips and pressed closer to me, her body hot in the chilly night air.

"This is close to where we first met, Andrew. Remember?" she whispered.

Numbed by the cold and shocked by the heat of her body I stuttered, "I . . . Prof. Vairaja said something but I never saw you . . . I . . . ."

She covered my mouth with her warm lips. Nara's tongue probed, those sharp teeth of hers scraping sensuously against my flesh. The erection I achieved was immediate and painful.

Nara guided me behind the hedges and pushed me to the ground as if I were weightless, then straddled me.

"Near here," she said softly, unbuttoning my trousers, "close to this hedge row. I followed you to your home. Later I had the girl who left after you had arrived."

Any questions I could have had about her meaning vanished as she slowly placed me inside her.

Nara rode me in an unrushed rhythm. She threw her head back and gasped as my hands slipped under and up her gown.

I had never been with a woman in this way. Adrianna and I were stoic in our belief of waiting until after we were married. Because of my inexperience, I came quickly. Nara felt my shudder and moaned, "No, not yet. Not yet."

Nara broke the kiss and grabbed my shoulders. She looked directly into my eyes. Her face strained to hold back the scream of pleasure but could not. As she cried into the night and thrashed against me, her nails dug deep into my back. She dragged them down and through my shirt.

After, we lay quietly on the cold earth. Nara positioned her face in the nape of my neck. "I know," she whispered, "that you would be sweet, but Charles won't allow it. He wants me to do it differently for you."

She nudged me on my side and pulled up my shirt. I offered no resistance even though the scratches Nara had inflicted burned. Then she licked the wounds like an animal. It made the pain more intense for a moment, but then the stinging subsided.

"Dear, Andrew," Nara said as she rose and placed her robe on over the gown, "take care on your journey."

"But, wait. What journey?"

Like a wisp of smoke she drifted swiftly from my sight. I was left exhausted and confused on the wet ground. I felt nauseous and disoriented but managed to put my shirt back on and button up my pants.

What had I allowed to happen?

I had betrayed Prof. Vairaja. I had committed an act that could destroy my relationship with Adrianna. And what if my parents should discover the gravity of my actions? They and Adrianna would be here another two days. How could I be around them and act as if nothing had occurred?

A faint line of red was lighting the horizon as I walked back to my lodgings. When I arrived and opened the door, I fell into bed a mass of aches and weariness, the scratches on my back throbbing.

Fatigue won out over the pain and I slipped into a deep slumber. I was awakened by the off-key singing of Brommel.

I moaned as I raised myself up and Brommel commented, "I didn't think you drank all that much last night, old man." He was putting on riding togs.

I placed my head in my hands and replied through a pounding headache, "I'm certain I didn't."

"You do remember, "Brommel continued, "that we are cutting classes to go riding in the country with your parents and Adrianna this afternoon."

If Brommel had mentioned this last night, I did not recall it.

"You were quite intoxicated when we got home last night, Thomas," I said, "The first thing you did when we entered the lodgings was lurch towards the bed and pass out."

He hesitated for a moment then said, "Oh dear, then it's possible I didn't mention the plans to you. Sometimes when I have too much to drink I only think I have said something. Forgive me for not telling you, Andrew. However, that does not alter the fact that they will be arriving soon, so you had better get up and going."

I felt horrid. "But what time is it?" I asked too loudly and a new wave of nausea and pain spread over me.

"It's just after noon. Your parents and fiancé will be here around one. We are to take a coach to a small riding stable just outside of London. Your father has an acquaintance who arranged this for us."

"I don't think I'm up to it."

Brommel shrugged. "I'm certain they will understand if you choose to stay in bed. I will be there in your stead."

I may have been ill and wished to avoid Adrianna and my parents so soon after my night of infidelity, but I had no desire to leave my fiancé in Brommel's company. It was obvious he was attracted to her.

Feeling as if I might vomit or pass out at any moment, I got out of bed.

"You are right," I said to Brommel. "I must go. After all, they will only be here through tomorrow."

"I knew you could do it," Brommel said with a slight grin. "By the way, I forgot to mention that Prof. Vairaja and his enchanting wife will be joining us."

Just the crowning blow I needed. Not only would I have to deal with being sick, I would have to remain calm in the presence of my fiancé and the woman who had fornicated with me like a wild creature on the university grounds just hours before.

Of course, the day could be nothing but disastrous.

Adriana and my parents, seeing that I was not well, insisted that I stay at home. Since my mother, and not Adrianna, offered to stay behind with me, I assured them with the lie I would feel better as the day progressed.

I made it through the bumpy coach ride, although I thought my head would be jostled from my neck. When we arrived at the stable, Prof. Vairaja and Nara were waiting for us. How she could appear so calm and rested after the wild night was a mystery.

When I said hello, there was no hint of what we had done in her eyes or actions.

"You look a bit pale, Andrew," was all Nara offered before joining the others in the group.

They chatted like communal birds and waited patiently as I forced myself onto a horse.

Even the slowest movement of the animal beneath me was irritating to my sorry condition and as the pace increased, so did my misery. I slowed the horse down to a walk and fell behind. Prof. Vairaja and my parents noticed that I fallen back. Brommel, Adrianna, and Nara were involved in a silly race. I could only gawk at them as they sped well ahead of the group.

I called to my parents and Prof. Vairaja to go on without me, and that I would catch up after a short rest. They went on, but at slower pace.

As I came to the crest of a hill, I discovered the racers had halted at the bottom of the hill's extended slope. The other riders were half way down and steadily approached Brommel and the two women.

Nara and Adrianna circled Brommel. I could hear their laughter. Watching the blatant flirtations of the two women sent a blaze of jealousy and anger through me, so much so that I was trembling from it. I recognized what was happening and calmed down. Envy was one matter, but I felt a violent urge toward Brommel, Nara, and my fiancé. That was just not my nature.

When Prof. Vairaja and my parents joined the others, they hailed me to come down. Instead, I dismounted, arranged the reins neatly around the saddle horn then passed out, falling into a swirl of lights and colors.

I returned to consciousness with the murmur of soft voices distant in my head. It was my mother and Adrianna talking. I opened my eyes and was assaulted by daylight. I turned away and found my father sitting by my bed in a chair. His head had fallen on his chest. He snored in convulsive spurts.

My throat felt dry and constricted, raw and in need of water. I tried to clear it as best I could. It was enough noise to get Adrianna's and my mother's attention. Even my father was stirred by the rasping sound of my cough.

Adrianna brought me a glass of water. When I tried to drink, it lodged like a knot of fire I could not swallow or cough back up. Eventually, I was able to force it down, but I felt no relief from it at all.

"Prof. Vairaja thinks you have come down with a respiratory virus," my mother said as she placed a cool cloth on my forehead. "He instructed you must be watched closely but that you are young and healthy and should be able to weather it."

"He recommended you stay in bed at least a week," Adrianna added.

I tried to answer but only produced a hoarse whisper.

"See here," my father chided, "Don't strain yourself, my boy. Rest. That's the ticket."

A sudden chill gripped me and was so intense the bed shook beneath me. It passed quickly, leaving me soaked in perspiration. Adrianna placed her hand over her mouth to suppress a sob, turned away and walked to the window to look outside.

"It was just a small one this time," my mother comforted me. "When you passed out by the horse, we brought you home immediately. You were in an extreme state of chills and fever. You were making no sense, talking about something chasing you in the fog. We undressed you and saw those horrid marks on your back and asked you about them. You babbled something about a hedge so we assumed you had injured yourself in a fall of some kind. Prof. Vairaja assured us the scratches had nothing to do with your current illness, but he told us to keep an eye on them should they become infected. It wouldn't do to have your system strained even more than it is already."

I nodded to her and began to drift off, lulled by the soothing nature of my mother's voice.

Next morning I did feel a bit better, especially when my father informed me they were going to extend their stay until I was back on my feet.

"It's unthinkable," he stated, "to leave you in such a sad state with only strangers to comfort you."

My mother tried to get me to take a little warm broth but I could only swallow a small amount. I craved sleep more than anything and seemed to do nothing but doze throughout the day.

When I awoke that evening, my parents were sleeping. Adrianna had taken my father's seat by the bed. She reached out and took my hand when she saw me stir. Her touch was uncomfortably warm, almost painful, but I was not about to let go.

"Feeling better, dear?" she asked and squeezed my hand.

I nodded I was, then asked her in my hoarse voice to bring me my journal. I wanted it near so I could write down the events of the past two days. I knew she would never read it unless I wanted her to.

I inquired as to Brommel's whereabouts.

"Prof. Vairaja offered him a bed at his and Nara's flat," Adrianna said. "He felt we were needed here, that family would be more help in your recovery."

It was just as well. I'm convinced Adrianna is developing a certain affection for Brommel. I can tell by the look in her eyes and her mannerisms when his name is mentioned. I know he is attracted to her. His clumsiness seems to vanish in her presence. Brommel is by far physically superior to me, and he does possess an animal nature that women would find stimulating.

Perhaps this weakened state has affected my imagination on the subject of Brommel and Adrianna. It's just the thought of losing her is more hurtful than any sickness.

Adrianna has finally fallen asleep in the chair. I will write what I can of the last two day's events before a chill returns and I ride a wave of fever into the empty land of sleep.

November 10, 1848

What has occurred in the last week is a nightmare.

They are all dead. All of my dears. All except me.

"It was the ether," Prof. Vairaja explained to the police inspector. "I warned Andrew's parents about its proper use for sedating their son if he became too violent from his fever. I told them it was highly flammable. Well," he continued, pointing to the burned rubble that had once been the lodging Brommel and I shared, "you can see for yourself how dangerous the chemical can be. If I had not stopped by to check on my student, I'm certain Andrew would have perished along with his parents and fiancé."

"Was there any one else acquainted with your student Andrew Morgan who might have been around before the fire?" the inspector asked.

"Only his fellow lodger, Thomas Brommel, but he has been staying in my home so Andrew's parents could have complete care over their son without interruption. I haven't been home yet myself to give the bad news to my wife and Thomas. We had all grown very attached to Andrew's parents these last few days."

However, I knew the truth. I was drugged but well aware of what was being said around me. Now that I am capable of writing, I will tell the story without fabrication.

The night I wrote my last journal entry with Adrianna sleeping by my bed, the fever and chills assaulted me again. My shaking was so severe that not only the bed rattled, the chair where Adrianna slept trembled as well.

She awoke with a start, looked at me and screamed. It was the last thing I remembered with clarity. Everything after was a jumble of blurred images and sounds. I heard my mother yell for someone to fetch Prof. Vairaja. I felt hands restrain me. I heard a distant snapping sound, like jaws opening and closing on each other. At times consciousness seemed close only to be replaced by a swirling maelstrom that sucked me into obscurity.

I was suffocating. I could draw no air into my lungs. Prof. Vairaja's voice came through the cloud. He ordered my parents and Adrianna outside the room. It was the last sound I heard before the buzzing in my ears lost its volume. Something sharp pricked my neck then there was silence. My struggle against the fever was over and I felt at peace as I was swallowed by a black cold void.

I came to in a large cage in the lab at the waterfront warehouse. My muscles were tender and sore, but I felt no fever or illness. I was more confused and angry than sick. Why had I been placed in a cage like one of Prof. Vairaja's animals?

I was naked and dirty. Something wet and viscous that stank of decomposing tissue was smeared all over my body. I felt my head, discovering a wild tangle of hair. As my vision cleared, so did the surroundings.

I was in a warehouse, but it looked different from the one I had been taken to before. The room was larger and more expansive from the ceiling to the floor. There were a number of cages, but they were bigger than the ones Prof. Vairaja had used for the baboons. They, like mine, were big enough for humans to move around in.

I stood and my body lost its stiffness. In fact, my muscle tone felt fluid and loose. The only discomfort was in my throat. I was parched and incredibly thirsty.

"It is your superior intelligence that is to blame." Prof. Vairaja's voice startled me. "I decided to stop using the baboons. I could get no new research advances from them. Humans, you understand, had to be the next step. So far, the others have not survived the infection and change." He moved in front of me. "I tried something different with you, Andrew. I wished to observe what would happen if the organism was introduced into your blood stream via a wound, like the scratches on your back.

"I admit I had reservations about experimenting with the one person I knew clever enough to help me with my research," he continued and walked to the center of the room. A figure lay there covered in a white sheet. Dark blotches had seeped through the cover, staining it. "I told you I would offer proof that most of the tissue cultures were infected with Nara's and my own blood," he said and pulled the sheet from the body on the floor. "Although you do not fully realize you are that proof, I will show you something you can observe and absorb."

I asked in a dry and painful whisper why I was caged and what he meant by me being the proof. When I realized it was Brommel who lay uncovered on the floor, I fell silent.

Brommel was gagged, his hands and feet bound. He was naked and appeared to have been in a vicious brawl. Deep bruises and cuts covered his body. He struggled against his bonds, great rivulets of sweat rolled down his face. As he stared at me, he tried to speak through his gag. From a shadowed corner, Nara moved toward him. She was dressed in a sheer gown similar to the one she wore the night we were together. Her movements were cat-like as she approached Brommel.

An expression of horror spread over his face when he heard her behind him. He flipped over on his side and stared at Nara. As she came closer, Brommel froze. She untied him, turned him on his back and removed the gag. He made no attempt to get away. The straps still dangling from his wrists, he put his arms around her waist. She straddled him as she had me behind the hedges that night.

They were in front of me and all I could see was Nara's back and rear with Brommel's legs protruding from beneath. She bent down and must have kissed him. His hands moved up her back and dragged off the gown. She placed him inside her with slow deliberation.

Their coupling was furious, their moans loud and full of pleasure. Nara's cries of ecstasy transformed to guttural growls of hunger as she buried her face in Brommel's neck. He wailed in pain and thrashed convulsively with Nara still grasping his throat.

The carotid fountain spewed from Brommel's neck when Nara released her bite for an instant before attaching again. The great strength Brommel possessed drained on the floor around him. He lay still, like a discarded rag doll. Nara's head jerked spasmodically. She resembled a shark as it rips and tears into its prey.

Brommel made one last effort to cry out, but when he opened his mouth a gout of blood was expelled, splattering him and Nara.

Nara looked to Prof. Vairaja. "Do we still want to keep this one?" she asked, her face and body gory with blood.

"Yes," Prof. Vairaja answered. "I still have use for him."

Nara looked frustrated and went back to Brommel's neck to drink any remaining blood.

It was as if I had witnessed the event through another's eyes. My thoughts were torn between horror and hunger. My hands gripped the bars of the cage. Drool hung from my lips. I smacked loudly. As much as I abhorred the thought, I needed to feed on Brommel's body.

Prof. Vairaja moved in front of me.

"You would have died had I not infected you with my bite. The inoculation of the organism through Nara's saliva into the cuts on your back did not have the result I'd hoped for. It was killing you instead." He looked at me and continued in a flat monotone, "Almost all the blood must be drained, the organism left with no rivalry for its take over of the host."

I heard cries coming from the other cages. Cries of fear. I could smell the living flesh trapped there. Prof. Vairaja unlocked my cage and swung the door open. The floor was cold on my feet as I ran to one of the other cages. I pulled at the bars. I wanted the food inside.

My mother screamed and gazed at me with disbelief. "Andrew, what is wrong with you?" She moved to the rear of her prison and wailed at me. "Go away! Please, my dear son, it is me, your mother! Please go away!"

I heard my father yelling from his own confinement for me to stop. From further back in the room, Adrianna's voice pleaded with me as well, but none of their appeals mattered. The haunting fact was that I still had the sane thoughts of a son as Prof. Vairaja opened my mother's cage and I hurried in. There was no stopping the action of my body, the entity that drove me was uncontrollable and starving as it tore my mother to pieces. Grunting with desire I drank her blood and gobbled down her flesh. It was an unholy communion of consumption. The agonizing cries of my father and Adrianna were distant and vague, no competition for the thrilling taste I could not get enough of.

I was then placed with my father. He fought but could not compete with the desire I had to keep on feeding. As much as I consumed I still felt ravenous. The miserable thing I had become seemed insatiable.

When I had finished with my father, I curled into the fetal position and wept at the despicable acts I had performed. Even as remorse assaulted me, even as the horror at what I had done burned in the vestigial human part of my brain, the awareness of Adrianna being in the room shrieked at me in my desire to feed once more.

"Andrew." It was Adrianna's voice. "Andrew, help me."

I looked up and could just make out the outlines and shadows of her face peering through the bars of her distant prison.

She had witnessed all, watched as I had killed and eaten my parents. For an instant, I felt a wave of affection for her, followed by a jolt of despair knowing she had seen me do those loathsome things.

I threw back my head and howled, "Adrianna! Adrianna!"

I got up and walked to where she was caged. I can only imagine how maniacal I appeared covered in gore. She tensed slightly, then placed her hands through the bars and held my soiled face.

"Whatever they have made of you, it cannot change my feelings," she whispered.

Tears streamed down my face as I placed my hands over hers. Then, I was jerked away and thrown to the floor.

"He must kill her too," Nara hissed above me. "There must be three bodies in his lodgings. These are not the usual dregs we kill, Charles." Nara stared at Adrianna with venomous hatred and said, "These are social brats. They will be missed. He must take her and finish her." Nara reached through the bars and Adrianna moved quickly to the rear. "If not, then let me have her."

Somehow, the monster inside of me was held at bay by Adrianna's love. I stood to challenge Nara when I was wracked by a coughing fit. Something had blocked my airway. I strained to expel whatever it was and, through great effort, was able to eject it. My two upper canines lay in a clot of blood at my feet.

Stunned, I stared at the teeth, oblivious to the fact that Prof. Vairaja stood beside me.

"Don't be concerned," he said, "they will be replaced with a stronger more efficient pair very soon."

"Well?" Nara interrupted. "Will he take her or will I?"

I was shaken and nauseous and made no move to intercede for Adrianna's safety. As it happened, there was no need to.

"Not just yet," Prof. Vairaja said as he moved to Nara, "I have something else in mind for her."

"But the bodies, Charles," Nara said, gazing with disgust at Adrianna again, "there must be three!"

"There are many her shape and size, many possessing the color of her hair," Prof. Vairaja said as he stared at Adrianna with distraction. "You know the type, Nara. The ones who sell their bodies. It will be easy to find a replacement."

"It should be her!" Nara was insistent. "She is his love! He must be made to suffer as much loss as we did!"

Prof. Vairaja placed his arm around Nara's waist and whispered in her ear. She eased a bit then said, "I will return shortly."

She brushed past me as if I were no more than the remains of my parents.

Prof. Vairaja turned and came to me. He had not lost his composure during the whole affair. How could the hateful thing that had driven me to murder be the same as that residing in him? Could he willfully control its needs?

I was sick again. If the organism was so unpredictable could it still kill me in the attempt to take over my physical being? I felt dizzy and was about to fall when Prof. Vairaja grabbed me. He took me to an examining table like the ones used in dissecting class and placed me on it. I started to convulse and vomit clotted blood. He placed an ether soaked rag over my nose and mouth.

"Don't be afraid, Andrew," he assured, "this is a normal reaction during transformation."

That was the last I recalled until regaining consciousness outside the burned dwelling where I heard Prof. Vairaja lie to the police about the deaths of my parents and Adrianna.

* * *

The world has turned upside down. I have been thrown into a darkness that is terrifying yet enticing. To die, to relieve myself of this corruption would be a blessing, but the drive to live, to breathe and feed is constant and overwhelming.

Prof. Vairaja convinced the authorities that he could better care for me at his home, that my illness had improved to the point where a hospital would not be necessary. Since Prof. Vairaja was a professor in the medical school, they trusted his judgment.

However, I was not taken to his home. Instead he moved me into the spice shop Nara operated. I was kept there for the next few days, fed raw bloody meat and constantly observed during my transformation.

I cannot remember all that happened during that period. My thoughts were always obliterated by a lust for blood. Eventually I began to feel calmer and more like my old self. My new canines had almost pushed through completely when Prof. Vairaja took me back to the waterfront one night.

"Your confusion has just begun, Andrew," he said. "Tonight we will find out just what you are becoming."

I did not respond. I was sullen, torn between emotions. Prof. Vairaja shrugged off my disregard and said no more until we had entered the warehouse. Once we were in the room were I had killed my parents, I was assaulted by the stench of human waste and fear. It maddened my hunger. I went from cage to cage for the source. I pulled frantically at the bars of the one where a huddled shaking figure crouched.

"Open it!" I screamed at Prof. Vairaja. "I am starving!"

I grasped the bars in an even greater rage and roared over the whines and groans of the food inside. The figure looked up at me. Adrianna glared with wild darting eyes. They had left her locked in there with nothing to anticipate but her own death. Remnants of decaying food lay mixed with piles of feces on the floor of the cage. The heavy aroma of ammonia from old urine was mixed with the musky smell of Adrianna's panic. She did not recognize me for the companion I had been. She saw only the thing that would kill and eat her. She screamed hysterically and battered her body against the bars at the rear of the cage in a vain attempt to escape. From the shadows behind her, Nara appeared.

I fell to my knees and wailed as I fought the torment of my hunger.

"Don't you want her blood?" It was the first time Prof. Vairaja had raised his voice in anger to me. He grabbed me and tried to lift me, but I struggled against his efforts. He released his hold and opened the door of Adrianna's cage. "Go in!" he commanded. "Her blood is warm, her flesh succulent. Go, Andrew! Taste her! She is no longer your love, she is your food!"

I was on my feet then, staring through the eyes of the thing I had become. I entered the cage and fell on Adrianna. I turned her pale face away as I prepared to tear open her neck. She made no attempt to resist.

"Andrew," she said in a whisper, "be quick."

Through her insanity she still knew who I was. The hunger that ripped my stomach with a thousand needles could not overcome my love for her. I released my grip and rested her head gently on the floor.

She gazed at me and pleaded, "No, you must kill me. This torture is too much to endure. Have mercy and kill me."

I could not. Even though the hunger was intense enough to blind me, I could not harm her.

"What is wrong with you?" Nara growled at me. "You are no better than the rest of us, no different. Never think you are."

"No, Nara," Prof. Vairaja spoke, his voice had calmed. "He is not the same. He is the bridge, the combination I have hoped to find."

So I had been another of Prof. Vairaja's experiments after all. Was it conceivable to hold on to one's humanity at the cost of the lives of others? Who writes the final definition of what we are if not ourselves?

"We will see," Nara spat out the words. "Observe to what degree the will can be tested by the need for life or death."

She walked to and opened the door of a cage just across from Adrianna's. What had once been Brommel staggered out.

He looked to be in agony, and when he realized the food that had been near, the food that had been driving him mad with hunger was in front of him, Brommel became alert, sniffing the air. His naked body was covered with grime, his countenance horrible to behold. Every creased line of his face was filled with rage and hunger. For one such as Brommel, one who held the hurts of his life inside, the transformation had probably been a welcomed one.

He rushed into Adrianna's cage. I blocked him. Brommel roared and grabbed me, forcing me to the floor of the cage. Before we had been changed, Brommel could have bested me with ease, but I was stronger now and could compete with his strength. We rolled, spitting and biting, using our new teeth to inflict as much pain as possible. At one point I felt my ear tearing away. An excruciating line of white hot spasm seared down my face, rage filled me as I pushed free of his hold and stood in front of Adrianna.

Brommel leapt to his feet. He opened and closed his mouth slowly, as if in indecision. He snarled, his face a mass of nervous ticks, his body, like mine, torn and bleeding. He rushed me again, but I was ready and swung him against the bars of the cage. I smashed his head on them over and over until blood gushed over my hands.

I knew I had dazed him and that I had little time to waste. I threw Brommel down flat on his back. He moaned and tried to gather his stunned senses. I sat heavily on him. A rush of air was forced from his lungs. I turned his head sideways to expose the pounding artery under the skin.

"Yes," I heard Prof. Vairaja say, "that is the thing to do. Go ahead, Andrew, kill your friend before he does the same to you and your love. Drink him then rip off his head and tear out his heart!"

I glanced sideways and found Adrianna watching intently. An insane grin was plastered on her face. I opened my mouth and let my teeth slide just above Brommel's carotid and experienced a feeling so repugnant that my stomach convulsed at the thought of drinking his blood or killing him. I trembled, stood up on wobbly legs and grabbed the bars to keep my balance.

Nara laughed obscenely. "The bridge you say?" Nara screamed at Prof. Vairaja as if she had won a victory. "Oh, my husband, this is not the one."

I was impotent. I could not kill Brommel. I could not save Adrianna.

Brommel regained his wits. I fell to my knees. He leered down at me, streams of red drying on his face. He brushed me aside. I placed my hands over my ears to muffle the struggles and screams of Adrianna, the groans and slurps of Brommel as he fed.

After what seemed an eternity, Brommel leaned and whispered in my ear. "I left some for you, my brother." I could hear the sticky grinding of her blood on his lips. "Just a little to slake your thirst."

I crawled to the side of Adrianna's lifeless form and lifted her head. I bore my fangs and stretched my jaws wide open, but it was not in hunger. Agony carried my wail of desperation across the room. Tears streamed down my face, their saltiness bitter in my failure to save her.

Prof. Vairaja appeared on the other side of the bars.

"It is your choice then, Andrew," he said.

Nara moved swiftly to his side and said coldly, "There is no choice, Charles. He cannot, must not. You see how weak he is. How much better would she be?"

He ignored Nara and placed his hands through the bars and held Adrianna's head up to me.

"You must take as much of what is left as possible," he instructed. "One can never get it all, but you must try to drain her as completely as you can."

The terrible realization of what he suggested stung me. Did he believe this would be a kindness, that I should wish to hold her hand and kiss her bloody lips as we fed together?

"Never!" I hissed at him through my teeth. "Never! Never!"

A flush of anger clouded Prof. Vairaja's face as Nara laughed and said, "I told you, Charles. He is weak, unappreciative."

"Then move away," he ordered, "and allow me to do what must be done."

It took both Nara and Brommel to pull me from the cage. Through my resistance and threats I watched Prof. Vairaja rip out Adrianna's heart and suck what blood he could from it and stared in abhorrence as he tore away her head.

I was dragged to the cage where Brommel had been kept. They threw me in and locked the door.

If there was any saving grace it was the fact I had not caused Adrianna to become a creature like me. The instability of the organism made the personality of the transformed uncertain. Adrianna could have changed into a monster like Nara, using sexual lust to lure and kill her victims. To save her this fate, I had to let Adrianna die.

I know now that there are no devils or demons, gods or angels. There is just the body and the chemical mechanics that stir it.

Whether I will ever write another entry in this journal will be left to chance. For now, I will put down my pen. Life as I knew it, lived and loved in it, is but a gloomy chamber of painful memories.

All the world is red.

All the world is blood.

May 16, 1938

To blow away the dust of ninety years, to pick up this journal once more is a laborious duty, but I have promised Peter I would write as much history concerning the last ninety years of my life as I can tolerate as we travel by ship to America.

Although Peter is not from my adoptive family of creatures, he has become a genial companion and learned much since I discovered him when he was brought to me for treatment as a boy. How his mother became a carrier of the organism was never discovered. It is amazing she was not exposed to the stimuli needed to change her. Peter's transformation was set in motion when he attended a boy's boarding school. He got into a fight and inadvertently tasted fresh human blood.

Being with him now, in his youth, I can't help but be reminded of myself after the death of Adrianna and my parents, and the fact that I was doomed to the company of Prof. Vairaja, who I will refer to as Charles from now on, Nara, and Brommel.

At first I hated and despised them. To be bound by a common hunger was disgraceful, but I was wrong in my judgment of Charles as he became a great friend and mentor. After completing medical school, I opened a small clinical practice and did further research with him on the organism infecting us.

My assessment of Brommel and Nara didn't change. They were nothing but selfish monsters.

After the tragedy befell my parents and Adrianna, her parents would visit me on occasion. They, as well as the authorities, believed the explanation Charles had offered about the fire. I was never too congenial with them. I think they believed my unsociable behavior a result of depression from my recent losses. By and by they tired of staying in touch with me. I heard less from them until they just seemed to vanish from my life.

That was just as well. My present company of Brommel and Nara discouraged me getting close to any one. Those two were always near by and hungry.

To this day, I have not taken another life. In the beginning, I would not go out hunting with the rest. I was still full of indignation and loathing for my fellow creatures and myself. It was Charles who kept me fed. Nara and Brommel chided him for it.

"Let him starve," they agreed. "He will come around soon enough if you do."

Charles ignored their comments and continued to share his kills with me.

There were so many lost and homeless souls in London, enough to supply us as long as we were careful.

Eventually, I found myself wanting to go out with Charles for the hunt, but I still could not take a life. I had no problem drinking the blood or eating the flesh Charles gave me, but he was the one who executed the kill. Nara and Brommel took great sport from my behavior, calling me the bastard coward and that I should crawl into a box and be locked up for eternity. Charles, however, said I was the perfect balance, the complete irony. He told me he had always been able to keep a degree of humanity about him but had never felt hesitation to kill and feed. I, on the other hand, was unable to give up my empathy for mankind. This, he said, made me the saddest creature of all, torn between the needs of the organism and my lingering humanity.

How many were there like us?

Charles told me he had seen others and that they seemed to stay in their own territory. There was never many of them, he said, because it was a general habit not to let victims transform, keeping our population low. In fact, over all these years, there was only one occasion where Charles allowed a victim to be changed over. The outcome of that mistake was death.

Ten tears after my transition, Charles and I were out hunting with Brommel and Nara, something we rarely did due to their rouge behavior. We looked for the usual class of prey: prostitutes, the homeless, and the dregs who peddled opium and hashish. The death or disappearance of such lower class citizens seemed to be viewed as 'just deserts' by the authorities and not investigated with any enthusiasm. I convinced Charles to start incinerating the remains. We installed large furnaces at his private labs for that purpose. To make feeding easier and more discreet, victims where brought back to these labs where they were drained, eaten and disposed of.

On the night we went out together, Brommel and Nara were in a particularly fiendish mood. They did not wish to return to lab with their prey.

"It takes away the rush, this stupid foreplay," Brommel said through his teeth. "Nara agrees. The food needs to be stalked and killed where it is, not invited like a guest to a party."

It was impossible to reason with them when their blood lust was this fierce. They had become more husband and wife than Charles and Nara had ever been. We did not argue the point and continued on with the knowledge we would have to be wary as we fed.

When the four of us were together, it was our custom to pay for two prostitutes or take two homeless citizens. On the night in question we were feeding on two prostitutes. Charles would alternate drinking with me until it was time for him to take the final, fatal drink. Brommel and Nara kept to themselves, moaning with pleasure as they fed.

When we had finished and were about to leave, a drunken laugh echoed down the alley where we had taken our victims. Walking with stealth toward the disturbance, we discovered a young prostitute. Her client was a big burly fellow. The odor of his unwashed body hung in the air. He had the girl pressed against a wooden fence. One hand covered her mouth as his other unbuttoned his trousers then fumbled under her dress. He was laughing all the while.

"You shouldn't fight, deary," he said roughly. "I paid for it and I want it right here. To hell with your bed."

The brute ripped off the girl's undergarments and forced himself into her while she was standing. Charles and I watched with indifference as he rode her. I heard Brommel and Nara whispering lasciviously behind us. The only sex acts Brommel was capable of by then were memories pooled in his violent brain. Nara was an altogether different bird. She stripped herself, yowled like a wildcat and jumped on the sweaty fellow's back. The girl screamed and slid down the fence. The man bellowed in rage at being disturbed. He swung in a frantic circle to throw Nara off his back, but she held on like a tick. The man lost his balance and tumbled to the ground. Nara released her hold just as she was about to be trapped under his weight. Before he could regain himself, Nara grabbed his still erect member and slid it into her. He never got to enjoy the moment as she tore into his neck to drain him.

It was her way.

Nara did not act in this manner every time she fed, but there were occasions where her sexual drive needed to be slaked along with her hunger. From what Charles had told me I gathered the organism affected females differently than males. There was a drive for propagation. The irony being that only a female born to a carrier could complete a pregnancy. Nara certainly possessed the need to reproduce but was destined not to be able to.

When the man ceased struggling, Brommel joined Nara. He needed no more food than he had already had, but he was not about to let another moment of pleasure slip by.

We had forgotten about the girl.

Frozen in place, she stared in shock at the nightmare unfolding in front of her. Charles pulled her up. She never screamed. He knew it was only a matter of seconds before Nara and Brommel would be on her when they finished their meal.

"Hold her," Charles commanded me. "I will try and stop them from attacking her."

The girl was so stiff it was like holding a stone figure. When I looked closer at her, I was stunned by her resemblance to Adrianna. I believe Charles had seen this trait as well and intended to somehow give back what had been taken from me. It was the only act of selflessness I would know him to commit.

He hadn't gone far when Nara noticed the girl. Brommel was under the influence, as we all had been at one time or another, of the alcohol in the man's blood and stumbled when he tried to get up and join Nara who never seemed to be affected by any foreign substance in the blood she drank.

"Give her to me," Nara said.

Charles stood his ground between Nara and the girl I held.

"This one is coming back to lab," Charles said with authority. "I need a human subject."

Nara glared with defiance. Fog had crept around her body. She was terrible and stunning at the same moment.

"Still searching for an answer?" She threw back her head and laughed. "Go ahead then, take her with you, but when you fail to find what you never will, remember, she is mine."

Nara dressed and helped Brommel up on his unsteady legs.

"The night is young," she said to Charles and me, "and we intend to enjoy ourselves some more. Unlike you foolish two, Thomas and I know the only answer to our existence is to feed."

They disappeared into the darkness of the alley and the mist.

By now the girl had passed out in my arms. We took her back to one of the waterfront labs and bled her. She was so terrified she made little effort to resist. Charles stopped before completely draining her. He placed her in a small room where we could observe her initial transformation.

I had never witnessed someone change before. It took days and was such a strain on the girl's physical body I was certain she wouldn't survive. Charles said one never knew if the victim would make it through the transition or not. Each individual was different in their biological makeup.

The girl endured but her temperature had been so high during the process her brain was damaged. She became as wild as the baboons we had studied and had to be fed and confined like them. It was depressing to look upon her beauty and realize the girl would not be able to carry on a simple conversation again. Nara was pleased that the girl would offer no competition for her and teased the unfortunate convert unmercifully.

It would have been better to kill our mistake, but none of us could take the life of one of our own. It was as if the organism recognized each brother cell that lived in another's body and provided a safety mechanism for survival. Even the girl, in her retarded beastly condition, never attempted to kill any one of us.

One evening Nara was in an especially foul mood and taunted the girl more than usual. Charles and I were examining some tissue slides while Brommel, waiting to go out and hunt with Nara, moped around the lab. Nara got so worked up in her baiting of the girl she opened the cage door to have some contact fun as well. Nara was not prepared for the quick reaction that followed as the girl rushed out and bolted for the door leading outside.

Chaos followed.

We tried to corner and catch her, but she managed to elude our efforts.

I have said that none of us would kill another of our kind but that doesn't mean we will not bite, scratch or struggle with a fellow creature if we feel threatened in any way. The girl inflicted several painful wounds on us all including a particularly vicious ripping of Brommel's face. He was enraged and shrieked in agony. Brommel grabbed the girl and tumbled into one of the laboratory benches, spilling reagents and knocking over a Bunsen burner. He and the girl ignited when the burner's flame came in contact with the stream from the spilt reagents. The two locked in a fiery embrace as they screeched and wailed in a spasmodic struggle against one of our few real enemies.

By the time we managed to beat down the flames, Brommel and the girl were dead.

It was the beginning of the end for the relationship between Charles and Nara. With Brommel gone, Nara had lost her companion and could not go back to the life she had shared with Charles and his passive personality. I would certainly be no comfort to her. Eventually she became a solitary feeder and kept to herself, living in the small spice shop she ran. Charles and I saw very little of her after the night of the fire.

Charles and I continued to study the organism. One night we fed on a derelict female who was pregnant. We had never tasted the blood and tissue of a fetus before. In the days that followed, we noticed our need for food was reduced. It was almost a week before we had to feed again. After that meal, our hunger returned to its usual pattern. Being men of science, it was obvious to us that the fetus had somehow prolonged our need for nourishment.

Charles had friends in the medical community and was able to acquire abortive tissue under the guise of research. After feeding on several meals of it, we were assured of our conclusion. The potent sustenance from beginning life could sustain us for up to two weeks, depending on the gestation age. The younger the sample, the more powerful it was.

For the first time in a long while, we felt a degree of freedom from the hunger. We spent many nights out mingling with the human race. We dressed in high fashion and frequented posh clubs, but after a while Charles became dissatisfied with 'the high life', as he called it, and wanted to do more studies on the organism's affinity for developing fetal tissue. If the material from humans was that nutritious, why not try substitutes from similar animals like the baboons he once used for experimentation?

So we took fetuses from a range of different mammals, but, as well as the unpleasant taste, our hunger was not put off as it had been with human tissue. Charles tried many primate species, but was met with the same result. Of all the species we tried, the only one that was even close was the blood and tissue from fetal pigs. It prolonged our hunger but only for about half the time compared to a human fetus.

When we were experimenting with the animal fetuses, Nara appeared one night. It had been a long time since we had seen her. Charles shared what we had discovered about feeding on a human fetus with her.

"To feed without hunting or killing?" she reproached us. "Why should I become lazy and soft like you weaklings? I enjoy the feel of fear in my victims, the smell of it. The rush of life as it flows into me while their heart still beats."

Nara was an ideal predator, but her irresponsibility and disregard for exposing us to danger was what made her a liability. I feared that she would come to a sorry end just as Brommel had.

Nara mistook one of the animal fetuses for that of the human one Charles had mentioned. She gulped it down, frowning at the taste.

"This?" she said with disgust. "This sorry tasting pulp? You can't be serious."

She walked to Charles and handed him a package she had held under her arm.

"I only came tonight to bring this to you, Charles," she said. "It arrived a week ago at the shop." She headed for the door, turned and added, "When are you going to accept the fact you are no longer human, Charles? You can't have a brother who is not a meal? I am sorry I found you both in a more pathetic state than the last time I saw you. Go back to feeding on that shit!"

He stared as she walked out the door. I knew Charles still felt what love he could for her. That is the reason he did not try and force her to stay with us. It would be like caging her, and that he would never do.

"Why don't you see what's in the package, Charles?" I asked to break the dark mood Nara had left behind.

The first box contained a second one, which held an ornate heavy necklace embedded with large green and red stones. There was also a small bottle with a desiccated insect inside. The wrapping paper was postmarked from Pasha, India.

Charles silently read a note that was with the items.

"So he is still alive," Charles said in almost a whisper, "after all these years."

It was his father who had sent the package.

"He writes," Charles shared, "that an archeological expedition discovered the temple ruins just outside of Pasha. He feared the necklace he had placed on the statue of Kali would be confiscated by the team, or that it might fall into the hands of thieves if he kept it himself. So he sent it along with our little friend, the insect I named the rhinoceros vampire, to me. How he discovered my whereabouts is a mystery."

Instead of trying to answer my innumerable questions, Charles gave me his mother's journal along with his own to read. It was the only time he had allowed anyone other than Nara to read his mother's, and I would be the first to read the writings of his past.

What a life they had experienced. To consider their history resulted from the bite of an insect vector and the possession of the necklace by a young British girl who had fallen in love with a dark man of India, a man whose brother was a merciless killer and the father of Charles Vairaja, was astonishing.

How ghastly Charles' father must be today if he still lived. His leprous body rotting away over the years as the organism kept him alive in a state of coexistence. The once feared and ruthless bandit Vairaja now a hulking shell, a ghoul who fed in graveyards.

As I read the journals over the next few days, Charles would wander absentmindedly in and out of the laboratory. He would pick up the necklace on occasion and hold it to the light as if hypnotized by the refractions from the jewels.

During the next year, Charles was persistent in his efforts to get Nara back in his home. The necklace had infected him with nostalgia for their past association. Sometimes she would come by the laboratory, but his adamant appeals for her to come home were always ignored. He showed her the necklace and she was callous in return, saying it was worthless to her now. She did, on one occasion, accept an invitation to dine with us on a meal of human fetuses although she commented it would probably be no better than what she had sampled before. Of course, as this was human fetal tissue, the meal was very pleasing to her. I gave her my portion as I was not particularly hungry that evening.

Within a day, Charles and Nara fell ill. I couldn't help but think it must have been something in the tissue they ate. I cared for them as best I could but could not stop the state of unconsciousness that befell them.

It was unusual for us to be ill. The organism was resilient to the foreign bodies that affected humans and other mammals. Some mutant form of a blood borne virus must have attacked their immune system. They eventually recovered but at a dreadful cost. Charles suffered irreparable damage and Nara was forced to live a sheltered confined existence. It was as if their years of postponed aging caught up with a vengeance.

Charles withered and became bedridden. He recognized Nara and me only on occasion. He was desiccating like the insect in that bottle his father had sent. The illness had targeted Nara's joints. She was still mobile but limited because of stiffness and pain. Her beauty faded away. She resembled a hag in a fairy tale.

Charles stayed in Nara's spice shop where she and I cared for him. I notified the university of his illness and explained the malady to be of unknown origin. Some of the faculty came to visit him. After seeing his condition, none returned. I suspected they believed it might be contagious.

The university, however, did grant Charles a stipend for a number of years.

I now had to provide their food as well as my own.

I usually had no trouble luring a victim to the shop where Nara could corner them. Her limited motion did not diminish her ability to make a vicious kill.

Over time I found it more desirable to bring homeless children to the shop where I could drug them. They were helpless then and an easy meal for Nara to feed herself and Charles with.

I could have continued harvesting fetuses, but since Charles and Nara had become ill after eating one, I was hesitant to use them as a food source. From what research I conducted on Charles and Nara, I strongly suspected a venereal disease had been passed on to the fetus from its parent and had somehow produced the devastating results.

Peter's parents had both died, so I adopted him. When he finished his medical studies he joined my practice. I involved him in the investigation for the safe use of fetal tissue. Over time we developed serological tests to screen patients before their abortions. We could not share any of our findings with the medical community. We existed in shadows and participated in what was needed to maintain our licenses, nothing more.

Our trip to America is a direct result of our experiments. I have read many articles on disease control from some of the top scientists there.

Charles is coming with us. I placed his shrunken body in a small box that I will declare as materials for research. I lined the structure with enough herbs and spices to cover the odor of decay.

Nara refused to come. She has infected a few children. Some survived and she plans to use them to help her find food. If they don't, she will fade away from slow starvation.

The hour grows late. I will stop writing. Perhaps I will continue making notes of our voyage. It all depends on my mood and just how well the food stores of tissue cultures we brought along retain their freshness. So goes the meal, so goes the mind.

May 21, 1938

Peter says the incident on board was caused by the tendency of my human traits to surface.

"It makes you vulnerable to the world outside our sphere," he said. "You feel sorry for mankind with its physical limitations. That is why you can never make a complete kill."

Perhaps Charles was correct when he said I was the bridge between two worlds. There is enough empathy in me to suppress the driving hunger inside. Although I have learned to drain a victim, I cannot take their life.

I've Peter to do that.

Yesterday I observed an attractive female on the upper deck. As usual, Peter kept to our cabin while I went for a stroll. I was enjoying the salt breeze on my face when I spotted her standing against the rail not far from me. She had short red hair and appeared to be in her early thirties. A summer dress lightly grabbed the curves of her body and danced in the breeze above her slim thighs. She smoked through a slender silver cigarette holder.

I was admiring her when she turned and caught sight of me. She didn't seem annoyed; in fact, she sent an engaging smile in my direction before she walked away.

That evening I was in The Promenade Room. An orchestra performed nightly there. That night they played one of my favorites: The Mephisto Waltz by List. The woman I had seen earlier on deck appeared by my table and asked if she could join me. I readily consented. She was bewitching in her new attire. A long delicate black dress embraced her and a dark white speckled boa curled around her neck and bosom.

I ordered champagne and explained I never took alcohol myself. The drink warmed her into talking. Her name was Elizabeth and she had spent the last six months in London. Her husband had been killed in an oil rigging accident earlier that year. As it was his company, she was left quite wealthy. She was now on her way back to Houston, Texas.

After the concert we strolled on deck. I fabricated a tale of my own life, adding enough truth to make it reasonable. We stopped by the rail and leaned against it. The sound of the ship gliding through the water was hypnotic under a half moon and a clear night painted with stars.

"It feels so wonderful up here," she said softly, "almost as if we were flying."

Like a melancholy phantom, her face shone with its own incandescence in the pale light. I bent and kissed her. She made no resistance and gave one in return.

Sex was an oddity for any male affected by the organism. One could feel passion but was impotent. However, our hands and mouths were quite deft at bringing women pleasure. As the soft feathers of the boa brushed my face, I thought of nothing else but taking her to bed. The last time I had felt such desire for a woman had been with Adrianna.

She took me to her cabin and slowly undressed in front of my adoring eyes. She was exquisite.

"I hope you don't mind," she said and wound the boa around her. "The texture of the feathers makes it better, more exciting."

I turned my back to prevent her from seeing the shriveled remains of my manhood as I undressed. As I sat on the corner of the bed, she pressed her breasts against my back.

"There's no need to be shy," she whispered.

I turned and kissed her neck. I moved gradually down. My tongue and lips explored her full breasts. Eventually, I reached the mound of auburn hair and the waiting sweetness beneath it. I moved her to climax with my fingers and tongue. After, she lay exhausted and content, her moist beaded body lovely in its heat and odor. I took her blood, weeping as I did. She resisted briefly and then slipped into the dazed state I had encountered with other victims. I stopped before mortal death would occur.

Elizabeth's breathing was shallow, her ashen skin cool. She was still striking even in her near death state.

I despised myself for letting passion control me, hated myself knowing I would have to ask Peter's help to save or kill her. I was taken aback when he refused.

"Were you seen with her?" he asked as I appealed to him.

Of course I had been seen. We had been around other passengers on deck and at the concert. God knows who saw me go in her room.

"Then we can't very well remove her head, can we?" he said cynically. "And if she is missed, questions will eventually be brought to our door, won't they? How could you be so irresponsible, Andrew?"

So nothing was done. Elizabeth would transform or die.

If Charles had been in his former state, he would have found a way to be merciful to Elizabeth. Peter, on the other hand, thought no more of the poor woman than he would a piece of lint on his sleeve. He would simply brush it away and go about his business. I cannot judge him. He is what he is. I sometimes wish the organism would have killed me or made me as ruthless as Brommel when I transformed. To be a contradiction is the cruelest fate.

May 23, 1938

Elizabeth was not strong enough to endure the change. At least she will not have to live at the expense of others.

I kept an eye on her cabin. The ship's doctor has been in and out of it. I imagine her cries of agony alarmed the neighboring cabins to alert the crew. I overheard fragments of a conversation between the doctor and the captain this morning. The doctor mentioned a dangerously high fever of unknown origin, central nervous system complications, and, as was to be expected since Pasteur's research, a similarity of symptoms found in those who had contracted rabies.

"I saw some bite marks," the doctor informed. "They could have well been made by a bat. As you know, these animals are well documented as carriers of the rabies virus."

She was taken out in a tightly wrapped sheet and transported to a quarantined area on the lower deck. The weather began to change as they took her away. I stood by the railing and watched the gathering clouds swirl in their black and gray madness. When the driving rain arrived, I went back to my cabin. Perhaps Elizabeth's betrayed spirit had delivered its wrath upon the ship as winds and rain of hurricane proportions developed this afternoon, forcing us to stay in our cabins out of the tempest's fury.

Peter read his medical journal while I took a long warm bath. I fell asleep after reading my own correspondences with medical colleges from Austin, Texas. Normally I do not dream, but this afternoon, with the storm howling around the ship and the guilt of Elizabeth's death still fresh in my mind, I dreamt deeply.

I was walking through the streets of London. It was night. Shadows followed as I traveled toward an unknown destination. The wind was moaning and pushed me forward with an icy hand. Suddenly, it stilled. A soft snow began to fall. A hooded figure approached through the swirling flakes. A sense of foreboding came with it as the form stood in front of me. The hood was pushed away by aged hands. Adrianna's cold countenance met my shocked stare. There was no warmth as she grabbed me. She laughed cruelly and opened her mouth, revealing jagged canines that were rotten and foul. She embraced me and drove them deep into my neck where she feasted like one who has thirsted for a thousand years. When she pulled away, Adrianna's face had changed. It was now Elizabeth who gazed at me. The ghastly appearance had vanished, leaving only the smooth aquiline features I had looked on with delight just days before. Her look was one of pity. Scarlet tears streamed down Elizabeth's cheeks as she backed away, holding out her arms as if to beckon me into the shadows. I stood frozen in place. I knew only despair waited for me there. The snow increased, obliterating the retreating specter. The large flakes were drops of blood and the end of all that was left for me as it melted in its crimson cold on the deserted street.

I awoke crying.

Peter did not hear me. He was asleep, his head placed in the cradle of his arms on top of the books spread out across the table.

I know that I no longer wish to appease my hunger. It will be painful and wretched, but as soon as we are settled and Peter is able to manage the clinic on his own, I will seal myself in a stone coffin and asked that what remains of Charles be placed in a similar resting place next to me. In starvation, I will age rapidly, soon becoming a mirror image of what Charles is now.

This will be my last entry.

None will win the contest for my being. The final choice is mine.

Forgive me all my loves, my dears for what I have done to you.

Forgive me, Peter, for deserting you.
Come now phantoms and guide my descent into oblivion.

DR. GLENN RUSSELL, ROUND ROCK, TEXAS

1997

1

After reading the journals, I knew what must be done.

Those who carried the organism from the beginning made a mistake. Charles Vairaja should have learned from his father who had no trouble realizing what he was. From Charles to Andrew to Peter, the aspect of our true nature has been shadowed by the useless research of what infects us. Are we to become fat and lazy like our human counterparts? Will we eat the high nutrient meals of fetal tissue and never hunt again?

As I see it, the organism is a blessing. The world is falling apart around us, becoming what we are may be the only road to salvation. The wars and genocide, the cost of fuels, the greed of those in power across the earth are human traits, and we are not human. To continue in the direction Peter would have us go, with politicians and drug companies, is the destination to our own end. When money and power become the motivators, even our super human physical characteristics will not save us. Our kind will be found out, hunted down and destroyed.

So, I decided to make my move.

I waited in the clinic parking lot. As was his routine, Peter stayed after all the others had left. I went in and found him in the room where the developing fetuses were kept. He did not seem surprised to see me.

"Finished with your pathetic afternoon of love?" he asked as he added saline solution to the tanks. "Did you really think I would not find out the woman was your ex-wife?"

"It doesn't matter," I answered, moving closer to him. "I killed her."

Peter turned and was a little surprised by my closeness.

"Oh? So I had no reason to worry after all."

"Certainly not. In fact, remember your predication about my personality? That I would be driven by the virus alone, that I would be able to kill one of our own?"

He anticipated my move and skirted away before I could grab him. He looked more thrilled than afraid.

"I misjudged you. I never expected it would be me," he said, bracing for my attack. "You are mistaken if you believe I will let it happen."

Peter lunged and locked me in an embrace of life and death. We rolled across the room. Several of the tanks were turned over, spilling their contents on the floor. He put up an admirable fight. He ripped two of my fingers away and gouged out a large portion of my left cheek.

But I was younger, stronger, and more determined.

I pinned him. His arms were trapped under my legs as I bent down and tore his trachea away with my teeth. Air and blood exploded around me. I continued to dig into his throat until I reached the cervical vertebra and crushed them. I decapitated him and left his body where it lay.

I kept a close watch on the clinic the next day.

Along with the clinic being closed down, the frantic movement in and out of the building told of the discovery. I saw Maria get in her car and approached before she could leave.

"Where have you been?" she asked, obviously distressed. "Do you know what has happened?"

I told her that I did then asked her to arrange a meeting tonight with the others at the tomb. I explained I had vital information to share about our safety.

They all showed. They mumbled, looking from side to side unsure what was to become of them with Peter gone.

I stood and told them to settle down.

"I am the one who killed Peter," I confessed.

There were shouts and curses thrown at me, but no one made a move to assault me. Their eyes were full of hatred and fear. I must have seemed a powerful and dangerous being to have bested and killed Peter.

"You must regroup," I said. "Join me and help establish a strong safe colony."

"But what about the fetal tissue?" one asked irately.

"Yes, how will it be supplied now?" another added.

"It has become a poor substitute and made us vulnerable," I answered. "We are becoming slaves to humans who will surely destroy us in the future."

My statement brought about even more outbursts and confusion.

I lost my patience.

"Then fight among yourselves," I yelled. "Go ahead and risk the doom of your existence or join me!"

I left them still arguing. Maria stopped me at the door.

"Wait," she said, our son cradled in her arms, "I will come with you."

2

Austin and its surrounding areas are honeycombed with caves. Most were discovered when a major highway was under construction. Spelunkers received a big Christmas present when the caves were exposed, and those in the tourist trade turned some of them into attractions for travelers.

For us, these caves have become home.

There are many yet untouched by man. These are where we live.

The most difficult adaptation was to the low light and, sometimes, total darkness, but over time we have adjusted. We can distinguish what humans cannot.

Our brood is a small one. Some of the clinic workers joined Maria and me, but most of them went their own way.

As a thin layer of fur now covers us, we have disposed of our clothes. Our hair and nails have grown long, our upper and lower canines extended. My genitals are beginning to grow back as they were before my transformation. I think my son will have brothers and sisters in the future.

Hunting is good and the food plentiful. In a world where babies have babies, children have no fathers, and mothers have no husbands, there are many who wander the roads. They are not missed. We stalk in a pack now. The kill ratio is more efficient that way.

My thoughts do not linger on worldly things. I am content in the arms of the Earth, the warmth of Maria, and the soft breathing of our son as he sleeps between us.

Tonight, above a dense forest of cedars just outside our den, a full moon rises against an overcast sky and peers through gaps in the banks of clouds. Our pale faces mimic it as we stare into the expanding ground fog where we wait, where we want.

ABOUT THE AUTHOR

Timothy Hobbs is a retired Medical Technologist living in Robinson, Texas. He has had short stories and poems published in *New Texas* (an annual literary collection of Texas writers) in 1999, 2000, and 2002, a short story and flash fiction piece in *Dark Tales,* a U.K. publication, and a short story in *spinetinglermag.com,* an on-line Canadian magazine. Tim's latest short story publication has been *The Visitor,* which appeared in the April 2013 edition of SOL: English Writing in Mexico. He has also published a short story collection, *Mothertrucker and Other Stories* and a novel *Veils* through Publish America in 2008. His novels *The Pumpkin Seed* and *Music Box Sonata,* and a novella *The Smell of Ginger,* were published by Vamplit Publishing in the United Kingdom and recently republished by Visionary Press Cooperative. His new novel *Maiden Fair* was published by Netherworld Books in the United Kingdom in 2013. Tim's author page can be viewed at Amazon.com.

ABOUT THE PUBLISHER

Visionary Press Cooperative is a totally new and innovative way of publishing. We are 100% member owned, controlled, and benefited. The goal of our co-op community is to publish entertaining Science Fiction, Fantasy and Horror literature for all ages

Visionary Press Cooperative
Denver, Colorado
http://visionarypresscoop.com
visionarypress@gmail.com

8466494R00088

Made in the USA
San Bernardino, CA
10 February 2014